David Boyle is the author of a number of books, including *Blondel's Song: The imprisonment and ransom of Richard the Lionheart* and other books about history and the future. He is a member of the Folklore Society and has a lifelong fascination for fairies. He lives in London on the edge of what was once the Great North Wood, now more commonly known as Norwood.

www.david-boyle.co.uk

LEAVES THE WORLD TO DARKNESS

David Boyle

The Real Press
www.therealpress.com

First published in 2007 by
The Real Press
The Red House, 56 Dale Park Road, London SE19 3TY
www.therealpress.com

Cover photograph by Ruth Potts.
Cover design by Andrew Hodge, 021 Creative

ISBN 978-0-9552263-0-4

Printed in England by Tandem Press,
82-90 Queensland Road,
London N7 7AS
www.tandempress.com

To Carol Cornish,

with love and very grateful thanks.

Acknowledgements

It is now a decade since I dreamed the end of this story, rather unexpectedly in the middle of the night, so there is a very long list of people who have played a part in its creation – too many to thank by name. Those who are not named here will know who they are, and I am still deeply grateful. But especial thanks to Carol Cornish for starting me down this path, for her suggestions and ability to inspire and draw out. To Kate Cutler and Gill Paul for their guidance and advice at different stages. To my mother for reading it through, and for many other things too. To Lucinda Cook and Julian Alexander for their encouragement. To Karen Sullivan for her expert and sensitive editing, though – because I did not always take her advice – I am solely responsible for the mistakes. To all those at the Folklore Society who, without knowing it, have inspired the writing of the book. To my partner at the Real Press, Andrew Simms, for moving me along. To Andrew Hodge for the cover. And, as always, to Sarah and Robin for encouraging me, for being there, and for a great deal more.

THE WESTON FAMILY TREE

John Weston
Gentleman Farmer
(1741–1805)

'Jo'
Farmer
(1777–1912)

Emma
(1792–?)

?

'Jack'
(?–1877)

Robert
Colonial Administrator
(1820–1851)

Edmund
Farm Manager
(1824–1860)

Joseph
Farmer
(1841–1895)

John
Banker
(1865–1916)

Gerald
solicitor
(1887–1918)

Edward
Soldier
(1889–1915)

'Harry'
Journalist
(1902–1979)

Jeremy
Banker
(1930–)

James
(1960–)

I

"A sad tale's best for winter.
I have one of sprites and goblins..."
WILLIAM SHAKESPEARE, *THE WINTER'S TALE*

Oberon, Surrey, October 1912

WHEN Harry Weston walked into the parlour and found his grandparents dead, he was not terribly surprised. When people are as old as they were, you kind of expect sudden death. Harry could hear it whispered around them, could sense the waiting in everybody's dealings with them – even a kind of impatience, as if the order of things was not being upheld and they were keeping the afterlife waiting.

Probably his grandparents had ceased to perceive these things decades before, but even at his age, Harry picked it up. He knew they were so old they had almost been forgotten.

He had gone there before anyone else in the house, as he always did. The cool morning sunlight was only just ahead of him as he pushed open the creaky old parlour door. The same door had been pushed open by generations of maids with china dishes, shepherds with blood and snow on their hands from the wintry fields, and boys back from the local hunt – right back to Cromwell's time when the old one had been splintered apart by angry soldiers.

And there were his grandparents in their two ancient chairs, staring out of the window across towards Saxon Wood, as still as ever – they always were still, as if even the slightest movement might tear their papery skin. But this time they seemed more than usually shrunken. There was an extra quietness about the room that struck him the moment he lifted the latch. And when he walked through, and heard his small feet pad on the linoleum, he could tell there was something missing, like a dog can tell if a house is empty.

Afraid for no obvious reason of making a noise, Harry tiptoed quickly across the room and grasped his Grandpapa just below the shoulder. There was a horrible crunch and a smell of something dusty and just a little fetid – or was that always there when he sniffed the air? To his horror, Harry realized his fingers had met in the middle, and the arm of the patched black jacket the old man had worn for decades was hanging loose.

Harry glanced at their empty faces and bolted. It was as if something had beaten him into the room some hours before, in the darkest part of the night when the oil-lamps were out – he was too young to have more than the haziest idea of what the house was like in the dark – and sucked the life out of them like a vampire.

And not just their lives, but their bones and gristle as well. Two crumpled tiny corpses they were: he could almost have folded them up and put them away in a drawer like a nightshirt. They had been so old, they had almost disintegrated before dying, and saved decay all the trouble.

But for all that, they had been the cornerstones of Harry's short life. And when the cornerstones disappear between one sunset and the dawn, as if on a kind of whim of the weather, ten-year-old boys are bound to feel a sinking sense of terror. Looking back from the benefit of the twentieth century, it seemed to him later that their deaths had marked the end of the underpinning of everything – though he knew, since they were at least 130 years old, that he was very lucky to have met them at all.

Harry lived in the countryside and knew all about death.

He had seen kittens drowned, dogs drop dead with exertion, old farm hands collapse alongside their bulls. He had seen pigs slaughtered in the yard outside, with their blood trickling down into the drains not ten yards from him. But then the bodies had somehow resembled the animals when they had been alive.

"They're just sleeping," his favourite of the family servants, Sophie, comforted him as he looked frightened into the farmyard. "Sleeping until the Lord wakes them."

His mother had constantly reminded him how frail the grandparents were. "They're so old, darling," she would say. "So old. We have to prepare ourselves."

But then Harry's mother was a great one for preparing herself – she shunned face powder because she said it was common, but spent hours in front of the mirror trying to achieve the same effect with unusual facial exercises. So Harry had taken her instructions with a pinch of salt, and – although he had in some ways been preparing himself his whole ten years – he had imagined there might be some warning. They would be ill, they would go one at a time, there would be time to discuss the prospect with them in their old-fashioned blunt way.

But there hadn't been. Somehow they had been living together for so long – married, in fact, for well over a century – that when the heart and blood of one stopped pumping and their brain stopped ticking, the mechanism in the chair next to theirs could work no longer.

"Oh I do hope not, poor old dears," he overheard Sophie saying to the cook later in the morning. "Wouldn't it be dreadful if one of them went in the middle of the night – you know how lonely it is in the middle of the night. And then the other woke, and – oh, it's terrible to think of."

"Well I don't think we need to worry ourselves about it," said Cook, glancing round to make sure nobody was listening, but without noticing Harry in the corridor – nobody ever noticed Harry in the corridor. "I happened to overhear Dr Hansen talking to the Mistress. 'No sign that one had outlived the other, even for a little while,' he said – and those were his exact words. Together in life as in death. Do you know, they've not left this house – to my certain knowledge – since the old century. They've never even seen a motor car, for heaven's sake. It was *time*, you know what I mean? It was time for them. It wasn't natural being so old. Let them rest in peace at long last, poor old things."

Throughout Harry's ten years, they seemed to have been in the parlour, with its old wooden sideboard and dusty pewter dishes, their rough wooden beds and eiderdowns in the corner and the smell of tobacco and snuff. They had been living there very gently, the faint breaths from their ancient lungs barely disturbing the air or fogging the windows.

They sat there like human furniture, as if they had grown part of the old wooden chairs with the big tall backs they had sat in for decades. They moved only a few feet from there to table and occasionally to bed, and back again at dawn. Sometimes they didn't even bother with that. They hadn't been outside for decades – they hadn't seen the sky, face to face as it were, or felt the breeze on their faces, in the new century. And to Harry, who had known only one century of steel and motor-buses, that seemed eons ago.

After breakfast every morning, he would take the last slice of jam on new baked bread and rush through into the parlour and watch their yellowed eyes light up, and the silver heart which Grandmama always hung round her neck glinting in the morning light. There would be a movement in Grandpapa's old waistcoat and her black lace full-length dress, and he would kiss them both on their wizened cheeks. Life would rush with him into the room, awakening the ancient beetles in the skirting board and the sleeping dust-mites napping between the floorboards – floorboards from trees that had last blown in the wind during the reign of Edward I.

Harry seemed a sailor-suited outsider in the stillness of their room. Because although he referred to them – as everyone did – as Grandmama and Grandpapa, they were in fact nothing of the kind. Or rather, they were something of the kind, but far more impressive. They were great-great-grandparents, and their extraordinary longevity was as much a mystery to them as it was to everyone else.

Back in their 80s and 90s – in itself an impressive age at the time – they were endlessly questioned about their recipe. And although they wracked their brains through the pipe smoke – both then still smoked little clay pipes, though they were extremely hard to buy – they could think of no adequate answer.

Once Harry remembered one of those rare occasions when the whole family joined them in the parlour, with the smell of buttered toast and the remains of the day sinking down behind the trees of Saxon Wood outside the window – and Harry's older brother Edward had asked the same question.

"Eh, what did you say, Sir?"

"I said, how do I get to be as old as you?"

He made no reply, but puffed at his clay pipe. The conversation had almost turned to something else, when the black lace next to him twitched and Grandmama's thin voice wafted over the teatime scene. "Cod liver oil. Cod liver oil," she said. She often said that.

"If you would live to my age, Sir, I will tell you what you must do," said Grandpapa suddenly, a wicked gleam in his eyes. "You must refrain from union with your wife entirely. I have not touched my wife since I was a stripling."

Harry didn't know what this meant, but the company froze. "Grandpapa, please! There are ladies present – and children!" said Harry's pompous oldest brother Gerald. His mother hastily began discussing the dinner.

Peering out from her hopelessly outdated black brocade, Grandmama had a far away look in her eyes, indicating that she was trying to remember if he had been speaking the truth.

"You know what," Edward whispered in Harry's ear. "I think they're so old, they've forgotten. What's more, there's nobody as old as they are who could say one way or the other if they're right."

"I'd wash their mouths out with carbolic," said Nanny

Butler in Harry's hearing. "Goodness knows the words they're filling the boy's head with." But the more they disapproved, the more protective of his grandparents he became and their strange talk of hunting and game pie.

"It's a sad business for a man to outlive his great grandchildren," said Grandpapa distantly during this period, and it was sad for them both. They sat in the parlour in the home they had known all their married lives and received no invitations and no visitors. Those who had been astonished at their reaching a century had assumed they had long since died. Only Harry and his family and their servants remained as witnesses to their continuing lives, and found that they never mentioned them when they were outside Oberon House, just as you rarely discuss your beds or chairs with anybody else.

And now they were dead. But exactly how old were they?

They were getting on in age by the time the government began to insist on the central registration of births, just as they were married before they began to register marriages, and neither could recall exactly. For as long as anyone could remember, they had bickered gently about who was oldest.

It was said that their grandson Robert had known their birthdays, but he had died in a cholera epidemic in Bangalore in 1841, and his young family had drowned somewhere in the Indian Ocean on the way home, and their coat buttons had washed up on the beaches of Madagascar.

And now it was impossible to know which was right. There was no record of Grandpapa's baptism in the local church, because of an unseemly disagreement between his father and the local vicar. Grandmama's church records had been destroyed in a fire in 1857, before anyone had bothered to look. There was a record of their wedding dated 1802 – at least it seemed to be their wedding – and there was no doubt that they were extremely old.

Through the great transformations of society, the Enclosures, the Napoleonic Wars, the Luddites, railways, bicycles, telephones, the Boer War, Grandpapa had sat in his parlour in his old wig, smoking his clay pipes, and discussing the meals he had eaten the previous evening. As the years wore on, he would describe in copious detail meals eaten a century or more before, the ale, the suckling pig, the roast lamb, roast ham, Bellamy's veal pies, bottles of porter consumed at a sitting, and the similarly gargantuan meal he ate a few hours later.

Neither Grandmama nor Grandpapa had been heard to mention God, except in oath, and they had given up going to church altogether in the 1860s because the sermons bored them to distraction. They had never heard of Darwin, believed that 'evolution' was a French spelling mistake, and never wondered whether or not the King James version of the Bible was the literal truth. It had never crossed their minds that it wasn't.

"Church? By God, no," whispered Grandpapa. "I can't abide it. I can't abide that sermonizing. It can send a fellow insane, Sir. It's for women, I say." And soon he was off to the story of meeting mad King George III, trespassing on his land, gathering information for one of his columns in Agricultural Magazine – and sent the King packing.

"Was the Magna Carta for nothing?" he wheezed. "He should have asked my permission. The man was mad even then."

And although their voices were barely audible, their memories of the distant past seemed undimmed. Grandmama would tell how her father refused to accept the loss of the American colonies: the mere mention of the United States would send him into a rage, a hatred made all the more intense when her brother lost his life burning the White House during the war of 1812. Though it wasn't the Americans that killed him, it was his insistence on bringing back a keepsake from the president's house while his men were trying to set light to the furniture.

Grandpapa also told a strange tale about age. He remembered hearing his own grandfather, reminiscing about how he had danced with the old Countess of Desmond, Katherine Fitzgerald – then a very old lady, famous for her longevity.

She in turn had told him about a court banquet she had

been to in her youth, how the heraldic shields had sparkled in the firelight and the minstrels had played through the night, and how she had glimpsed Richard III presiding at the great oak table, handsome, genial and straight-backed. In those few long lives, a human connection with the history of England.

"Not a hunch-back at all," said Grandpapa happily again and again. "And if you ask me, the rightful king. Precious little has gone right with old England since Bosworth."

"I sometimes think," said Grandmama in Harry's other ear, as her husband completed the old tale for the umpteenth time, "that as I lie here and listen to the wind and the noises of the house, that there are lamps flashing outside the window. On and off I watch them, but do you know, I believe they are day and night rushing past. Just the sun and the moon coming and going on their journeys. Time goes faster when you're older, you know. It hardly seems yesterday since I was up there on the hay-rick making the May sweet in his arms for the first time."

Harry didn't know what she meant, but knew that this was exactly the kind of talk his parents disapproved of him listening to, so he pretended to take no notice – filing the phrase away in his mind like a jackdaw for examination later. He knew he needed to be careful if his mother would allow him to carry on spending hours in the parlour, sitting on the old green linoleum, drawing pictures of dreadnoughts in collared crayon.

"They're his flesh and blood," she used to say. "And they won't be there forever."

Actually there was every indication that they would be there forever, dreaming of rabbits and game pie and frosty mornings in hunting pink. It was now nearly half a century since the varnish on their chairs had been replaced. And then suddenly they were gone – an aching void in the parlour, a lingering whiff of bodies and smoke, though the daily business of the house seemed to go by unconcerned. Or almost unconcerned.

By mid-morning, there was a crunching on the gravel drive. Harry looked up from his lesson out of the upper window to see the big black carriage and a man in a lugubrious black tail coat, holding a battered top hat in his hands, and fingering the rim as he was let into the house. His colleagues had pasty white faces and hung around the back door, smoking and guffawing as they stubbed out their fags on the gravel.

A little later, Harry crept down to the parlour corridor to see the final coffin being shuffled away through the curtains and outside – probably the first time the old couple had been anywhere near the wind for a decade or more. He could just overhear the two men left behind in the parlour as they tidied up.

"Blimey, I never seen any as old as they looked. Proper Pharaohs weren't them both? About ready to fall to dust if you ask me."

Suddenly the loss hit him in the stomach and the tears rolled down his face. No more lying in the parlour while they dozed. No more mornings with bread and jam. No more looks of delighted recognition in their eyes. No more old-fashioned clothes. Why couldn't they have just said they were going?

When the undertakers had sloped away, he peeped in through the parlour door – and found he daren't actually go in. The old chairs were still in front of the window, but it was the first time he had seen them empty. The drawing he had made of the knights of the Round Table was still on the floor where he had left it a week before, and just between the two chairs was an old clay pipe.

Hot tears flowed down his cheek and he slipped quickly out of the back door and shot across the yard to the cold reassuring privacy of the lavatory, with its old newspaper and heavy green-painted cistern.

He pulled the chain and watched fearfully as the water in the bowl rose, wondering for a moment if the death of the central pillars of his life had undermined the laws of nature and the water would just keep rising. Then, yet again, he heard adult voices outside. It was one of the undertaker's assistants chatting up Sophie. They evidently knew each other from the village.

"I bet they could have told a tale or two," he was saying.

"They might have done at that. There are so many old tales about this house." The undertaker blew his nose horribly.

"Oh yes, what then?"

"I don't know if I likes to say," she said giggling a little. "There was something about some poet. They don't like to talk about it because he knew the lady of the house of something. Wrote her a poem, and there was something queer about it. Old Martin the gardener, he told me about it once. They don't like it mentioned."

"Sounds like he had his wicked way with her," the undertaker's assistant leered.

"Get away with you, Fred! There's no need for cheek." They both giggled out of earshot. Harry peered out of the lavatory door, afraid that the process of dissolution that started that morning when he bounced into the parlour had carried on – afraid that the laws of nature that held Oberon House to its course through the centuries were becoming unstitched. And in a way, they were.

II

'I know not why I am so sad; I cannot get out of my head a fairy-tale of olden times ...'
HEINRICH HEINE, *DIE LORELEI*

London, April 1998

I NEVER met Harry Weston, and I'm sorry for it. I don't like to regret things, but I regret that. By all accounts, he was a wonderful, kind and wise old man of the old English school, with nicotine stains on his fingers, a smile in his eyes, the smell of whiskey on his Harris tweed and a twinkling pretence at stupidity and conservatism. He might have explained some things that would clarify the peculiar events I'm about to describe. But he died nearly three decades ago as I write, and back then in the 1970s, I wouldn't have known what to ask.

No, I never knew Harry, but I knew Oberon House once and I knew his grandson James. If it wasn't for James, I don't know if I would have developed what became an obsession with the poet Byron, his times, and his enticing but elusive link with the house – before I felt quite as strongly as I do now that we follow these traditions at our peril. I don't know if I would have studied art history or specialized in the Romantic Movement, or ended up renting old master drawings to the boardrooms of financial service organisations, if it hadn't been for James and his stories. Maybe I would: it's a living, after all.

I'm certainly not ashamed of what I do. It keeps me in cars, and there's a kind of satisfaction watching my pictures adorn the walls of those pompous here-today-gone-tomorrow edifices, with all their smoked glass and fake antiques. Not to mention forcing art onto those board meetings, with all those short-sighted suits focusing on the short-term and the bottom line. It's a small contribution to corporate ethics.

I adopted James, just as his family kind of adopted me. I had mislaid my own family along the way, and maybe I felt in them some echo of my own rootlessness, brought up – as I was – by aunts, friends and institutions. Knowing James and knowing them, I was bound to know Oberon House. I had never seen it in those days, but I was instructed to peruse endless ancient lithographs, forgotten newspaper snaps, blotchy watercolours, old fading photographs of Edwardians playing tennis in long black dresses.

And I heard about it – God, did I hear about it. That was what knowing James was all about. If Chekhov had set his plays in late twentieth century England, and chosen the Weston family as subjects, Oberon would have played the same role as Moscow – the distant phantasmagorical focus of his characters' snobbish hopes.

One day, one day, James' stories implied, Oberon House would revert to the family – I was never entirely clear how – and then peace would reign in southern England, the Fisher King would be healed, and plenty would return to the land. And I got caught up in it, too. I came to inhale the old stories that filtered down to me, via old Harry, I assume. Now I can't forget them. I have long since forgotten my father's face the last time I saw him; I forget now what my mother said to me before she disappeared off on a shopping trip to Paris from which she never returned. I've forgotten what the first poor girl I seduced looked like; I've even forgotten my original intention to be an art historian. Yet somehow I still remember how the vicar of Oberon munched his way through a whole hog during a lengthy sermon in the cold winter of 1792.

I know when the stocks disappeared from the village, during a night of Restoration revelry after the hunt. I know when the last wolf was seen in the nearby woods, sloping through the shadows with its ribs showing and its eyes glowing with defeat. I know about the recruiting rallies held in the ebbing summer of 1915, attracting those whose names now appear on the Oberon war memorial, with its forgotten names and initials, still in rank order as they died. I know about the German bomber that crashed into the lake in 1940. I know about the strange medieval wall paintings in the Saxon church, pointing out the different sins possible with each different body part.

The stories must have played an important role for old Harry as well, because they seemed to stay real for him long after he had forgotten everything else about his life. There he sat in his old people's home in Pinner – municipal, as the Weston family had long since run out of money – with the urine-soaked smell of hideous green 1950s armchairs and the game shows continually on the large TV set, and the view of concrete and drizzle outside. There he sat in his final years, and dreamed of a lost – and probably fictional – version of England of carts and squires and dew and ancient tales of kidnap, smugglers, press gangs and fairies.

Fairies seemed to feature more often than was entirely healthy. There were the villagers, year after year, dancing outside the village on balmy summer nights, to ward off the threat of goblins, will o' the wisps and abductions of unsuspecting children – or the disturbing thought of a changeling, the soulless lump of wood substituted for a child. Last time I visited there, some years ago now, the village store was still draped with faded, unsold Arthur Rackham prints, or pamphlets explaining the significance of the local festival every June, celebrating those former residents said to have been stolen away during the previous centuries.

It was probably never like that anyway, but his old stories of the Domesday Oak were true enough. In those days it was there beside the Oberon churchyard, by the old iron gate which led to the footpath at the back of the house, because I saw the drawings – one by Stukeley in the seventeenth century – with its vast great trunk tangled and blackened along the ground.

It was the arboreal equivalent of Harry's own long dead great-great-grandparents in its age. Every Oberon tale involved meetings by the oak. Every illicit love affair was consummated under the oak. The initials of boys were carved into it for centuries. The recruitment rallies for Crêcy and Harfleur took place underneath it, just as they did for Ypres and the Somme. Nobody knew how old it was, but it was rumoured to have been planted in the reign of Alfred the Great. And who knows, maybe it was.

It was a kind of virtual home for all of us, this mythical, unforgotten and inaccurate Oberon, with its beating heart of a house outside it. And because I wanted a home – though the Oberon wolf wouldn't have dragged it out of me – I adopted it as a kind of focus for my own hopes, too. James had that apparently solid, reliable past which seemed to beat away, reminding him who he was. I envied him that. Perhaps if I'd realized that at the time, things would have turned out differently.

But there was another reason why I began to feel such an affinity with Byron, as much as the house. I was born with one leg just slightly out of kilter with the other, and suffered a childhood of specialists, traction and strange hideous Victorian contraptions strapped to my legs. It wasn't the so-called 'club foot' that gave Byron his limp and his lifelong chip on his shoulder, but it was bad enough. I blamed it for everything that went wrong with my life, including the disappearance of my parents. I imagined that they were as bored by it as I was: brought up in an endless procession of hospital waiting rooms and a faint smell of disinfectant.

When I discovered at the age of sixteen that Byron could be a romantic hero and rake, and yet be regarded as a 'cripple' by the critics and the public, it gave me a surge of fellow feeling with him – driven into exile, as he was, by pious debtors and moralists.

We live in a similar moralistic age now. And like all periods of suffocating morality, we are convinced that morals and ethics are loosening everywhere we look. In Byron's day, sex before marriage was frowned on – for women at least – but afterwards, there was at least some respect for extra-marital passion. Now look at us – rigidly controlled serial monogamy until your wedding, then anything outside your padlocked front door is condemned as sleazy, undignified, immoral and damaging to the children.

So if my mother disappeared off to Paris for passion, good luck to her. She might have written, but what's most important? You've got to live. And she's provided me with a built-in excuse for my many failings ever since. Most mothers couldn't say that.

But most important, I was fascinated by the fact that James' old house – not that it was his at that stage – had that small, though forgotten, place in romantic history. Byron himself had visited after getting back from his grand tour to the East in 1811, stealing the heart of one of James' ancestors and leaving behind a poem to her. It was a major reason for studying him as a student.

As an adolescent I was steeped in Byron. I imagined myself with my own collection of Venetian whores, telling tall tales with the Shelleys far into the night, or deflowering the elfin fireball, Lady Caroline Lamb. I had always liked that epithet 'elfin' – though there's more than a whiff of child abuse about it when it's used in that context. I like its hint of knowing innocence, of the unworldly, and I've found myself attracted to the 'elfin' in all its forms ever since. But I've had my own Caroline Lambs, too. You often run across them in art dealing rooms, with their hair and their ambition. I've had books, bottles – even once a baked haddock – flung at me in my time. And I suppose, if I'm honest, it was the elfin in James that attracted me to him when we first met.

I knew James longer than almost anybody, since the day when his serious eyes first regarded me across the playground. He had a grave kind of innocence which I felt – wrongly I can see now – that I could mould into a follower of mine, a collector of my jokes and tall tales and an admirer of my ten-year-old wit. I don't remember how we became friends, but soon his father was dashing us off to watch *You Only Live Twice* or *Oliver!*, before catching a plane to a business meeting in Paris or Amsterdam. The connection with Paris was enough for me. For all I knew, my mother was still wandering along the Champs-Elysées with her shopping bags.

We were recognizably English when we first met, with our little upper lips stiff, and our atheistic middle class encyclopaedias of bible stories 'told to children' and our Blue Peter-inspired willingness to build a new world out of silver paper and sticky-backed plastic. But there was also something different about him. He was a little bit vague, fey even, with his brown eyes staring into the middle distance – not quite part of the world, with his faint odour of stale underwear.

By the time I discovered that my mother had married a cattle-rancher and gone to live in Argentina, and my father had gone to the lengths of dying to wriggle out of responsibility for me, I knew James' family better than I did my own. By then James had lost his father, too, abandoning himself to his secretary one delightful spring morning when the taste of coffee had undermined his defences. That brought us together, too, though we never talked about it. You didn't, did you?

In later years it was our common inability to make a relationship last longer than five and a half months. Mine exploded in jealousy and betrayal – I swapped the roles each time, just to ring the changes; his just petered out in confusion and frustration and the sound of front doors banging shut in the dark. I was constantly enraged by my last relationship, while James was hoarding old lipsticks as keepsakes and dreaming of what might have been.

The first time I ever heard of Oberon House was also my first defined memory of him. 'My family has a big house, too,' he told us all in the playground. He wasn't usually as forthcoming, and you could see he immediately regretted it. We had been boasting about the respective size of our parents' mortgages, in the way ten-year-olds do, recycling the overheard tittle-tattle from their parents' gossip. I remember that we had ignored James until then. He was one of our quiet followers in those days, as we stood around the tarmac in break time after downing our regulation third of a pint of milk – in those days before Mrs Thatcher became Secretary of State for Education – and hanging around the ivy-covered wall of the old church next door.

'Oh yes, so where is this house then?'

'I don't know exactly, but ...' Another major tactical mistake.

'What! You don't know? Whose is it then? Your Dad's?'

'No, it's empty, but ...' We shared our derision at the whole idea and went happily home that evening to our semi-detached suburbs, with apple blossom on the pavements, and parents tearing the skin from each other's faces in blazing row after blazing row in the kitchens.

Somehow the mere existence of Oberon House, crumbling away under the care of some faceless solicitor, seemed to give James a sense of ownership. Connected with his grandfather's stories – the long-flannelled tennis parties, the arrival of the first farting petrol-smoking motor, the clip-clop to church – it provided a kind of backbone to James' life, and through it, eventually, to mine. The sense of tragedy seemed to give him meaning, too – not just for the house, but the sad fate of the village as well. He wove it together with his own disappointments to give him a studied air of satisfactory melancholy.

But then James was also having a long random rococo kind of career. He went from filing clerk to library assistant to sales assistant to leaflet deliverer to law student to journalism student to charity volunteer to night-watchman to simple collector of 20p second-hand books – which covered every wall of his flat – every one of them unread. He spent a number of years on the dole, before drifting into reviewing films for giveaway magazines aimed at the Australian market in London. The rest of us flocked to the heated embrace of the City of London or even Wall Street, and the gargantuan accountancy firms that currently run the world, force-feeding ourselves with bizarre rules and popping out as qualified accountants wearing shirts with exactly the regulation width between the stripes.

While I was covering up for my slight limp by being as outrageous as I could, James was dreaming his way through his life, until that letter arrived and changed everything. His father was abroad, his mother concerned with other things and he had no brothers and sisters. He never seemed to care that he was almost alone, apart from a few distant relatives – and old Harry in Pinner. He never seemed to feel furious and abandoned, as I know I did. He never really seemed to care about his unusual appearance – thin and elongated like a dried-out pixie, which used to attract unflattering comparisons to characters in *Star Trek* – any more than he used to care about the way I walked. He just somnambulated through it all, with me and our small circle of friends.

'Get yourself a girlfriend, for God's sake!' we would tell him. 'You need someone to take you in hand. Get you up to date. Stop you listening to those terrible Irving Berlin records.'

'I don't think girlfriends and me mix very well,' he'd say. 'Caroline didn't like my taste in music much, so she just left. Nor did Frances, come to think of it.'

I think James was a challenging project for them. Some of them even claimed to like the music of the 1930s musicals that he played the whole time. Some of them even sang along to 'My Funny Valentine', which he whistled the entire time, driving most people around him to abstraction. But they never lasted long. There was something lost about him that repelled almost as soon as it attracted. He was such an anachronism. Something inside him seemed to imagine that the past was as real as the present, where his ancestors and relatives – long dead – crowded in on him. As if part of him still suspected that the great dances at Dorchester House included him, or the gaslights flickering across Hyde Park, and carriages at midnight were still among his most pressing concerns, or that the world had not actually changed completely. Oberon House was part of this continuing dream, and it had a sense of mystery. Not just that, but a good old-fashioned copper-bottomed mystery, too. It was just one of the stories that James and his family used to tell, but for me it was always the over-riding one. And, as I got older, it assumed an increasing hold over my mind. It was the poem.

If Byron really had left a poem behind him somewhere in the house, it hadn't come to light for generations. I think the Weston family assumed it was somewhere among their family papers, if it existed at all – and if it was ever dragged out it would at least prove the Byron connection. But for me, it represented the chance of academic glory. It would belong to the period when Byron had been first writing *Childe Harold*, before the day he said he suddenly 'woke up famous'. If it was a poem of any length, I could use it to re-interpret his development as a writer. I even had the thesis – all I needed was the evidence of the poem to prove it. I could even write a book about it, which would make those sneering art auctioneers behave with a little bit more respect. When I was starting out as a research student, I imagined the poem coming to light and making me famous. In later years, trying to establish myself in the art hire business – I left academia after a little trouble involving a student – I imagined it adding a kind of academic glow to what was basically a white van delivering pictures to pinstriped idiots who didn't appreciate them. Either way, I wanted it.

But whatever my reasons for wanting the poem, it was missing and that was mysterious in itself. If the verses were found, would they reveal hidden byways of the Weston family – or might they, in fact, set out in black and white the truth about Byron's growing incestuous passion for his sister? I still wanted to be the one to unveil it to the world.

But time plays tricks. And when it isn't playing tricks, it changes things. Look what it did to the village of Oberon. It was still picturesque, no doubt, rather like those forgotten villages around Heathrow between the motorways, which were kept in aspic from the moment the airport arrived so unexpectedly at the end of the war. There was still a whiff of 1930s suburban respectability. But the insistent carriageways speeding the traffic and buses to Gatwick had already obliterated one of the pubs, and a good chunk of the houses. The roar of the traffic echoed round the remaining buildings, shaking the black timbers for most of the daylight hours.

They echoed right up to the edge of the churchyard, and among the bits and pieces sacrificed to progress was the Domesday Oak. It happened to be in the way of an arterial route to the airport in 1966. Now the lorries carrying packaged food for flights to New York and San Francisco trundle along where it used to be. I make the journey quite often myself. I should probably feel guilty about this too.

But then time isn't what it seems. 'Look at it this way,' said James one day. 'I've met a few people – other people's grandparents, people like that – who were born in the nineteenth century. I was born in the middle of the twentieth, and we'll soon be living through the first few years of the twenty-first. And probably before I die I'll meet children who will live well into the twenty-second century. That's four centuries at just one remove. Pretty good for three score years and ten.'

'But it doesn't matter,' I said. 'It doesn't mean we live any longer or build better lives. It doesn't mean anybody else does. All these long memories, dynasties, traditions that seduce you, can drag you down in the end. You have to shake them off. You've got to throttle them off, or they drag you down with them. Anything else tastes of death. It's morbid. You'll end up like your granddad.'

But then suddenly, out of the blue, time hadn't changed the world as much as I thought. At the ripe old age of 35, and barely employed, James suddenly found himself the possessor – if not exactly the owner – of Oberon House.

III

'There never was a merry world since the fairies left off dancing, and the Parson left off conjuring ...'
JOHN SELDEN, *TABLE TALK*, 1689

Oberon, October 1912

IT WASN'T until some years after their death that Harry understood quite how much of an embarrassment his great-great-grandparents had been to the household. They were barely mentioned in front of the posse of servants, governesses and nursemaids who passed through the house during those early years of the twentieth century. Their names did not pass people's lips during those summer picnics by the river, with the wasps buzzing around the butter and the stiff backs of the men bent carefully over the hampers. Nobody spoke of them during those long, drawn-out Edwardian breakfasts, with the dishes along the wall – at least on the rare occasions that Harry was allowed in from the nursery, watching the silver knives and forks making short work of the kedgeree and scrambled egg.

They had been so important in his life, yet there was hardly anybody to talk to about them, and the number of people he could converse with seemed to narrow as he got older. The local tradesmen, who he had ragged with when they had come to build shelves or mend pipes, soon started to doff their caps to him in the village – even though they were three or four times older than he was. His circle of acquaintance was anyway pretty narrow 30 miles south of London. He had barely been up to the capital city – the imperial city as he kept being told – with its great port, heavy banks and thick burly policemen.

He could only remember going there twice. Once to watch open-mouthed as Gerald du Maurier romped through *Peter Pan* as Captain Hook, and once to gaze at the white lights along Harrods before Christmas. He had never been on a bus, still less the underground.

But somehow his great-great-grandparents had not been part of this genteel world. It wasn't so much their embarrassing longevity, though anything so flying-in-the-face-of-nature had to be slightly ill-mannered. Nor was it their strange mixture of generations and crumbling physical state – that was downright respectable, and the old house resembled them in that regard. No, it was their language and their behaviour.

'Don't you let them go teaching you their nasty habits,' one fastidious nanny had said to Harry, as he tripped down to their parlour early in the morning. And once, though only once, he had overheard a nursemaid complaining about his Grandpapa spitting on the floor. Mostly the servants avoided them, and seemed a little fearful of them – like an old flag blackened with age and history. They sensed something disturbing about them, just as they sometimes did the house. More than a few had left suddenly complaining of strange noises in the night, of midnight footsteps, and children weeping in the still, dark hours.

Harry sensed none of this. Nor had his Grandpapa ever seemed to generate enough energy to spit while Harry had been around. Though in retrospect he could see him swilling saliva around his mouth in preparation, before evidently forgetting what he was intending to do and swallowing it – or letting it drool out of his mouth like a lugubrious bloodhound.

It may have been a good thing that the old man had given up spitting, because it sometimes seemed as if it had been the bile that kept him going so long. It lent him an occasional moment of thoughtfulness that seemed to sit uneasily with the rest of his crumpled personality. Because Grandpapa still seemed to be able to hate with a great passion. The only thing was that he hated things that Harry had never heard of, and which, as he discovered later, had mostly gone the way of all flesh. He hated the machine-breakers. He hated the highwaymen. He hated the French. And most of all he hated the whole tribe of poets and writers of all descriptions, with their opium and their sideburns and their airs.

He was aware somehow that these things had gone, but they riled him all the more somehow for having escaped his reach. They remained alive in his mind, however long their bodies had mouldered away in vaults. He loved to be read to, but would accept only two things, both read to him every day by a bored servant – the *Book of Common Prayer*, including regular selections from the 'Thirty-Nine Articles', and the *Police Gazette*, the horrific tabloid packed with the most lurid and unpleasant murders of the day. To Grandpapa, the *Police Gazette* was one of the miracles of modern life – he had never used the electric telegraph, still less set foot on a tram car – but this confirmed his worst view of human nature with relish.

Most of all he reserved his bile for poets. Head-in-the clouds, ragamuffin adulterers, word-perverters, un-English reprobates, there never seemed to be a verb in the sentence. It had become family policy not to mention poets at all, for fear of these tirades. But Byron's name, on the rare occasions it came up – and in a life of at least 130 years, it was bound to come up now and again – reduced him to a white-faced rage.

There was one exception to his loathing, what Grandpapa referred to as *The Elegy*.

'The finest piece of doggerel in the English language,' he said. You could hear him whispering it quietly to himself sometimes on summer evenings, when the rest of the household was gathering for dinner and the sunlight was still glinting a little on the weeping willows by the pond. Gray's *Elegy* was beyond dispute. You could never so much as mention a possible rival – not that Harry knew many: his own favourite was the 'Charge of the Light Brigade'.

'Why don't you go and recite it to your grandparents,' his

exasperated mother would say as he began with his *half a league, half a league*. But Grandpapa would have none of it. After the first fusillade, the blood would filter down the ancient veins and reappear after a long absence in his face, and he would explode in a reedy voice, high and trembling.

'Wolfe!' he would interrupt, as if Tennyson's masterpiece was some kind of challenge. 'Wolfe!'

General Wolfe, he would explain for the umpteenth time, recited the *Elegy* to his soldiers before battle. 'Gentlemen,' he said as they waited in their boats below the fortifications, 'I would rather have written that poem than take Quebec.' Having reminded Harry of the story, there was then a silence that brooked no interruption. Maybe he would tell how the news came to his father at the village blacksmith, and how – some decades before his own birth – Wolfe's heroic sword was returned to his Surrey home. Maybe he would let the occasional tear slide down his ancient cheeks, with his wife beside him entirely oblivious to his ranting, like a Siamese twin, attached but separate from the mêlée.

But later, when the excitement had died down, you could tiptoe into the parlour in the evening, with the shadows from the last light of the day, and see that Grandmama was snoozing by the angle of her head. And there was Grandpapa's hunched figure dwarfed by his high-backed chair, whispering quietly to himself about the curfew, the lowing herd and the ploughman who homeward plods his weary way. 'And leaves the world to darkness and to me.'

And now the old man had left the world to darkness, taking his wife with him. He could hate, thought Harry, but he must have loved his wife – though he certainly never used the word. Had they loved all that time, and if they had – how awful it would have been to be separated by death. Could love last forever? In the early mornings in Oberon, with the old elm trees, it had always seemed to Harry that everything could last forever. Now, for the first time in his short life, he doubted it.

Just before death, they had been even more bird-like than before, as if they were hardly there. As if coming down into the room with a song and verve and noisy dash and not knowing they were there, you might not have noticed them at all. They seemed almost at one with their ancient chairs, and now they might as well have been. Harry ran down the end of the garden to the weeping willows beyond the old pond and sobbed.

There was so much he could have asked them; so much he wished he had known. It seemed unforgivable for them both to leave suddenly, with no hint or warning, though as he had been taken up to bed the night before, passing the old hunting prints and hartebeest on the stairs, he thought he could hear – in the faint echoing distance – the familiar night-time rhythm of Grandpapa and the *Elegy* tolling the knell of parting day. As his tears seeped into the dew and banged his fists in fury at the clump of grass, he cast his mind back to his last evening with them.

If only he'd known it was the last time he would see them alive. If only he had hugged them both and told them how much he loved them. Instead Grandmama had said: 'Now you run along, er ... Jack, James ... I mean Harry. Go have your tea and don't forget your lessons.'

'Lessons! It's teatime, silly!'

'Teatime, my . . . I do get juddled,' she said, her voice cracked and broken with 130 years of use. And he remembered when he had come to say goodnight to his Grandpapa, he had seemed more confused than usual, misty-eyed almost, his ancient waistcoat almost swamping him now.

'Goodnight, Grandpapa,' Harry had said and he hadn't responded.

'I said, goodnight Grandpapa!'

Still no response. His ancient ancestor seemed to look a little through him, staring out beyond the trees. And then ever so quietly, and gently, from the very back of the throat, he whispered: 'Emma!'

IV

'If thou'rt of air let grey mist fold thee,
If of earth let the swart mine hold thee,
If a Pixie, sink thy ring
If a Nixie seek thy spring.'
SIR WALTER SCOTT

Oberon, April 1998

WHEN Byron unexpectedly inherited Newstead Abbey, it included lines of grimy but disturbing portraits of his ancestors – murderous ancestors, some of them – but otherwise the place was crumbling around him. He ran up huge bills and invited his friends for strange all-night parties, dressed as monks, drinking wine out of skulls. For some months, he lived openly with one of his favourite servant girls.

It was different for James – he wasn't the type for orgies. But from the moment the letter arrived, his fascination about the idea of the house rapidly became obsession. I can still hear him maundering on about the wooden staircase or the crumbling roof. He saw himself less like Byron at Newstead and more like Charles Ryder at the gates of Brideshead, mumbling 'I have been here before.' He had done no such thing, and much as he wanted his genes to leap at the sight of their heritage, I don't believe he felt any spark of recognition as he drew up in his battered Metro at the gates to Oberon House.

As he peered through them for the first time, he told me he could see the lush vegetation had long since forced its way up through the tidy gravel, which must once have resounded to the echoes of the wheels of carriages crunching over it up to the front door. The brambles had entangled themselves over and over, leaning on each other to toss their arcs many times his height. I think it was the prospect of tidying it up that really excited him. As if this was the planet and it was his task to play God enough, slowly but surely, to put it right. Until it gleamed with self-satisfied precision like an old grandfather clock.

Though James had failed to hold down a conventional job for longer than two months, he was motivated by the idea of creating order from chaos. His flat swung between the two from week to week. His hair was usually uncombed, his shirts un-ironed, but he longed for a tidy life. He made lists of things to do and crossed them off one by one with great satisfaction. Here was a chance to tidy his life up completely, with one Herculean effort to put right a kind of exile. He was Moses returning all his mental baggage to the Promised Land.

'I'm coming home,' he said to himself, as the wafts of honeysuckle hit him from the driveway. I think he always hoped for that elusive whiff of homecoming or a distant beckoning sense of belonging – a sense that under these bushes his ancestors had deflowered the milkmaids. But, as I say, I don't believe there was any such thing.

Even so, it was an important moment for him, and he described it to me in detail. He went back to the car, shifted the old cheese-and-onion crisp packets, newspapers and half-read books into a special box he put aside to tidy away such detritus, and pulled out from underneath the letter from the London firm of solicitors which had brought him down. James had always known it was possible that the lease of the house would revert to the family, but he had always done the calculations incorrectly. He had expected it to happen in at least 10 years' time. It seemed hardly to be credited that nobody could think of a use for a country house near Gatwick Airport, and yet judging by the rampaging undergrowth, they hadn't for a good decade or so. He had also feared that the rumoured 'understanding' that the house would revert to his family was the kind of gentlemen's agreement from another age which had long since been driven out by the power of modern business.

Yet here it was, and he had shown me the letter.

'Dear Mr Weston,' it read:

I write on behalf of our clients London and County Property Market Ltd, to whom the lease on Oberon House, Oberon, Surrey, reverted on the death of Mr Hubert Fay. This is to inform you that their lease has only a few years left before it is due to expire and, because of the current state of the property market and the current divestment policies of our clients, they will be surrendering it. The property has therefore reverted to your father, Mr Jeremy Weston. Since he is abroad, he has asked us to contact you directly, since I understand that he intends you to arrange the sale of the property. Doubtless you will realize that the property, having been unoccupied for a considerable period – though it has been the subject of basic maintenance in accordance with the terms of the lease – is in need of some redecoration. Doubtless you will not be unaware that Oberon House, though in the possession of our clients in recent years, was formerly in the possession of your family. I would be grateful if you would contact us forthwith to arrange a visit.

Yours sincerely
Foster & Foster, Solicitors

We could hardly have been less unaware of Oberon House. I had never been there myself, but James had even driven past one sweltering afternoon with his father, at least a decade earlier, although they had got no further than the village pub. His father claimed he couldn't bear to see the old place dilapidated, though as far as I knew he had never seen it in any other state. It seemed impossible that he could ever rescue whatever remained of the bricks and mortar inside, yet – since the moment he had received the letter – James had been utterly determined that it should not be sold.

When I saw it properly myself, a week or so after James arrived as its owner, it was almost frightening to see how overwhelming nature could be, with its vast layers of suffocating leaves and its tangled undergrowth. I shook the gate and there was the rustle of an animal escaping deeper into the brush. Then suddenly, through the bushes, the clouds opened for a second and the morning sunshine shifted round, and there was a glint from the great line of windows which I knew from old photos were over the front door.

It was almost a welcome, I felt, and probably all I could expect in the circumstances. The house seemed suddenly more aware, and so did the greenery around it. As if an army of unseen eyes looked dispassionately at me with my hand on the rusty metal gate. I ignored it, but decided to get to the house the way I had been told – round the back.

If the building had been anywhere else but deep down a country lane, it would have been vandalized, squatted and probably burned. But I knew that this had not happened here: the solicitors had sent regular caretakers, none of whom had stayed long, but they had made sure the roof was repaired where necessary, and that the rooms were occasionally heated at the dead of winter and that the fabric remained watertight. Processions of carpenters and builders had made the trek over a couple of stiles to get in through the back door to keep the house up, or so James told me. Through him, I also knew that, although the downstairs had been used for most of the century as a kind of New Age adult education centre, nobody but caretakers had even attempted to get into the house by way of the drive for nearly 25 years or so.

So knowing that James had gone this way a week or so before, I picked my way over the stiles, through the cow pats and flies, and along a muddy track through the woods. And there it was at last, battered and picked at as if the old house had suffered a severe attack of eczema, almost held up by a rash of ivy, but standing nonetheless and familiar from all those lithographs and Edwardian photos that Harry used to keep in an old Harrods biscuit tin. It had a roof with enough pitching to make you seasick – enough to win a Civic Trust award. It had three tall and heavily patched chimneys, but the plasterwork between the windows seemed to be giving way and the old mediaeval slats were becoming visible underneath.

I had heard from James the night before. His lists of things to do had multiplied to the extent that he now had a list of lists, and had even tried to put together some semblance of accounts and a budget. But where was he going to find a quarter of a million pounds, he asked me? His father had already told him in no uncertain terms that the building must be sold as soon as possible. As far as I knew, his savings amounted to a £430 overdraft and his prospects were unappealing. I could imagine him standing in the porch in the evening light, barely noticing the breeze on his face, and dreaming his way through the options in his usual way. The options would be circling his head – even the small ones like whether to call Abigail and invite her down, whether to start ordering milk, whether to leave his small room in London.

'Bring your shears,' he had said to me on the phone.

'I don't have any shears.'

'It's a figure of speech. It means prepare for undergrowth.'

'Well, as long as there isn't undergrowth in the bedroom, I'm happy,' I said.

'There isn't a bedroom. But joking apart, can you bring a paintbrush?'

I had not welcomed the idea of having to paint. My sole aim of going down there, apart from catching sight of a place which was almost as much in my blood as it was in his, was to remind James about the Byron poem. I did also want to get out of London, do a bit of work somewhere quiet and contemplate the usual wreckage of my emotional life. I expected an amusing weekend. I thought it might stoke up my supply of disparaging anecdotes, which I could enjoy with others who knew James as well as I did. I wanted to be able to tell the 'real' story of the dream house. The great drive leading to a semi-detached. The garden gate that said 'Dunroamin'. The monstrous Victorian red brick monstrosity trying to blend in with the landscape.

I knew I would also spend my weekend lying on a patch of grass, watching the leaves sway over my head, and talking about relationships and why they didn't work, in the kind of wistful and nostalgic way that James used to inspire. We did have the late night conversations about women, and the people who had slipped through his fingers – and those who had been deliberately dropped from mine. But I wasn't able to tell any of those disparaging tales, though I had pictured myself in Hamptons or the Hungry Otter with a bottle of red, telling Jan or Patrick about them.

Still, Oberon House was smaller than some of my mental pictures. It seemed to be held together by exhausted pieces of crumbling mortar, with nothing left but the will that says to them 'hold on'. Yet there was something magnificent about it even so, as it glowed there in the evening light. The otherwise of the style, I found the three-foot path which had been cut for me by James and his strimmer, with the undergrowth towering over me on the other side like a jungle.

'Dr Weston, I presume,' I was preparing to say when I reached the house. But by then I had seen it and the great window above the old door glinting in the setting sun and I didn't know what to say except to start the equally magnificent calculation about what it would cost.

Ancient alcoves in the front looked gloomy somehow under their oak beams and, across the west side of the house, overwhelming the rusty drainpipes, the ivy had taken over completely. It swirled up the masonry like General Wolfe assaulting Quebec. Then above the main door, under its own pitched roof, were the glinting windows of the great light room that Harry had reminisced about so often – the one where the family had watched the sunset and sipped gin and tonics, and which had once charmed the greatest romantic poet of the age.

With the paints in hand, I struggled through the back door, which was badly warped and needed all my strength to force open. Inside, the dust was horrendous and it lay in mounds over the kitchen. A long-impotent Aga stove slouched in the corner of the room. A mouse skittered away. My footsteps showed in the linoleum floor as I walked through the room, through the green painted door with a great black metal hook on the back, and into the body of the house.

The dustsheets were everywhere, like great Antarctic mountains still and shivery to the touch, but the dust was less all-pervasive. There were one or two minor chandeliers done up in bags, and even a few pictures on the walls – most of them covered in the same way, as if they had been censored by some long-forgotten governess. The few that remained uncovered were mainly hunting scenes: wild English parsons gallivanting over hedgerows, big red-cheeked magistrates cavorting around fireplaces with great flagons of beer in their hands, or the traditional Edwardian 'Stag at Bay'. And, over the stairs, hung all that remained of the head of a hartebeest.

I pushed open the door of the main room, and caught the faint whiff of the atmosphere of parties in days gone by. Here held the moment of a hunt outside, champing at the bit, the copper horn above the fireplace, and the ladies wandering along with poetry books in their hand. Because although this was a long low-slung English manor house in the old style, full of whooping and dead animals, I kept remembering it was a house of some poetic pretensions. I pulled back the shutters and the fitful sunshine shot in like a ray gun, with ancient dust floating in the light like an armada of midges.

In the doorway was pinned a pencilled note, just readable: 'Mr Brice,' it said peremptorily – who was he? 'Please see to the broken window in the Smoking Room. The rain is coming in. Also you have not given me details of your account for January.'

It was dated 16 March 1963, more than a quarter century earlier. A shiver went down my spine. I couldn't read the signature. So the house had not been entirely neglected, just unloved. But now there was James, with his far-away look and his tapes of Fred Astaire.

It was hard to know where to start when almost everything you touched in the old house crumbled to dust. James had put up a camp bed in one of the bedrooms and began to make a list of things to do and neighbours to contact. There was a knock on the door which heralded Mrs Jenkins. She turned out to be the local busy-body, who ran the local post office in Oberon village – I discovered later that she read the back of all the postcards which went through her hands.

Then there was a visit from a stiff couple who lived nearby, who seemed to think we might like to borrow their garden shears, which they waved menacingly in the doorway. Both fumed silently when the other spoke, and they seemed to have been enjoying a healthy argument as they came up the path.

'Oh, yes, I'm sure you'd like to buy our raffle ticket, wouldn't you,' said Mrs Baldwin, just as they turned to go. James fumbled in his pocket. 'It's just the usual local do.'

She wrote in his name and address and handed it over, putting the £1 coin firmly in a very tiny purse. James looked at the prize list.

'But it's for the Conservative Party,' said James.

'Yes, of course,' she said, looking a bit bemused.

After they had gone, I looked back at the crumbling house.

'My God, James. You'll never pay for this, will you?' I exclaimed encouragingly as I saw him come round the back of the house in paint-bespattered overalls.

'You sound like my mother. In fact you sound like everybody.'

I hate it when people say things like that to me. I go to enormous lengths not to sound like everybody. But as he showed me the old place, as it juddered when our feet banged the creaking staircase, as the small clouds of dust rose from the ancient linoleum, I was pretty sure that everybody was right. It seemed such a long way from the old stories I had heard. Of the Edwardian cook who had gone mad, and raced naked across the rose garden, pursued by the gardener with a large cloak. Of the occasional masked parties almost two centuries earlier, and all the little details about hunting tales, nurseries, enormous wardrobes and beauty spots.

And furthest away of all seemed those stories of the heady

and romantic summer between phases of the Napoleonic War – as the family followed the contradictory rumours of the progress of Sir Arthur Wellesley in Spain – when the greatest poet in the land had spent a month there in secret love.

'So this is the scene of the Byron seduction,' I said, shifting the conversation over to the missing poem.

'That's right. You remembered.'

'I remembered a bit. Remind me.'

'Oh, I must have told you before. Byron caught sight of the daughter of the house at a ball at Holland House in London, tracked her down and installed himself here for the summer to wage war on her virginity. I think there was some kind of relation who knew Byron's lawyer. I don't know when it was exactly, but I imagine it in late summer, with the cattle wandering idly by, and the two of them wandering around the nearby woods – in those freer days before chaperones. There's a story that he would gobble down candles to prove his love for her at the height of dinner, and she'd sort of laugh and shoo him away.'

'Did he get her in the end?' I asked. 'Did he penetrate that English veneer and roll up those corsets under the Domesday Oak?'

'Do you mind! You're talking about one of my relatives.'

Actually, history never related the answer, nor what became of the girl and whether she died an old maid, or a plump disreputable figure, clutching the picture of Byron to her bosom. All it said was that the romance hadn't worked out – it never even reached his biographies and within months he was trapped in the spiral that took him into the arms of Caroline Lamb, his own sister Augusta and into a disastrous marriage.

'What about the poem then?' I asked. 'Isn't it time we found it?'

'I suppose. It's time for rather a lot of things.' He looked sadly at the crumbling plaster ceiling above us.

Another low-flying airliner bound for Gatwick passed over the house with a roar, but as far as I was concerned it was the poem that counted, no matter how sad the linoleum turning up at the edges, or the dusty sheets dragged over every chair and picture. Though the heavy leaden black-painted drain pipes were hanging hopelessly off the walls outside the windows, I had to keep my mind on my key objective. I saw that, behind the shutters, there were pieces of unkempt ivy and clematis, which threatened to blot out the sky completely – blotting out at the same time whatever tenuous connection with reality still remained and plunging the old building completely into its dream world.

James was still in his own dream world.

'You know, I can almost feel my genes tingling, walking through here,' he said.

'Are you sure it's not hay fever?' James sneezed.

'No, this is where I belong. It's kind of seeping up through my legs as if I've drunk too much. I've never really belonged anywhere before. Certainly not in Earl's Court. No, I owe something to this place. However long it takes, I'm going to do my duty by it. I'm going to carpet it, clean it, and if it takes me the rest of my life, I'm going to bring it back to its former glory.'

'Then sell it,' I said, unused to self-dramatisation from James. At this point, a stairboard broke under him and he grasped the banisters, smacking his palms together to knock off the dust.

'Why does this always happen?' he said, with a characteristic note of self-pity, and pushed open the first bedroom door.

It was dark inside and old crates were piled right up to the ceilings, with cobwebs falling from them like a tropical rainforest. The remains of moth-eaten clothes seemed to creep between the boxes like cement between bricks, spreading like surf across the strand. Papers were also sweeping in layers across the floor.

'Maybe that poem's here somewhere still,' I said. 'Then you might not have to sell it. It would fetch a pile from an American university.'

James stopped still for a moment. 'I couldn't sell Emma's poem, though, could I?'

'Emma? Who's Emma?'

Emma was Byron's lover, of course. I should have remembered, just as I remembered the main problem about this mythical verse. Nobody has ever seen it. In a family that remembered too much and felt too little, there was no anecdote about elderly aunts and uncles dragging it out of cupboards for their perusal, no picture of it being carefully unfolded from the dusty pages of the family bible. In fact, nobody had remembered meeting anybody who remembered seeing it.

'Maybe it was buried with her,' I said. James still said nothing, but fingered the dusty papers on the sideboard thoughtfully.

The evening was drawing in, and we wandered down to the George & Dragon, where he told me about Abigail – how he would paint the bedroom before she came down to see it. How he would rig up a proper stove to cook her dinner. Abigail with the flat chest and dull, flat approach to life. I made snorting noises about his girlfriend.

'Oh I don't know. I just don't seem to be able to inspire her,' he said. 'What's the matter with me?'

'I don't think she's the kind that inspires easily.'

'Nonsense. It's always the same,' said James, reassuringly himself.

I stayed up smoking on my makeshift camp bed in the hallway of the old house, then I blew out the candle and listened to the strange noises and creaks from the ancient wood contracting in the cool air. I dreamed fitfully of Abigail and James, and about my daily routine foisting lithographs on to pompous charlatans for their fake wood-lined offices, until I drifted off completely. Then I dreamed about it all again.

I don't know if it was an hour that I slept for – it could have been more – but suddenly I was awakened by a faint noise that could not have been a creaking building, however ancient. In fact it sounded like weeping.

In a second I was wide-awake and searching for my lighter. It wasn't just weeping. It was the thin, hopeless weeping of a child, at dead of night. And it was a chilly, chilling sound.

There was definitely no child in the house, I knew that, and as I searched my memory about whether I had somehow forgotten one, I felt the hair on the back of my neck tingle. At last, after an agony of searching, I found the lighter, lit the candle and listened. It felt like five minutes but was probably much less. Nothing. I searched for the torch, flashed it around the staircase and into the old kitchen, then hurried back to bed.

As I lay there with the candlelight flickering on the rafters and cobwebs, I tried to make sense of what I had heard. Then it struck me that I had heard something else as well as a weeping, despairing infant. It was on a different frequency, so I hadn't immediately recognized it. I had heard, ever so faintly, a distant, cajoling, desperate adult voice calling back – searching even. Though I could barely remember my own mother, I knew what it was. It may not have been real. It may not even have been human, but somewhere in the old floorboards of the house, I had heard a mother's voice.

V

'She is the fairies' midwife, and she comes
In shape no bigger than an agate-stone
On the forefinger of an alderman,
Drawn with a team of little atomies
Athwart men's noses as they lie asleep.'
WILLIAM SHAKESPEARE, *ROMEO AND JULIET*

Threadneedle Street, London, September 1912

WITH every passing year, the gold settled a tiny bit further into the stone floor of the vault of the Bank of England. It sat there for decades – the solid wealth of many nations – barely even glinting, the great solid anchor of the British Empire. Golden ingots melted down from the treasure brought from the New World by the Conquistadors, turned into holy icons by the goldsmiths of Europe, plundered by Sir Francis Drake, now cornerstones of the heavy Edwardian buildings of the City of London. And if you drew a line diagonally up from the gold in its blue metal cages, just 100 yards or so away, were the offices of Granite & Partners, investment bankers.

Inside, up the wood-panelled staircase to his office, walked John Weston, Harry's father, his mind filled with historic stories from the Italian Renaissance. It was 10.16 am according to the railway station clock, with its Roman numerals, which hung in the foyer of their Threadneedle Street offices. The office black cat shot up the stairs ahead of him, and as he breathed in the familiar banking smell of ink and cigar smoke, Mr Weston shrank inwardly to see how late he was. Over an hour. He should be setting an example.

'Family business, I'm afraid,' he said to his chief clerk as he removed his top hat, and brushed the dust and horse dung from his shoes and trousers. 'Has the telegram arrived from Cincinnati yet?'

'It has, sir, and it's on your desk. I hope your family is well – no illness I hope.' The chief clerk of Granite & Partners had a morbid and fearful fascination with disease, and collected Victorian medical dictionaries with disturbing photographs, kept shut away in his home in Penge.

'No, no, all well, I'm glad to say,' said John Weston, noticing only a moment's regret that he was denying his great-grandparents. But if he was honest, their bizarre longevity had embarrassed him more than anybody. They were an uncomfortable reminder of his family origins. Although it was perfectly acceptable for him to have yeomen farmer forebears, who had sworn and hunted their way through the eighteenth century, it was another matter perhaps to have them still in the house, liable to leap out – or so he feared – like unquiet ghosts to point the finger. Or spit in the soup, heavens!

But John was a thoughtful man, an admirer of Mr Asquith's and a reader of avant garde novels by Mr Joseph Conrad, and he realized the stupidity – not to mention the indignity – of his embarrassment. But he was embarrassed nonetheless. Outside the window in three short blasts, a taxi horn blared like a farmyard animal greeting the dawn. He looked out into the street, and caught a glimpse of the bag lady on the steps of the Bank of England, to whom he had slipped a shilling on the way to work that morning. She seemed to be counting her money.

Back in Oberon at the same time, Harry was dreaming unwillingly through his morning lessons. A cockerel had been crowing regularly all morning, and it dragged him back to consciousness each time, together with the memory of the empty room and the coffins arriving. He had heard his mother giving instructions to the servants. 'They're laid out in the Blue Room upstairs, so I want no noise down that corridor.'

As soon as he could escape after lunch, he ran down the lawn and lay under the old willow tree staring at the sky. He could see the leaves weeping above him, with the sky glinting through the lugubrious branches, and could feel the cold spiky grass against his cheek. Why hadn't he said more to them the night before? Why didn't they tell him somehow that they were never going to see him again? It seemed such an abrupt departure – rude almost. So unfair.

He had only the haziest idea of heaven or life after death. From the descriptions he had heard, it sounded like a cross between his expensive private school and matins at Oberon Parish Church – all praise and prefects with wings. It could have been calculated to annoy his Grandpapa. It seemed such a communal affair. Dull and matey and completely without privacy. Completely un-English, in fact.

He thought of his grandparents arriving at the Pearly Gates with their bags packed, thrust into this mêlée of singing, and his heart ached for them. Or worse, if there was no heaven and no God and evolution was right, as his brother Gerald had often told him, then they were completely alone and dark and lost. How could God encourage them to love each other and get married and live happily with each other, only to tear them apart when they were used to nothing else? Love was such a fraud. Everlasting love just wasn't everlasting, was it?

Or could love last forever? He knew sometimes it didn't last very long. His parents' maid Milly had loved the telegraph boy from the village for about two months, before she transferred her affections to the chauffeur. And then there was Mr and Mrs Ford in Oberon, the local grocers – he'd had gone off with a girl called Mildred. Or so he'd heard when listening into the conversation downstairs.

'Only 16, she was,' Cook had said. 'Ruined. Ruined.' That love hadn't lasted either. It was a perplexing business.

Even at his age, Harry could see that a number of the regular couples who sat in front of them in church didn't like each other very much. Mrs Jeffrey had been red-faced with rage through the final hymn only last Sunday for some reason, which seemed to be connected to her husband's hacking cough. He would have liked to have asked someone about it, but he couldn't form the question into words. He didn't dare ask his parents about love, and asking Mr Phillips, his long stringy tutor, was obviously out of the question. Somehow he preferred to avoid the topic with his brothers too.

He lay on his side and looked at the horizon over the hedge through the grass. One stalk seemed almost to reach the clouds, and a bright red ant had just made it to the top. Then he turned his attention to the other mystery that weighed on him. Who was Emma? Even the thought upset him again, and he glanced back at the house to make sure there was nobody in the vicinity. There was only the postman arriving for the second time that day, and making his way towards the back of the house. Why was that name on his grandfather's lips before he died? It must have been important. For all Harry knew, it was his last word.

Harry stopped sobbing and thought carefully. He had never heard the name before. Had Emma been someone in the house? Was the maid called Emma? Harry had once possessed a toy dog he had christened Emma. It had accompanied him everywhere until one ear had got almost rubbed away. The local vicar, an amateur water-colourist, had even attempted to lend it dignity in a frame and the picture still hung in the nursery, specially touched up by the artist to make it clear he was not attempting to paint a real dog. But no, it couldn't be that Emma.

Emma Hamilton, Nelson's beloved, Harry had heard of and knew that his Grandpapa had disapproved of her for sapping the resolution of the great hero. And he wondered also if it might be a kind of title like 'Nurse' or 'Governess'; was Emma the name you called someone you loved so much that you spoke their names – like both his grandfather and the hero of Trafalgar – on their deathbed?

It hadn't been until after the funeral was over that Harry dared ask what Emma meant. Something had prevented him doing so before, as if it had been a special intimacy between him and his beloved Grandpapa. As if the farewell understanding words he wished they had given him before shuffling off were somehow contained in that one name. If only he could understand what the name meant. But unless he knew that, it was hard to unravel a meaning specifically aimed at him.

He was aware that the answer might well lie in the category of something he was considered too young to know – and there was already a long list of those, like the precise 'trouble' that their maid Rose had got into, and what his father had meant when he described Lloyd George as 'a bit of a goat'. It was a mystery, and if Harry was honest, he knew the word had not actually been addressed to him. He felt in his heart of hearts that his grandfather had been in a different world already when he said it. Much as it hurt, Emma was not a message. But it was a clue to something nonetheless.

'Who is Emma?' he asked his mother as they walked, in black crepe, back from church after the service, with both coffins in dark wood alone next to the altar. Dust to dust.

'Emma who, dear?'

'I don't know. Emma someone. Grandpapa said "Emma".'

'Said Emma what? Sorry, dear, I don't understand the question. Oh goodness, there's one of those terrible reporter chaps who were at the church. Don't look at them, Harry, it only encourages.'

The word had already gone out that an elderly couple of unprecedented age had passed away. Consequently, two dour-looking men in tight-fitting jackets, bowler hats and obsequious manners had slipped in at the back of the church during the service. They had been doing rather more than the traditional noting of names after the service. The sunlight was filtering through the trees, and the cows were contemplating the earth. In those days before tarmac on all but the biggest roads, Harry was scuffing his shoes in the dust. He kicked along a small stone in the manner of a Bolton Wanderer at Crystal Palace. His nanny, some way behind, looked at him disapprovingly.

'Stop that!' said Gerald, his grown-up brother, down with Edward from their London digs. 'You're supposed to look sombre. People expect it.'

He patted Harry on the back with an officious grin, jingling the change in his pockets. Harry walked back in step. He could see the reporter, his body language as servile as he could make it, waylaying members of the family. His mother climbed up into the carriage.

'Old? No, I don't know exactly how old. Look, this isn't a very good time at the moment. Would you mind?' Gerald was telling the reporter. As Harry climbed up next to his mother, he could see his other brother Edward walking on by himself, his tears rolling unrestrained down his face. Harry shivered with embarrassment and looked away.

'Mother, are you allowed to cry at funerals?' asked Harry in a whisper, wondering where his handkerchief was. He had made strenuous efforts not to do so, and with success, even when they watched the coffins disappearing into the ground.

'Of course you are, dear,' she said. 'But most people prefer not to put their feelings on show. It can be a little vulgar to display everything in public. But your brother is upset. He loved your grandparents very much.'

'I did too,' said Harry.

'I know dear. I think you're being very brave. Very brave indeed.'

'But do you think people will wonder if I never did love them because I didn't cry?' The tears seemed to have let up their pressure on his eyeballs and Harry was getting worried that he was being hard-hearted. He was aware of the fishmonger's boy staring at him from the side of the road.

'I certainly don't. They know you prefer to keep your feelings private. It is best to keep them private, you know. The other people don't talk about you and it helps you keep up standards. You can't run the country or command a battleship if you're in tears all the time, can you? It isn't very manly.'

'Won't Edward be able to command a battleship then?' Harry knew Edward's ambition was precisely that.

'No, Edward is a brave young man. He's just different. You're both brave. Very brave indeed. Now what did I do with my smelling salts? Have you seen them? Edward? Oh, he's not here ...'

Actually, Edward wasn't sure what he wanted to do, but vaguely dreamed of going to sea. He wanted heady adventures plundering the Spanish Main with Drake, or tracking the North West Passage with Franklin, though preferably coming back alive. He had followed the progress of Scott's Antarctic expedition with enormous interest. His face had begun to show the first hints of red-blooded bloating that would become apparent in early adulthood. His allowance – such as it was – didn't allow him anything much more adventurous than music halls and swooning over the latest actresses. While his brother loved to shoot, Edward wanted to hunt – not so much to kill the foxes – but to appear in his pink-coated finery and leap hedges. The rest of the time, he spent goading Gerald. And Gerald was astonishingly goadable.

Some hours later, with his father turning over a new blotter in the City of London, Harry wandered through the stables and out through the cucumber frames. There seemed to be a heavy damp in the air now that evening was arriving. He wanted to be alone, but underneath the oak tree by the gate to the woods, he found Edward – large and bluff somehow even in back view, but quiet. He was puffing on a small pipe and staring across the field on the other side of the track. It was getting cold, and a haze was rising up on the other side of the field like a mist.

'It's the end of an era, you know. Nothing will ever be the same,' said Edward half to himself, without looking up.

Harry loved his brother, who seemed to fill whichever canvas he occupied at the time with his echoing laugh and big leather boots. He stood next to him and followed his gaze across the fields, where brown and white cows had chewed calmly before being led off to the barn for the evening milking. A family of rabbits were in the distance, playing between the corn and the woods. Apples bulged on the trees around them. The whole world seemed to be pregnant with the future. He didn't know what to reply.

'Edward, do you know who Emma is?'

'No,' said Edward absent-mindedly. 'I don't think I know anyone called Emma, except perhaps this girl I knew at Browns Hotel in London. But I don't think you'd know her. Or Emma Lushington, of course.

'Grandpapa said her name.'

'Did he?' Then he came to life suddenly. 'Did he, by George! I don't suppose he'd know the girl in London either, but you don't think he meant great-great – lots of great aunts Emma do you?'

'I don't know. I've never heard of her.'

'You know, our long forgotten ancestor who disappeared? We were never allowed to talk about it to them, though I was never quite sure if they remembered – or even if the story was just made up. Yes, Emma disappeared. She was the one who loved Byron.'

'Who's Byron?'

'Byron? You know Byron. Childe Harold to the dark tower came. Byron the great lover. Don't tell anyone about this conversation, incidentally, or I will get into trouble.'

'Why?'

'Well. I don't think I'm supposed to talk about lovers to ten-year-olds. Anyway, Emma was Grandpapa's sister – if she really existed. How strange that he should suddenly mention her. What did he say?'

'Just her name.'

Harry told him about his last conversation with his grandparents, and how distracted they had been the day before they died, and the single lonely, distant memory expressed in a simple word. When they had finished talking, the day was a little darker and the evening clouds were mingling in pink over Harvest Hill. A few old men trudged by with baskets of vegetables under their arms. To Harry, it wasn't just the dusk of his childhood. Sitting there under the old oak with Edward as he reminisced – barely aware of where he was or that Harry sat beside him – it was also, it seemed to him, the dawn of adult life. Edward's face was reflected in the light of the dying sun, as they chatted on about growing up, his future and of Emma, the ancestor who mysteriously disappeared.

It was a sad but magical moment. Harry never forgot it. Long after Edward had been killed at the battle of Loos, he remembered it as if it carried the last of the old world with it – the world he had lost forever when his grandparents died.

VI

'But, spite of all the criticizing elves,
Those who would make us feel, must feel themselves...'
CHARLES CHURCHILL, *THE ROSCIAD*, 1761

Oberon, May 1998

THERE was a musty smell the next morning, and a letter. And suddenly in a flash, came back the memory of the night before. For some reason it was the faint mother's voice that echoed through my head, rather than the child I knew I had heard. The child was part of some kind of echo from the past, but the mother sounded real.

As I considered it in the cold light of day, I could see the letter through the door and down the corridor from my hard mattress and sleeping bag on the floor. As I stared towards it, half asleep, a mouse shot across my line of vision. Half an hour or so later, as I wandered through the house in my boxer shorts looking for an adequate bathroom, I glanced at it. It had a London postmark.

'Did you hear anything last night?' I asked James in a nonchalant way later.

'Like crying or something.'

'Crying? No. What do you mean?'

'I thought I heard someone crying, that's all.'

James made a dismissive kind of gesture. 'Oh, people have

always heard things here. I wouldn't worry. It's the floorboards creaking or something. Every floorboard here has a story to tell. Here, read this.' He handed me the opened letter. I had been tempted to open it myself, but couldn't think of an excuse. It was from his erstwhile girlfriend Abigail.

'Dear James,' it read:

Congratulations on getting into the house and I'm sorry I couldn't be there with you. Now that you've got a home, it seemed like a good moment to say this. I don't think we're going anywhere. I had high hopes of you – and of course I still do as a wonderful friend – but you've made so little effort and I've been wondering all this time whether I was having any impact on you at all. So I think this is best. It's probably more painful for me that it is for you, but there it is.

Love, Abi

James looked green and was staring out across the woods. I wanted say good riddance, but stopped myself.

'More painful for me than for you! Who does she think she is? Wackford Squeers?' James didn't reply or turn round.

'You know, I really wanted to carry someone over the threshold – anyone really,' said James slowly, still ignoring me. 'She's right of course – I haven't tried very hard. But I did kind of want to show her down here. For the first time in my life, I really feel I might belong somewhere.'

'You know, there are compensations to being single,' I said hopefully. 'You suddenly have choices and you don't have to worry about someone else – two careers, two people's health. There are other possibilities. It's not all bad.'

'It's true that Abi wouldn't have liked the dry rot here. Or the wet rot, come to that. In fact, it's hard to think of a kind of rot I don't have to contend with in this building.'

I knew how he was feeling. I knew he had imagined that Oberon House would be a new kind of life for him. I think it was almost erotic: he imagined wandering through its stately rooms, his wife at his side, his dog barking in the distance outside. Like those pompous landowners you see in front of their land in Gainsborough portraits, with their entailed wives.

He wanted something of that kind of magic in his own life, but somehow never dared look for it in his own generation. Sometimes it was staring him in the face – possibly even in the shape of Abigail. Though, if we're frank about it, Abigail wasn't really the magical kind. They had met in some god-awful office, where they had overlapped for about a week. I think it was a roller-towel laundry. He was trying to earn some cash; she was starting at the bottom in order to work her way up. Whenever I came across her, she seemed to be nagging him – and for some reason, my appearance would send her tight-lipped into the kitchen. Abigail didn't approve of me – and who could blame her: I didn't approve of myself. But this kind of Puritanism didn't endear her to me either. I took against the way she pulled her hair tight back into a bun. It seemed to symbolize her attitude to life.

Magic is sometimes a bit difficult to find when we're so cynical. But then cynicism is my problem. I didn't think James is cynical enough; that's his. He waited for life to summon up his hopes when the rest of us know perfectly well it just isn't going to happen. Looking back, the rift between us would never have opened up if it hadn't been for James' hunger for magic.

He moped about for the rest of the day, too limp to finish painting the front door or mending the broken window. Without his direction, I wandered with a scythe through the few paths hacked in the brambles and small trees that had once been the lawn and fell asleep in the sunshine under an ancient weeping willow at the bottom of the garden. I could see the new estate in the distance across the fields, and it depressed me. I dreamed fitfully of Byron and the poem, imagining I had found it in the kitchen drawer, along with all the old cutlery.

I woke up feeling damp and looking for the sun. I made my way back the path I had cut, with the brambles re-forging their manacles again across the gap, and I could see that James had a visitor.

'Jess,' said the visitor, shaking my hand with a suspicious grin. I could see a dog collar just behind a flowery kind of jumper, which looked as if a wild animal had vomited on it. He stared at me with a kind of knowing look, and had evidently decided that James and I were gay. 'Down for the weekend, then.'

Was this a question, I wondered? The answer seemed so obvious it hardly seemed worth asking.

'That's right,' I said, speaking very slowly and – I hoped – irritatingly. 'Down for the weekend.'

'I was just telling James about the local custom. First week of June. Put food out by the front door. For the Dance,' he said.

'What dance?'

'Little people, you know. Tradition round here.'

'You mean fairies? You don't think maybe Gatwick Airport rather cramps their style?'

'Well, I prefer to think of them as kind of nature spirits, myself. But I wouldn't worry if I were you. Nobody has seen them for about four centuries. They used to come out and dance together in early June, so they say. The locals would put food out to bring themselves luck. We call it the Dance.'

'Oh, you're from round here, are you?' I asked, suspecting a weak spot.

'Well I'm from Monmouth originally, in fact. Been here two years. Look after eight parishes.'

'Eight! Exhausting.'

'Ah well,' said Jess, although I wasn't sure whether this was in agreement with me. 'Come along to the festival,' he said, turning his attention back to James. 'We'd be delighted to see you.' He strode off with a backward wave and the air of a man with eight parishes on his conscience.

I noticed Abigail's letter in James' hand. 'You weren't going to ask Jess' advice about the letter were you? I don't think he likes girls.'

'Of course not,' he said, looking shifty. 'I was just tidying up.'

A few hours later, and there was more evidence of James'

hunger for magic. I caught him putting a bowl of milk outside the front door. Other people would put one out for hedgehogs perhaps – that's humanitarian, or at least sentimental. Only James could put it outside for the little people. I shook my head sadly and took another swig of whiskey.

'You're surely not using that cracked old plate, are you?' I said as he came back. 'Those wispy things I used to see in Arthur Rackham pictures of Kensington Gardens couldn't eat out of that hideous yellow.'

Mr and Mrs Baldwin were round again the next morning.

'Ah, the vicar's got you putting things outside for the Dance, has he?' said Mrs Baldwin, fiddling with her scarf. 'It's lovely to revive these old traditions. He's so modern, isn't he?'

'Modern? He's practically pagan!' spat her husband. 'We'll be sacrificing sheep next.'

'Oh nonsense,' she said, with a little giggle. 'I'm sure Jess doesn't know how to kill a sheep.'

I was less sure about this. They claimed to have visited to find out whether James needed any more coffee, or some other such lame excuse, but it was obviously that they just wanted another look. They seemed rather a forlorn sight, as they wandered back over the stile, lashed continuously together in mutual dislike.

'That's the reason I couldn't hack it with Abigail,' said James as we watched them bickering themselves into the distance. 'We'd have ended up like that.'

I know what he was thinking. I know he was mentally flicking through all his recent relationships with regret, and it annoyed me because I never allowed myself to do the same. Relationships break. It's like cups and glasses. They break. There's nothing you can do except get out the dustpan and brush and reach for another one. I can see why James was so wary of reaching for another one each time, but I didn't share it. I knew he would be thinking of Sara, with the green eyes and the strange taste in underwear. Or of Jackie with the sports car, who had thrown a blancmange at him when they had split up. Or Josie, who just cried and cried.

'It's a sort of family curse,' he said to me once. 'I want to put it right.'

And although I ridiculed the whole idea, I could see what he meant. You see, it wasn't just James' father who had disappeared off during his childhood. James' grandfather Harry had left his wife and children for a whirlwind romance in post-war Germany. Harry's father John had left in mysterious circumstances before the First World War. John's father Joseph had left his wife and children and gone to India in 1868 for fifteen years sending a regular remittance back home, before returning to inherit Oberon House. Joseph's father Edmund – the brother of Robert who had died in Bangalore – had been a real reprobate, and had joked about selling his wife at the local fair in the 1850s. But then, he was extremely drunk at the time. Edmund's father Jack had been a strange man, elfin in appearance according to the family miniatures, who would simply walk away from the house and farm for weeks on end. Sometimes he would be gone for years, returning with tales of mermaids, strange humped creatures, endless deserts and magicians, while his sturdy and exhausting wife ran the estate without him. It was even said that he had lived for years in a small village in the frontier lands of America.

But that was the limit to the curse. Jack's father, Old Jo Weston – Harry's Grandpapa – had never left his wife's side. In fact they were married for well over a century, sitting on high-backed chairs next to each other in the parlour of Oberon House as the years went by – a strange tale of extraordinary longevity which I can't say I believed.

'But even they died in the end,' said James miserably. 'Even they couldn't quite manage everlasting love.'

'What are you talking about? It isn't like that. It isn't even *about* that. We all just have to do the best we can. If you want everlasting love, you might as well forget it.'

'I know that. I just don't want to fall foul of the family curse, that's all. I don't think I could bear it.'

He seemed so helpless, staring again out at the hopeless profusion of plant life that had once been an Edwardian lawn.

I almost forgave him everything, but you can't wait around for these things to sort themselves out by magic. If love dies, then we have to live with that, or we'll die, too. And I've never known a love that didn't die soon after being exposed to the light. I carried on drinking whiskey until the sun melted into the Downs and the sound of ducks flying back to the pond echoed through the great window above the door, like angels roosting on the roof. It seemed such a long way from my office routine in London, the pile of post, the draft agreements and the lunch appointments in the traffic.

'It isn't really a curse, you know. It's just the way life is – it's difficult to be with one person for decades.'

'Of course I know,' said James dreamily. 'I just don't want to try it at all unless I *know* it will last forever. What's the use of love that dies when you die? It's like the death of a civilization.'

'Even civilizations die. I don't think I'd enjoy women if I didn't have a damn good idea the relationship would unravel relatively soon. Sometimes it's only real if it's going to end.'

'Oh, maybe, maybe,' he said staring out into the dark. I stared at the peeling, faded ceiling and felt generally giddy.

'You know I *have* heard something strange in the night,' he said suddenly, as if we had still been discussing it. 'I don't really know if I'm hearing it or not. But it's as if there's something unfinished about the house.'

Unfinished? Unstarted more like. I'd never seen anything more dilapidated.

'I lie there in the dark after blowing out the candle and wonder what the creaking is and where it's coming from – whether it's the roof or the staircase or the trees outside or just the memories locked into the bricks – and I wonder whether I'm hearing human voices. But even if I'm not, I can feel what they would be thinking. It's a search, isn't it? There's something about this house that's constantly being searched – or needs to be searched. There's some kind of secret here. Maybe that's what I'm looking for.'

'I wasn't aware you were looking for anything, except

everlasting love,' I said, emptying the whiskey bottle, and knowing that I was about to launch a major search myself. As far as I was concerned, deep in the night, after a bottle of whiskey, and despite all my childhood jealousy of James for having it in his past, Oberon House seemed to be the loneliest place in the world.

VII

'Who of late for cleanliness
Finds sixpence in her shoe...'
RICHARD CORBET, CHAPLAIN TO JAMES I,
THE FAIRIES FAREWELL

The City of London, September 1912

IN HIS wood-panelled office in the City, John Weston fingered the manila envelope with distaste. It was the unexpected resignation of one of his most trusted employees. Still thoughtful, he called for his hat and coat and stepped into the cacophony of the street, with the horseshit, the clouds of omnibus fumes and the noise of shouting traders. As he hailed a cab and instructed the driver to take him to Jermyn Street – he was a reliable creature of habit, and he always lunched with his mistress on a Wednesday – his son Harry was coming as close as anyone ever had to witnessing the Dance.

The City to Harry was clerks and stockers and jobbers, hurrying home in their bowler hats by soot-caked steam trains every evening, dreaming of bonds at four percent. For Harry it held up the world outside. The world inside had been supported by the ancient love of his grandparents; theirs was a kind of starlight that lit everything else. Yet he would never hear their infuriatingly familiar stories again. Never ask them what they felt and remembered. Never feel their uncritical love again. It all seemed such a terrible waste for them to have loved each other for a century and then to have gone.

This wasn't a matter he could ask his parents about, but there was somebody else. He may have smelled of manure, he may have had no recognizable place in the class system, but Harry trusted his advice: Josiah Goodbody.

Josiah had always been there for Harry – a bit like his grandparents. He was one of those spare and uncategorisable people you saw around the village, like the boy who sat by the road staring at the traffic for so long that people used him as a landmark. He remembered him being there from the earliest days of his life, but in all that time, he never remembered him doing any work – just sitting in his leather jerkin, under the oak tree at the end of the nearest field, occasionally muttering to himself.

It was a solitary kind of friendship. He knew his family would not approve of him talking to Josiah, so he never mentioned him, nor really asked himself what his station or purpose in life was. He could even have been a member of the household staff – one of those servants who was barely ever called upon to work, like the chauffeur. He could possibly have been a neighbouring farmer. He did almost nothing; sometimes he said even less – but sometimes he never stopped. But being in Josiah's gnarled and saturnine presence seemed to make Harry's heart beat a little faster and the sinews which held the world together seem to flex themselves.

Josiah did not speak like other people. He seemed to know the answers to obscure questions that nobody would ever think to ask – like the real reason hares dance in the moonlight. He also knew the most outrageous stories.

'Have you heard this jest, young man?' he would chuckle. 'Have you heard the tale which set the church bells a-jangle? About Old Mrs Jeffers and the broom handle? You haven't ...?' He would guffaw explosively with an evil leer.

'Tell me this, young man. Answer me this riddle. Why do crows gather on the topmost bows of the old oak? Come tell me that. Why do bulls go a-rutting on Sundays?'

Harry let it all waft over him, like sitting in the field and letting the full force of summer wash him full in the face. Josiah's conversation allowed no deference to class or youth, and although he barely understood him and found him occasionally frightening, he seemed to Harry almost part of the field system itself. Sometimes Josiah looked even older than his grandparents – and sometimes he seemed invisible until he emerged from the tree as if he had been there all along. His head seemed full of riddles and gossip and disorder, a kind of scatological Falstaff of the woods. There was almost nothing he was ashamed to say in front of the boy.

'Are you blushing now?' he challenged. 'And all because I let slip a word like rutting. Well, there's rutting all around you, I can tell you, even in the big house. Even in your big house.'

'I'll take you word for it, Mr Goodbody,' said Harry, who had no idea what rutting was.

'Josiah, Josiah. Now what about today, eh?' Then he would outline some jape on the villagers or people of the big house. The mud-splattering of Mrs Jenkins' washing on the line, the maddening of the calf down by the church, the further confusing of old Mrs Heffer, the spreading of dog shit by the back doorstep of Oberon House ready for when the housekeeper sat there for her morning smoke.

They were all pretty oafish stunts, of the kind a retarded teenager might dream up, but Harry laughed and laughed and wondered often how they came to pass – as they invariably did. Did Josiah carry them out himself, or did he bribe the local youths to carry them out for him? Or were they – in Harry's wilder fancies – carried out by a gang of desperadoes with Zapata moustaches hiding in the woods under Josiah's leadership? Or did he just know? The woods could conceal a whole prisonful of escaped convicts – a whole army, as indeed it had centuries before when the Vikings and Saxons squared up for the ancient and decisive battle of Ockley.

'Don't you ever do any work, Josiah?' Harry asked once. 'When do you get all these things done?'

'Work? Oh, I always work. Don't you see the flowers

opening in spring and the leaves mouldering away in winter?' And Harry laughed again at a job so onerous that the seasons did it for you.

He had not really expected to see Josiah as he walked sadly through the fields after lunch. But there he was in his jerkin and old hat, his yellow skin glowing as before and his patched old trousers as foetid as ever. He was apparently as jobless as usual, silent – as if he had picked up Harry's mood. 'You're a right one,' he said eventually, 'that you don't welcome your old Josiah. It's a special day today. Now why don't you hear my riddle: what's cool as a mouse, as cramped as a louse ...?'

'Josiah,' said Harry interrupting, a lump growing in his throat as he put the question into words. 'I have a riddle for you this time. Can you answer my riddle, because I really want to know the answer? Can you tell me if love lasts for ever?' With an immense effort of will, he managed to stop himself sobbing.

'Ah well, now you're asking,' said Josiah, looking serious for a moment, his creased eyes closing like a crocodile in the sunshine. 'Does love last for ever? That's a question. That's *the* question.'

'So what's the answer?'

'Oh, there's an answer, mark my words,' he said. 'But I can't tell you what it is. You'll have to find out.'

'That's the kind of thing that everyone says, Josiah. I thought at least you would tell me. I need to know.'

'What? Tell you in your pinafores, with your crumpets by the fire and your nursemaid and your "I'll see you alright my man and keep the change", and all the time the smell of grass in your father's gunroom? Tell you what it takes a lifetime and a deathtime to know? And what makes you think I know anyway?'

'You do then? Everyone knows, don't they? It's just another thing I don't understand.' And Harry looked away in embarrassment as if he had been caught taking too many sweets from the tin. And the field creatures popped up out of the dirt for a moment to see if there was going to be any more answer than that.

There was none. 'But I will tell you something for nothing, young man,' said Josiah softening a little. 'You go back home by Saxon Wood and One Tree Field and you'll see something that will make you forget all these daft questions. Oh yes you will.'

So Harry did, but a strange thing happened on the way home which put Josiah's instructions, and his failure to answer the question, right out of his mind. He missed the stile into the wood. He had climbed over it, scraped the mud off his boots on it countless times, and looked at the ancient yew hedge running on either side of him in defiance of passing time. It was just a matter of following the hedge along until you found it. But there he was right at the end of the field, and there had been no stile.

It was towards the end of a sweltering afternoon. He carried his jacket over his shoulder and had rolled his sleeves up to keep cool, but the haze over the fields which seemed to have stunned the cattle seemed also to have seeped into his brain. Hot summer smells almost choked him with their strength as he retraced his steps. Still no stile.

The sun beat down as Harry made his way along the apparently unending hedge, looking out for familiar twigs and branches. Had he seen that tuft before the stile before? Had he seen that dead pigeon? Then suddenly there was a sparse bit of growth at knee height and he pushed his way through, with dust on his hands and a stray thorn in his knee.

He got to his feet with a whiff of nettle and the distant smell of rotting mulch which hit him in the face. Yet now he was on the other side of the hedge, almost in the cool of the ancient Roman wood, there was the missing stile just ten feet from him. He shook his head to clear it and peered over it, prodding at the mossy growth on the wood. Across the field, the cows still chomped away, flicking the flies backwards and forwards, just as they had before.

As he strode along the path, with the trees and rabbit warrens breaking into what had once been a Roman road, he felt a little giddy. The expected cool from the canopy of trees seemed absent, and a warm musty breeze blew in his face. It smelt like elderly strawberries and vinegar and long dead pheasants, not exactly what you would call a pleasant smell – one you might expect when summer had gone on far too long. But it was compelling, fascinating. It made his mouth water. It made his loins stir in a way they never had before. It was embarrassing, and it made it difficult to concentrate or remember quite where he was going. He reached into his pocket and squeezed the lucky marble he carried with him on one side, and his list of battleships written out neatly on the other side.

His feet trudged through the brown dust and twigs on the forest floor, aware that the sun was breaking through the canopy above in great long shafts of light and heat. Then a strange thing happened. He realized this was no breeze that was blowing the fringe out of his eyes, but a tune. It was music. It was notes, dancing between the trees, not air at all. It had a beat like a jig with a hot sweaty, mournful quality, like Bombay on a sleepy afternoon. It lifted Harry's spirits and made him walk with his chin in the air and a sparkle in his step, while inside he struggled to keep conscious of what was happening. It was downright naughty – but where was it coming from?

The green foliage twitched, but Harry seemed to be alone. In a kind of dream, he looked around the glade, and as suddenly as it came, the music faded away, the pressure lifted, the shafts of light spread themselves more evenly and the birds started to twitter again. He walked quickly along the lane and back to the house, past the rusty plough and the battered milk churns and Mr Casey pushing his bike with his postbag over his shoulder.

As he walked up the back steps to Oberon House, his memory of the incident was already different. It was not so much music that he had heard, but colours he had seen, shades of green in circles around him. Not animals or insects as much as clothes, flashing in the corner of his eye. It was a disturbing memory, and he lay awake in the nursery that night, listening to the gurgling pipes, the squeaky floorboards and the faint tones of his parents talking on the floor below, trying to make sense of it.

He told almost nobody, and the few times he was tempted to do so, he found he could find no words to describe it. There seemed no category under which he could file it away for safe-keeping, so it hung around in his mind, reminded of it by odd sights – the flash of a woman's hat in a London tea-room, or the sense of exultation he felt as he stood in a bombed-out church in Hamburg a generation later. By then he rarely thought of it, but wondered – though he had been thirsty, hot and barely awake as he trudged through the woods that day – whether maybe he had seen the Dance after all.

VIII

'But now kan no man se none elves mo,
For now the grete charitee and prayeres
Of limitours and othere hooly freres,
That serchen every lond and every streem,
As thikke as motes in the sonne-beem,
Blessinge halles, chambres, kichenes, boures,
Citees, burghes, castels, hye toures,
Thropes, bernes, shipnes, daieries –
This maketh that ther ben no faieries.'
GEOFFREY CHAUCER, FROM *THE WIFE OF BATH'S TALE*

Oberon, June 1998

THE MOMENT the news reached England that Byron had died of fever in Greece in 1824, his friends all met together and ritually burned the manuscript of his autobiography. The first tentacles of Victorian middle-class respectability were beginning to flex their muscles, and no doubt they felt they needed to protect his reputation from the happy recounting of incest, whoring, homosexuality and loving defiance of rules. But even so it was one of the great acts of literary vandalism of all time. Somehow searching for his lost poem seemed, in a small way, to be redressing that great wrong. No matter that I wanted it for very different reasons from James, it still felt a little like a crusade.

'Well, it's never going to be in there.' I followed James through a small trapdoor in the upper corridor, with the torch playing over ancient linoleum. We peered under the roof. It was dank and dark and dripping like the inside of a whale. The light surfed across great heavy cobwebs, like joints of meat, hanging from the rafters.

'Well, you don't know, do you. It was obviously hidden somewhere.'

'I feel like I'm in somebody's stomach. If anyone left the manuscript here, it will have been digested by now.'

It was the first weekend of the Great Poem Manuscript Search. We began with a cup of tea and chocolate biscuits, then set to almost with enthusiasm. James had decided that the only solution to his problem was to find the missing poem, and auction it to rescue the house. The irony of a search after our conversation a few weeks before was lost on neither of us. I had heard no more weeping in the night, no more mothers looking from room to room, but the memory of that maternal searching in the dark stayed with me. I thought of it at unexpected moments – on the underground, brushing my teeth, queuing at the bank. I thought of it as I watched a young mother in a skimpy skirt bend suddenly over her pushchair to kiss her sleeping child.

Neither of us believed the poem would fetch enough money, even if we did find it. I had even talked to my ex-girlfriend Mary, who happened to work in an auctioneers near St James' Square, about what it might be expected to fetch. She said it depended. It always depends, doesn't it? Everything always depends – and even if it didn't, she reckoned it would be unlikely to fetch the six-figure sum James had dreamed of. It could be a lot, but it wouldn't be enough. It hardly seemed worth taking the poor girl out to lunch and re-igniting her hopes.

I was even less sure how I would have the benefit of discovering the poem from an academic point of view if it was immediately sold, but beyond telling James that I hoped it would help make me an academic reputation, we had never really discussed it. I hoped the answer would be obvious when it came to the point. I was also fed up with London, with its ozone in the back of the throat and its faint alcoholic morning-after headache. I also had my reasons for avoiding my own flat now that my relationship with Angelica had broken down enough for her to phone me depressingly every evening. So it suited me to leave the familiar washing up and undeodorised atmosphere of my bedroom as often as I could. And although I sometimes feared the Byron poem was James' monstrous deceit perpetrated on himself, and the manuscript pure moonshine – part of a hereditary fantasy of his family that I could not share – I still enjoyed the idea of a hopeless search.

There was something boyish about it that attracted me, like hunting for buried treasure. I felt like a cross between the Famous Five and Huckleberry Finn. And spending my weekends and days off in James' house searching for an ancient piece of paper was better than my usual thirtysomething quest for money and then, of course, for love. I preferred to poke around in attics. Or to re-open the shutters on either end of the great window to let in even more light than before. I had lent James my squash racket in the hope that we might get out of the house occasionally, but we never did.

It was obviously going to keep James happy for months, when some might say – the neighbours for example, with their brushed vowels and hedge-clippers – that he should have been spending his time creosoting the fence or plumbing in a new kitchen. But there was almost no money for that: I had been chipping in myself to buy paint as a kind of weekend rent. And there was a continual battering from estate agents eager to take on the sale. Letters from Lane Fox and Knight, Frank & Rutley poured in through the post, including mock-ups of how the advertisement would look in *Country Life* ('Superb country house set in four acres, needs some repair') or long descriptions of the value of exclusive properties so near to Gatwick. 'I think we could probably get a pop icon here,' said one agent who came round in Wellington boots, perspiring with cool excitement. 'It would be perfect for someone like Sting, for example.'

James put their letters in a pile on the floorboards beside the front door. At night the mice danced across them, leaving their droppings neatly behind them on the envelopes. Probably they did so as we walked carefully across the floorboards under the roof, noting where the rain had caused great forests of vegetation, noting the nests of rodents and where the owl made a temporary home in the chimney piece. It was like Bishop Berkeley's tree in the quad which disappeared when no-one was looking. Somehow the house had been alone for so long that you had no idea what might be going on when you turned your back.

I had never counted the rooms upstairs and I suspect I would have come up with a different number each time, because some of the cramped servants quarters under the ribs of the house looked like cupboards. Neither of us was very systematic about the search. We looked where we felt like next. It is strange when you are looking for something you want very much. It is much easier, somehow, to carry on searching in the same place over and over again, because it seems so certain to be there, than moving on to somewhere less likely but still possible. Before the roof and the ancient barnacled dry-as-dust water tank, we had been through an attractive-looking door on the upper landing, with faded paintwork, as if it had once had a nameplate screwed to it. Inside, it had been piled with furniture and heaps of what had once been old curtains, on which the moths had gorged themselves. They must have tasted enough William Morris print to give them a queasy feeling at the thought of any more, because the curtains fell to dust in our hands. We bundled what we could into black plastic bags.

Most of the furniture was rotten or pitted with woodworm, but there were papers inside the drawers of the first piece we rescued. There was a moment of excitement – though how we could have expected Byron's thoughts to have been left in a green-painted Edwardian dresser, I can't imagine. Then we read what it said.

'Oberon House Weekend Course – 30 September to 3 October 1956: Course Leader: Daphne Malvern-Hope,' it said with a long list of participants with racy ex-RAF names and handle-bar moustaches. And at the bottom: 'Please ensure after meals that you pass all crockery to the end of the tables. It makes clearing away much easier and saves the efforts of our skeleton staff.'

There were some guide books in the same drawer, some newspaper cuttings of articles by John Betjeman and an old pamphlet by Sir George Trevelyan. It clearly dated from the days when the ground floor had been used as a venue for adult education. We had only searched one small part of one room, but James felt like giving up.

'This is absolutely bloody hopeless,' he said, leaning against the bed. 'We'll never find it.'

'Your family were hardly going to stash it away in a drawer, were they? Come on, we've only just started.'

But however much I enjoyed the process of looking, there was also something painful about it. It reminded me of everything I had ever lost, from my car keys right through to my parents. Every drawer we opened hurt a little, although it also pulsated with possibility. But I enjoyed chatting away to James about women. I wanted to tell the story of Angelica and how badly I'd been treated. I wanted to describe how she had accused me of falling in love with every woman I met, and how the accusation had reminded me suddenly of James.

'What else do you expect me to do?' he said when I had accused once him of the same thing.

The night before, we had walked into the village so he could phone Abigail, as he did every weekend. There was still no telephone in Oberon House, and the evenings were still cold enough to need central heating in a telephone box. He also phoned her when he went up to London either to sign on the dole or to do a little of the proofreading work which seemed magically to keep him in rent money.

'How's Buckingham Palace?' someone said as he slipped into the phone box in Oberon village. It was a young man in a baseball cap and baggy white trousers, with the sleek air of the City of London. We both stared at him for a moment. 'I'm

Geoffrey Baldwin. You know my parents, I believe,' he said vaguely indicating the rose-covered walls of the house belonging to the Conservative couple, a house which I gather had belonged to the local wise woman, who cured warts and lovesick girls, two centuries before.

I was immediately irritated by him. 'Buckingham Palace is cold and wet, thanks very much,' I said. The man ignored me.

'The reason I'm asking is that I was wondering whether you were interested in selling. I know a place that size must be something of a burden, and it is potentially locking up a great deal of cash. Let me give you my card. I think I might be able to help.'

Before James was able to give his customary denial, Geoffrey had gone. And with a frisson of horror that Geoffrey and his City friends might buy his home, James dialled Abigail's number. I waited my turn outside. I assumed he reached the usual answerphone at the other end. When they had been together, with Abigail still absent, he had felt resigned and exhausted, assuming she was having more fun somewhere else. Now that she was failing to return his calls – probably couldn't even if she wanted to – he felt abandoned and despairing. I heard him take a deep breath ready to leave his message. But before he could work out what to say, she had clearly burst into the message.

'Will you stop calling me!' she said in an aggressive phone hiss.

'Why?' asked James.

'Why? Why? Didn't you get my letter?'

'You know I did. That's why I'm phoning you.'

'Listen, James. This is really hard for me, you know. I've stuck with you these last few months because I thought you needed me, but now I've taken the decision – whether you need me or not – and I just want you to accept it. OK? It's hard enough without you pestering me on the phone.'

'But I'm not pestering. I just ...'

'You're on the phone. I broke up from you weeks ago. That's pestering. Take it from me. Did you call me up when I *hadn't* written to you? Did you heck! No, you're stalking me by phone, so just stop.'

Bang! The receiver went down. James looked confused and a little battered. 'For some reason, since I came down here, everyone is treating me differently,' he told me. 'It's disturbing.'

'Well, you're different now.' And he was. He was more focused somehow, more clear-sighted about what he wanted. His tatty jeans walked with him with a little spring. His shoulders spread back. I found I liked him more. I even enjoyed listening to his stories.

At the end of the day, we would drag down a cheap bottle of wine from what had once been the kitchen, light a candle upstairs under the great window, and wait while the smell of elderly red grapes wafted through the room. Great pinks and dark blues streaked the skies outside. I could hear the ducks twittering again as they flew low over the roof on their way to wherever they went at that hour. I felt we were like two bachelors, but I think James was feeling something different. I think he was seeing something different to me, too. Where I saw dilapidated staircases and rotting window frames, he saw the hunting parties scraping their boots, the unmarried daughters gathering around the tea and the cavaliers hiding their rosaries. Where I saw decay, he just saw a glorious past.

In days gone by, this difference in perception would have irritated me, but I think I managed to derive a warm sense of belonging – distant and unsatisfactory though it was – just because he felt one. So I was prepared to tell stories half the night, and to travel down there in the evenings at weekends and carry on the search. He told me about his final rows with Abigail, like the one about having children – as if someone who could barely hold down a short-term contract of a day or so could ever afford to have children. As if the man who never combed his own hair, and whose car was so rusty that you could see the road through the floorboards, could ever manage to bring up a family. But then, as James told me, he had no idea the conversation was even about children at the time. It had seemed to be a mild chat about the politics of education, but

Abigail had taken it to mean he had no intention of having children, and accused him of being 'a piece of jelly'.

I told him in return about my extraordinary rows with Angelica. About how she upturned the spaghetti on my head in a restaurant in Camden Lock when I admitted to sleeping with an off-duty policewoman I met in Chicago. About how she returned all the letters I had ever written her in a bundle, which I had inadvertently left under the front seat of the car where the garage mechanic read them. About how I missed her.

'But you've got to come to terms with the truth, haven't you,' I said, after my third glass of wine. 'Nothing lasts for ever.'

'Doesn't it?' said James, looking around him.

Still awake in the early hours of the morning, I found myself wondering whether I was right. Then, just off the edge of my hearing frequency, and quite unexpectedly, I thought I could hear somebody calling. When I strained to listen some more I could hear nothing but the normal swaying of the old house in the wind. When I lay down and tried to go to sleep again, I could hear it again. Hear *her* again, maybe, heart-breakingly but systematically tracing the steps through the house of our own search. It sent a chill down my spine and I pulled the pillow over my ears to cut out the sound.

The next morning I dismissed it again. I had heard nothing definite, and I had drunk a great deal. I could never have stood up in court and say what I had remembered. But this time, James came down looking ashen.

'Did you hear it?' he asked. 'That music in the night? It must have gone on continuously from 1am to 3am. I thought I must be going crazy.'

'Music? No, nothing like that. You must have dreamt it.' James looked relieved.

'You're sure?' I nodded my head and set about the new day.

There was a misty haze across the overgrown lawn the next morning, as I stood in my shorts at the back door. It was going to be warm. It was also the day of the village festival, and a motley pile of bric-a-brac had arrived on trestle tables outside the pub down in the village. Soon I could hear the distant crashes as James shifted the piles of boxes in the next room on our hit list. When I got upstairs, he was deep inside a battered black metal trunk, with the box of keys he carried everywhere with him – knowing that one of them was likely to fit.

'Amazing, some of this stuff.' James seemed to have recovered himself completely. 'Look, this must be something from the military college at Sandhurst. It must have been some kind of exercise they were doing. It's full of coloured maps about the Battle of Waterloo. And this is a set of King's Dress Regulations from the First World War. Weston, E: 612347, it says. It must be Edward's – Harry's brother. Amazing.'

'Aren't you having breakfast?'

'Is there any?'

'What do you mean: is there any? I'm not making it, I'm just wondering whether you are?'

Since I had paid for the box of food I had brought down for the weekend, I didn't feel I should have to cook it as well. But before long I was as engrossed as James, as we blew the dust from the old books – Ernest Dimnet's *The Art of Thinking*, Volume II of *The Imperial History of England.*

'Did I ever tell you, there's supposed to be some kind of passage from here?' Actually, he never had, in all the years of obsession about Oberon House.

'You mean a secret passage? You know perfectly well you haven't. Where is it then?'

'I've no idea if it exists. I just read something, that's all.'

Taking a break from shifting boxes from room to room, James had begun catch the bus into Guildford to spend time at the local history library. His car had finally broken down and there was no money to repair it. The first bus of the day was at something after 11am. There was no bus timetable – and no bus stop either – but the locals knew that the bus stopped by the large oak tree in the main road. The only service back was at 1.30, which gave him only about an hour at the library, plus the reality check which came from a walk through the shopping centre and some deep breaths of diesel fumes in the high street.

The bus journey seemed to follow exactly the same pattern each time, he explained after his third visit. The same people sat there in the same seats. He found himself sitting next to two elderly men, one of them miserably staring at his shoes and the other one engaging him in unwelcome conversation.

'Have you heard the one about the man who goes into a café and says 'One crocodile sandwich and make it snappy!'?'

'Er, no thanks,' said James. It was like being squashed between Tigger and Eeyore.

Once inside the library, he went to the place on the shelf he had left the day before. This one, he told me, was a volume in red leather called *County Byways* by Canon Eric Micklethwaite. The book had an air of not having been glanced at by any living being since the Boer War, but this turned out to be wrong. James found an old pressed bus ticket costing 1d.

He had been through this same process as many days as he could spare. He had started by reading Pevsner: no mention of Oberon House at all. Then he read obscure volumes of local history by obscure clergymen, and many of them referred to the same story – of a mysterious tunnel under the house. It seemed to have been common knowledge among antiquarians. There was one eerie story in particular about how it seemed to lead nowhere, how it had been used during the Civil War for hiding cavaliers, but by the eighteenth century had become a mysterious venue for parlour games.

Canon Micklethwaite went further than most:

> It is said that Miss D——S sent down her favourite spaniel Quantock – named after the renowned Somersetshire hunt – and that the party of investigators at Oberon House followed the noise of its barking across the lawn and grounds of the house, until the sound suddenly fell silent. And no member of the company dared to follow its path.

It was the same story again and I could imagine the scene only too well. The hot summer sunshine and the parasols on the lawn, the birds chattering away in the background, the men dressed like cut-down versions of Beau Nash or maybe Captain Hook, as they called for hush – pressing their ears to the grass. And there was poor Jane D——S – she was bound to be called Jane – comforted by her sisters as the shame-faced party wandered back to the house, a little white in the face.

But glancing back at the page, James told me he noticed there was a footnote:

> See the tale of Byron at Oberon House in John Davenant's *Mysterious Tales of Surrey*, 1859, pp 20-24.

It was this kind of discovery which made his lunchtimes in Guildford worthwhile. A small tingling sensation must have run up and down his spine like an Oberon mouse. Did they have a copy of Davenant, James asked the fierce-looking woman on the desk? And after a gesture towards the index cards, and armed with the shelf reference, he went quickly back to the shelves.

'It isn't there,' he said to the fierce librarian.

'It *is* here,' she said, as if he had been expelled from kindergarten. 'But somebody else probably has it out.'

'What, that old book? I don't expect so.' The librarian gave him a look.

'You'll just have to wait. That's all there is to it.'

With great irritation, and looking at his watch, James wandered along the handful of readers straining to see what they were reading. There were the usual mournful clutch of recently unemployed people with nowhere better to go. One was snoozing in front of the newspaper. Another elderly man seriously needed to blow his nose, but seemed unwilling to do so. There was only one woman.

She looked sharp and intense, her dark bobbed hair clutched in one fist. A large duffel coat seemed to engulf her. But she did seem to be reading an old volume of some kind.

James hovered shyly, wondering what to say. She ignored him.

'Excuse me,' he said. She failed to look up. The books wafted around the smell of wet dogs. 'Excuse me, but I wonder how long you might be reading that particular book.'

'Is that any of your concern?' she said without taking her eyes off the page. She was American.

'It's just that I had hoped to look at it myself, and ...'

'I'll be done in 20 minutes,' she said, looking up at him for the first time. 'It took me ages to find it and I don't really want to stop now. OK?'

Before she buried her head in the print again, James noticed a pair of piercing brown eyes and just the smallest flicker of a smile of collusion.

'OK then,' said James. 'Right.' He wondered how to point out that his bus would then be gone and he would be forced to wander the streets of Guildford all night, but decided against it. She read on.

'Can I ask what you're working on?' He was unsure whether he was annoyed or genuinely interested. The fluorescent light beat down on them with all the heaviness of after lunch. The elderly man finally wiped his nose.

'Well, the sooner I read this, the sooner you can have the book.' She still did not look up. James wandered back out into the drizzle, wondering why he felt so offended.

'I felt really annoyed,' he told me with surprise, as we heaved the last sideboard out of the way in one of the smaller bedrooms. 'I never usually feel annoyed. I just thought how rude she was. I wish I didn't have to look at the book, but I must know what it says.'

'I think you thought she was attractive. That's why you told me about her hair.'

'Nonsense. I hardly find anybody attractive these days.'

Behind the sideboard in the corner of the room and covered in one of the dustiest dust-sheets I had ever seen, with earwigs crawling out from underneath, there was a peculiar item of furniture, overwrought and rococo, with a tower of tiny rounded drawers.

'You know what that is,' said James. 'That's what they used to keep beauty spots in during the eighteenth century. I wonder what it's still doing here. It's probably worth a bit.'

We got rid of the remaining cobwebs and peered into the liver-stained mirror, and opened one of the drawers, and there they were. Small dots, black and red, like the kind of sticky markers you can buy in modern stationers – as if they had last been seen by the bewigged and powdered lady who last wore them. I peered into the blurred mirror, wondering whether the lady with the beauty spots and been the last one to look into the glass. And whether it was her who was disturbing my sleep.

James held one up to the dying light outside the window. And as he did so, a shadow seemed to cross the room for a minute. As if the lady had peered back down into life to see what we were doing with her boudoir.

A mouse skittered down the corridor outside. 'I rather like the mice,' said James. 'They keep the place alive. They're like a soul left in the house.'

IX

'Pinch him, pinch him, blacke and blue,
Sawcie mortalls must not view
What the Queene of Stars is doing,
Nor pry into our Fairy wooing.'
JOHN LYLY, *THE FAIRY REPROACH*

Threadneedle Street, November 1912

THERE was an empty chair at the dinner table in Oberon House again. Once again Harry's father was delayed in the City, struggling by new electric light to keep the wheels turning at the family bank. He had received the letter from one of his junior associate partners, explaining that he had resigned from his position because he had run himself heavily into debt investing in South American railway stock. Attached to the note had been a large manila envelope sealed with old-fashioned wax. With heart beating unevenly, and the sweat building inside his wing collar, John Weston reached inside and pulled out the beautifully designed but worthless share certificates. They seemed to glow in his hands with their intricate lines, and carefully rendered Spanish, like unfulfillable promises. He reached for the telephone.

'Operator. I wonder if you could connect me to Mr Jordan's home number, if he has one.' As he hung the receiver back on the hook, the room seemed to swim slightly, with its leather book-bound walls, its sherry decanter in the corner, its green baize desk and pristine blotter. He could hear the rumble from the street outside, as his eye fell on the smiling but fading photograph of his wife staring upwards on their wedding day, as if contemplating the effects of eye-drops.

Then he pulled out a large sheet of company paper, opened his pen and as he wrote, he knew with a sinking heart that it was pointless. The phone rang.

'Yes. You're sure that the number is no longer used? Thank you.'

He turned back to the letter. 'My dear Jordan,' he had written, surprised at his own effusiveness. But then it was a kind of pleading letter:

> Having received your message of the 18th, let me say at once how distressed I am about your decision. Nobody has worked more assiduously for the bank than you and my best wishes go with you at this difficult time. I know, also, however, what an advocate you have been for these stocks in recent months. Could you venture to reassure me that none of the bank's money has been invested in the same way? You can imagine my concerns and the urgency with which I await your reply. I am entrusting this letter to a member of staff and would – for obvious reasons – be grateful if you would give it back to him, with your answer, once you have read it.

He wondered how to sign off the letter, and having caught himself wondering, signed it simply: 'Yours sincerely, John Weston Esq., Senior Partner and Chairman'.

John already feared the worst, and when the faithful member of staff returned with the same note an hour later, explaining that the house was locked and looked abandoned, he had some evidence to support his fears.

The bank had limited liability, but one of the conditions of directorship was that they should be major shareholders and major customers of the bank. If the bank was insolvent as a result of these rash investments, then James and his co-directors could well be ruined. Their children would be removed from school. Their whole universe would crumble. It was a potential disaster that would cast an enormous cloud over his already complicated life with its delicate checks and balances. His home, his wife Eleanor, everything he cared about, would collapse with him, and not just those aspects of life the world saw.

Jenny would go too: bankrupts do not keep mistresses. And those wonderful evenings in her small flat in Jermyn Street, the meals at the Criterion, the music halls, those careful compromises, those stolen fleeting moments when he was supposed to be visiting some dull smoky city, would be smashed beyond repair.

She was his mistress in the conventional sense, but their relationship did not fit into the usual mode of Edwardian infidelity. For one thing, she was not married, though she had been – her husband had been killed during the relief of Kimberley. There was no veneer of respectability to sink into. Jenny lived off her widow's pension from the Army and painted pictures that earned a little money, supplemented by the occasional sewing. John was unclear how she managed financially before he came into her life, and now he paid most of her rent. The relationship appealed to his sense of the unconventional. It made him feel bohemian, and he needed that after a heavy day at the bank. But actually it was her company rather than her body he craved, her delicate smell of rose petals, the sense of ownership with which she removed hairs from his frock coat – and their gentle arguments. He had never even considered arguing politics with a woman before, still less the details of trade union reform and Home Rule, but with Jenny it seemed quite natural. But if the next few hours went the wrong way, all that would disappear.

He had called a sombre meeting of the bank's directors the following day, a Saturday.

'You must realize,' said Sir Richard Wallop, his grey beard reflecting in the polished table, 'that if we continue to trade while we know ourselves to be insolvent, then we face prison as well as ruin.'

'They seem pretty similar to me,' said another director, picking at his fingernails in a way his colleagues considered ungentlemanly.

'But we have no evidence either way. This fellow Jordan – any news of him incidentally?'

John Weston shook his head ever so slightly. 'This fellow Jordan may have covered his tracks well, but he may not have used the bank's money at all. We're not going to know until next week. It would be pretty perverse to suddenly announce this difficulty to the world – or the Bank of England at any rate, with the risk that the news may leak out – when actually there may be nothing wrong.'

A young man in a wing collar piped up: 'Do we have a better price for these stocks now? Is there any hope there perhaps?'

'Through the floor, I'm afraid. They're absolutely worthless.'

'Well, gentlemen. I don't know about you, but I think any kind of public action at this point would be premature, until we can see the extent of the bank's exposure.'

'I agree,' said John. 'I have no firm evidence that Jordan has been embezzling the money of the bank. We have scrutinized the books and found nothing. We risk the future of the bank by making an announcement that anything is wrong. I simply have a concern, that is all, which it was my duty to pass onto you – despite the unusual circumstances of this meeting. I realize, of course, that having told you, you will not be able to claim – should anything be amiss – that you had received no warning. But being gentlemen, you would, I am sure, not have even considered doing so. The responsibility is upon me, but I recognize that the feeling of this meeting is probably to open as usual on Monday. But I could not, as I am sure you understand, have taken that decision alone.'

A silence fell around the table as he spoke. Bearded long dead directors of the bank peered down disapprovingly from their portraits around the walls. The naval battle over the fireplace stuck motionless as the cannon balls raged over the

French flagship.

'That is my proposal. May I have a seconder?'

At the vote, five hands went straight up. Three more followed more tentatively.

'And against?' Two hands shot up. John did a mental calculation.

'So you're abstaining, Woolley, am I right?' Woolley said nothing.

'I take that as assent.'

'You can take it how you like,' said Woolley menacingly, his whiskered face red and bulbous. 'Nothing, absolutely nothing has been said here about how a senior clerk – alright, more than a senior clerk – one of our most trusted servants – could have invested the bank's reserves in so extraordinary a manner. If indeed he *has*, though I feel sure this meeting would not have been called unless our esteemed senior director had more reason for believing so than he is letting on.' He pronounced the word 'esteemed' with emphasis and irony.

'So now I am going to be ruined, and not one word has been said about fault,' said Woolley. 'Not one word.'

'I said at the start of the meeting that, as senior director, I take full responsibility,' said John, his eyes downcast. 'I put my resignation as a director at your disposal.'

'And a fat lot of good that is going to do us now. You got us into this mess, you can damn well get us out.'

Silence descended again on the meeting. John cleared his throat. 'I shall endeavour to regain your trust again. We meet once more at Tuesday at 9am. In the meantime, I don't have to tell you the consequences of a word out of place in this matter. I am aware that many people in this room have considerable investments in this bank, and I must remind you that we stand or fall together. Any alteration to your investments could spark a run. We can't be too careful.'

Banging his books on the table, Woolley stormed out of the room. As the great wood-panelled door swung shut he shouted after him: 'A pity you didn't take your own advice a little earlier.'

John Weston struggled through the weekend, taking long walks through Saxon Wood at Oberon House. He was especially attentive to Eleanor. He engaged Harry in a rare conversation as they inspected the stables together. He collected some of the most private family papers and locked them away in the most secret place in the house he knew. And all the time, the decisions echoed back and forth through his head.

They did not know, actually, whether Jordan had invested the bank's money in South American railway stock. But he was extremely suspicious that he had done so, given Jordan's demeanour last time they had discussed such matters as risk and high returns. There had been an air of over-confidence and collusion about him that had been disturbing at the time. There was something about his letter as well. It seemed almost craven, and demanded somehow to be read between the lines. There were no serious discrepancies in Jordan's accounts, and yet there was something odd about them. All his investments, though perfectly legitimate, seemed slightly extreme.

So here was the dilemma. If they revealed there may be a problem, they faced a run on the bank, one of those tumultuous terrifying events where nothing could be certain. If they kept quiet, they faced arrest – especially if there was evidence that they had covered up the fraud and carried on trading illegally. Now that he had called the meeting of directors, but had not been entirely frank with them, he was probably the only one liable for arrest – but that was hardly a cheering thought. Even so, to risk ruining the bank when there may be nothing wrong at all, seemed foolhardy in the extreme.

We just have to get through seven more days, he said to himself. Seven more days. But Saturday's evening newspaper, which he read as he shuddered home from Victoria Station, had given him no comfort at all.

The body of a man, believed to be the missing bank clerk Mr Henry Jordan, of Great Ormond Street, WC, has been found in the Thames at Westminster Bridge. It is believed that he had been dead for some days.

Jordan must have known what he had done. John Weston sat forward on the edge of his first class railway seat and read and re-read the article. He could feel the hairs on the back of his neck stand up. Yes, Jordan knew and his life was about to change. As he arrived back at Oberon House and clip-clopped through the gates, he could see Harry fishing in the big pond at the end of the garden. He knew Gerald and Edward would be arriving for dinner. His home, his world, seemed calm and rational. He also knew it was poised for disaster.

The first inkling of trouble came at 1.30pm on Monday. The cloud no bigger than a man's hand came in the shape of a knock on the door. A deferential clerk in a frock coat sidled in.

'I think you should know, Sir. Mrs Adamson has requested that we liquidate her entire investment.'

'Today?'

'Yes, Sir.'

'You mean immediately?'

'Yes, Sir.'

'Thank you, Edgar.' He sat alone at his table and could hear, as if he was the only one that could hear it, the sound of beating wings. We have two hours before we can close, he calculated. If we can make it, we may have some chance. He looked into the street at the passing cars and trams and the Bovril advertisements on the other side of the street. It looked calm enough, but there did seem to be more people than usual hurrying up their steps below.

Feeling unusually calm, he called his most senior officials into the office.

'Gentlemen,' he said. 'We may be in for some difficulty this afternoon. Mr Graves, would you very discreetly and very carefully contact the police and ask them to send some constables here at once. But make sure nobody overhears what you are doing. Mr Jephson, please take an assistant with you and deliver a note which I have prepared here, for the chief cashier at the Bank of England. Impress upon him the urgency of his advancing us more cash, and report to me as soon as you have a reply. Mr Ovens, please put your best man on our back door and make sure nobody enters that way. And close the side door. And most important of all, act with calmness. It is absolutely paramount that we should continue to re-assure our customers of the safety of this bank. That will be all.'

Alone in his office for a few minutes, he thought of his family – remembering that there was a special dinner for Gerald's birthday that evening. Harry would be joining them for dinner for the first time, like a grown-up. It was an important occasion. He wrote out a telegram to his wife:

'MAY BE SOME TIME. WESTON,' he wrote. Then realizing it sounded a little like Captain Oates at the South Pole, he screwed it up. The noises coming from outside made it clear that it was now too late to write another. He grabbed his top hat and made his way quickly downstairs.

'Edgar, close all the cashiers but one. And do it discreetly.'

As he did so, the raised voices in the street seemed to grow louder. A horse whinnied unexpectedly. The great reassuring glass doors to the street were being held open. As he reached the ground floor, he realized it was too late. The tumult was upon them.

'Mr Phillips, would you be so good as to call the police,' he said as soon as he saw that the constables had not yet arrived.

He had never witnessed a bank crash, though he had been brought up with stories of them. As a young man, he had read Dickens' account of the banking collapse in Philadelphia. The whole thing offended every sense he had of what it meant to be British. Order, decency, drains, starched upper lips, the whole basis of his life in banking threatened to unravel in a few hours of orgiastic panic. If this had been the *Titanic*, he could have conducted an orderly queue for the lifeboats and gone down with the ship. But somehow loss of life was outweighed by the terrible fear of loss of wealth.

By the time the police had arrived, the storm had broken. The small hallway was a mass of rage. You could see fury and fear on every face. Some were pushing. One old lady in a hat was swinging her umbrella and banging it on the desk. John watched in horror as the crowd jostled in from outside, and was calm enough to take in the strange mixture of perfume smells mixed with panic – which wafted through the black and white marble entrance hall.

He stood on the counter, shaking and trying to make himself heard above the crowd.

'Ladies and gentlemen!' he bawled. 'Ladies and gentlemen, I am a senior director of this bank and I beg you to be patient.' He glanced up at the clock. It was still only a few minutes past two. They weren't going to make it. 'We have the funds available to satisfy you all. We are going as fast as we can.'

'Why do you only have one cashier window open then?' This unleashed a further roar from the frustrated crowd, but he hushed them again.

'To speed up the process, I will be asking you whether you will be prepared to accept cheques. Although we have the cash available, it isn't necessarily on the premises.

'I don't want your worthless pieces of paper,' screamed a woman in a feather boa. Someone screwed up a piece of paper. Someone else threw a banana. John leapt down behind the counter and the police formed up in front of the desks. This was the signal for an almighty push from the door. John could see the desperation of the people forcing their way in, the rewards of years of work disappearing before their eyes. Some respectable gentlemen in top hats, some bowler-hatted clerks, a few in fox furs and every one of them with that same look of dread – the dread of poverty in the days without a welfare state, when the workhouse beckoned for the failures of the world. If the bank foreclosed, it would mean ruin for more than just the directors.

It was the dread of the park bench in the rain, of the poorhouse, of nameless Dickensian characters, segregated by sex, when a man's wits as much as his class was all that lay between him and the gutter – and where a woman's husband's wits might be all that lay between her and prostitution. Or worse, of the dreadful degrading mortuary underneath Tower Bridge, where the bloated corpses lay, having thrown themselves in despair into the river.

Gathered together into one mass of people, this dread had the power of an avalanche and the human terror of a riot or mass insanity. John cowered behind the counter, noticing inanely that wood chippings from the desk now clung to his jacket, while dust from the floor marked his trousers. He must remember to have words with the cleaner. He shook his head, as if to dislodge his wandering thoughts. The bank was finished and he was facing the same terrors as everyone in the crowd.

It was also his fault. He should have listened to reason. He should have urged the directors to make a public statement and close the bank. He thought he could get away with it. He had shown cowardice, and now he had destroyed his own life. Goodness knows what his debts would be – and he might have to face prison, too. Their carefully constructed home, his wife and her beloved necklaces, Oberon House and the estate tended for generations, and Harry – with his peculiar enthusiasms for children's stories and folklore. It was Harry's expectant face that seemed to cause him the most pain. He did not believe he could ever face his son again, and the calamity which would befall him. He could not bear the simple unreconstructed old-fashioned shame of it all.

When the bank had been closed, John addressed the staff in a haze. He explained their predicament: that the bank would have to close for a week and might not re-open. As he took one look behind him before locking his office door for what was probably the last time, and glanced at his pocket watch, Edgar handed him the information that he had been dreading.

It was true. Two million pounds of the bank's stock had been invested in a bubble railway scheme in Latin America. The losses amounted to more than their entire reserves. He should have known, and the question of when he did know would – likely as not – figure heavily in his trial and the trial of his colleagues.

It was drizzling when he reached the street. The horse-cars

seemed to make a dull sound on the road. The air tasted of dung. Great skirts of women billowed as he walked painfully by. At home at Oberon House, Harry would probably be sailing one of his boats in the lake. Eleanor would be going through the details of dinner with the cook. Gerald would be already on the train. Edward would be striding across the fields with the dogs. But John decided not to make his usual short walk to catch a hansom to his train at Victoria. He wandered along the river wondering what to do. At Southwark Bridge he watched the barges passing underneath and felt the temptation to throw himself in. He realized it would only heap more dishonour on his family.

From Charing Cross, he tapped the new imitation of Edward I's enduring stone tribute to his dead wife, and wandered on through Trafalgar Square. The newsboys were shouting about a bank panic in London and his pace accelerated as he made his decision.

X

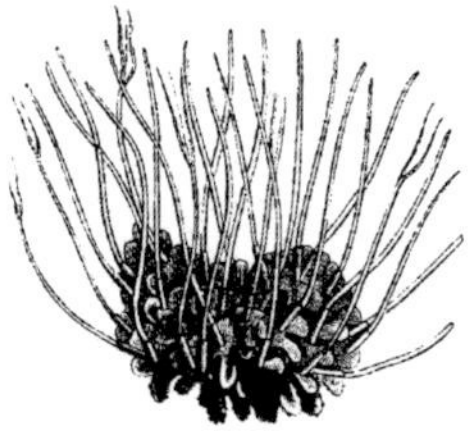

'He lay stretched on his back, pinned to the ground, while the biggest of the spriggans danced on his nose with shouts of laughter. At length the spriggan shouted, 'Away, away! I smell the day!' and disappeared. The miser found himself lying stretched at the foot of the mound covered with dewy cobwebs.
CORNISH LEGEND, FROM KATHERINE BRIGGS'
A DICTIONARY OF FAIRIES

Oberon, June 1998

EVEN when he was earning money from his best-selling poems, Byron was always tortured by debt. He had to leave the country quickly for his Grand Tour in 1809 at the age of 21, in case his creditors thought he was escaping his vast outstanding borrowings of £12,000. Only selling his home at Newstead Abbey would allow him to escape his debts, but this would not take place for almost another decade. When he left the country a second time, and his reputation for 'nameless crimes' crashed around him, the bailiffs seized everything he left behind. What were the nameless crimes? Well, not just brutality with his wife, incest with his sister and homosexuality, too – but one titled ex-mistress caught him in the act of seducing her 11-year-old daughter. It is hard to think of anyone less like Bryon than James, but I think maybe they both used to agonize about money and decisions about their blessed houses in similar ways.

James had, by now, moved out of his rented room in Balham and settled into the disorder of Oberon House. I watched him take out a clean piece of paper one morning – clearly a difficult process as he set down his morning cup of tea and rummaged among the cardboard boxes containing most of his possessions. The third box finally yielded a pile of old paper, and half way down the pile, past all those other notes of football scores, shopping lists, notes for film reviews, agonised draft letters to Abigail and others like her, past the unused doctors' prescriptions and the disorganizes receipts, he finally found a clean sheet.

I watched him rule a long line down the page. Then he wrote a small word 'bad' at the top of the first column and 'good' at the top of the second, clearly writing as tiny as he could from some morbid fear that I would see what he was doing. I pretended not to notice.

Under bad, I could still see him write the word 'alone'. Then he stared into space a bit and wrote '£4,000 credit card debt', followed by 'Abigail', 'eczema' – which he scrubbed out again – and finally 'need for £120,000'. Under 'good', he wrote in much bigger letters 'Oberon House', then he went back to the bad column and added 'structure'. Then in the good column, he wrote 'family' and 'Susie'. Then he folded up the piece of paper neatly and put it in his pocket. The old nut tree outside scraped the window. It was drizzling.

Taken together, this was not a very impressive comparison. He had some assets that would cost him a great deal of money, and the debit side went not really far enough. It seemed to hold out little hope of saving Oberon House – let alone transforming it into a home. We both needed to face it, James had insufficient money but he also had insufficient skill, passion, imagination and insufficient human ability to create the relationships that might fill the house full of people.

Put like that, it was obvious he should take his family's advice and sell up. And yet, and yet, I enjoyed my visits to the house and maybe this really was a way of discovering who he was. I knew it was more than bricks and mortar to him. And when the strange Baldwin couple arrived once again at the weekend, their beady eyes scouring the view behind his shoulder, he invited them in.

'Come along in,' he said. 'Can I make you some tea?'

Not suave exactly. Not exactly charm school, but not vintage James either. And maybe Susie's presence on the list made a difference to the balance.

Yes, Susie. I've been dreading her appearance in the story, for reasons that will become apparent. But there is no doubt that, if it was not for Susie and her particular gifts, James and I would still be struggling along with our paintbrush every few weekends, in that strange camaraderie that men have between them – part intimacy, part competition, part honesty, part deliberate obfuscation. If it was not for that dull elusive book in that miserable municipal library, then Susie would never have appeared in either of our lives.

Yet you never can be quite sure. Destinies have a habit of happening anyway. If you avoid it one way, by staying rigorously at home and leading the healthiest possible lifestyle, they tend to catch you unawares – on whatever parts of your Achilles heel remains exposed. Maybe Susie was my Achilles heel. Maybe she was James'. But either way, he had gone back to the library again – this time borrowing my car (his had disintegrated by this time). Again the wafts of wet dogs and stale tobacco on the air, but again the book was missing, and a moment's irritation began to swell in the pit of James' stomach. And there was the girl, just as out of place among the old codgers in their macks snoozing over the daily papers, lines of snot emerging like glaciers from their noses.

She was still buried in the Canon's elderly masterpiece.

'Excuse me, but are you going to be able to let me have a quick look at that sometime today?' James had taken ten minutes and three practice bombing runs to make that statement. She looked at him with a patient and amused expression. He could see the bulge of her breasts under her white shirt.

'Anybody interested in this old book must have an interesting story to tell,' she said. 'How about you buy me a cup of coffee.'

Across the table, the old man with the runny nose had perked up and was staring with a mixture of jealousy and shock. James mentally fondled the few coins in his back pocket, went slightly red, looked at his watch – pretending too late that he was just scratching his chest – and agreed. He kicked himself all the way down the stairs to the cafe outside.

Susie was doing a PhD thesis on Byron, as it happened. It was no coincidence that she found herself immersed in that book. She was chasing down a fleeting reference to the poet spending a few stolen weeks in the late summer of 1811 immersed in Surrey, before his marriage and while Napoleon's troops prepared to march to Moscow and where, perhaps, he had devoted his considerable creative skills to seducing the daughter of the local squire.

Susie had been sent over for six months by the University of North Carolina as part of some kind of exchange programme, and she described this in great detail – the loans, the instructions, the arrangements for living, the link with London University. But all James could see were her eyes, he told me, which seemed to laugh while she was saying the most serious things. They drank the coffee and tea he ordered while James explained about the house, his parents and his inability to settle in one job. He even told her about Abigail and her eyes sparkled throughout.

'I can't believe I've met someone with an English chateau,' she said, with a hint of irony. 'Why don't you open it to the public like Blenheim or Chatsworth?'

'Because it's about to fall down, quite apart from anything else. And I couldn't stand all those bored T-shirted kids coming around and their whispering parents saying "just look at the workmanship on that". Ugh!'

Susie laughed full-throatedly, like a chortling Canada goose, as if giving him permission for bad behaviour.

'You're a snob, aren't you,' she said. Her eyes dared him to agree.

'No, I ...' said James, thinking of his kitchen and the pictures on the wall and the rickety old chairs, like a land of lost content. 'I don't think so.'

She laughed again. She laughed a lot. She laughed more than anybody he had ever met. Abigail had been so depressingly serious. His girlfriend before that was a furtive type with a constant expression that implied she had been foully insulted. That must be why he fell for Susie and her eyes, and her fund of anecdotes about her home town – St Paul, Minnesota – and the exploits of the St Paul Saints baseball team, and the crocodiles in the Mississippi and the snowploughs in the shopping streets. She even carried a guidebook for the Minneapolis Museum of Modern Art in her bag.

The Canon's book was less helpful than you might expect. It confirmed the old stories about Byron's visit to Oberon House, mentioned that there was a letter in existence from Byron that mentioned a 'pretty peach, weighted with virtue' who lived there. The letters were not quoted any further and the Canon was ambiguous about where they were, but he wrote about the relief he felt about this friendship after the death of his mother. It explains that Byron's 'friendship' was returned, and quoted him as interpreting this further: 'Friendship is a dangerous word for young ladies,' he wrote. 'It is Love full-fledged, and waiting for a fine day to fly.'

'A dangerous word,' repeated Susie. 'We must be careful of each other.'

These few snippets of the conversation I had from James, as he breathlessly described Susie to me a few days later, when I escaped again from the world of fine art and fake wood-panelling. I've no idea, apart from that, what they talked about. What did they have in common, after all? There was Susie, attractive, bright, sophisticated – as sophisticated as you can be when you come from Minnesota – just out of a five-year affair with the president of some miserable IT corporation. Someone who could hold her own in conversation anywhere from a new age revival meeting to a boardroom. A law degree already under her belt. And a student loan which put her at least

$80,000 in debt. Someone who had known the worldly frisson of having sex on your boss's desk.

And James – well I loved him as if he was one of my limbs – but with the best will in the world, he was about as sophisticated as a chip sandwich. He had never stuck at anything. He hankered dog-like after all his few precious women, and he had barely travelled outside south east England. All he had was this bizarre unquenchable pointless devotion to a long-extinguished dream. A house – but one that looked like Brighton's West Pier after a particularly heavy storm.

To James, she seemed like a miraculous creature culled from a medieval bestiary, something carried back from one of Gulliver's travels. He had never seen anything like her. But why did she like him? I spent some time over the next few weeks trying to work it out. I mean, what had James got to offer a sassy American girl with dark red hair and an occasional knowing, faraway look in her eyes? It struck me that maybe she liked ineffectual Englishmen, or to be more accurate, Englishmen who needed re-arranging. Perhaps James was a project.

'Look, this is what you need to do ...' I heard her saying down the corridor, in her gently cajoling mid-western way. And yet, there was something else about her, too. It may have just been that she was American that she seemed so out of place. She seemed to come from somewhere so distant from Surrey that it was hardly on the same planet, yet she didn't behave like an outsider. She hinted once at some kind of Oberon link in her own ancestry, but I never quite pinned that down. And she looked at James and she seemed to know: as if she knew she had awoken him from a long sleep – and it was seeing that small transformation that drew her to him.

I wondered these things when I first saw them together, in the bedraggled kitchen of Oberon House, where James had set himself up with a Primus stove and camp bed, a trestle table and candles, surrounded by empty beer bottles and ancient milk bottles, still with what had once been milk residing in them, and generating the creature from the white lagoon.

When I came in, she had her head back again and was laughing uproariously.

'You're so damn English!' she said. 'No self-respecting man wears grey socks. No self-respecting man wears grey anything.'

'But I only wear grey,' said James. 'So that rules me out.'

Maybe this extreme unsophistication attracted her all the more. Or maybe it was the thought of staying the night in a dilapidated house that Byron once stayed in, and which barely seemed to have been re-decorated since.

She got up with an open smile as I walked in, brushing her red hair out of her eyes with one hand and shaking mine with the other. I noticed two large silver rings on the fingers of the hand I shook. Her papers were strewn across the table. I could see her strange, rounded, awkward hand-writing on screeds of paper.

'We've been talking about dreams,' said James, barely taking his eyes off her.

'Oh, dreaming,' I said, with an unpleasant expression, setting down to can of lager. 'Did you dream about me?''Not about dreams,' said James. 'We're talking about Dreams. Susie has Dreams.'

'James,' she said in a quiet and urgent tone of admonishment, looking embarrassed. 'I just dream some peculiar things, that's all.'

But that wasn't all. Susie dreamed about lost things. She claimed not to know how or when, and they were never very important things. But steadily through her life she had dreamed about people's missing spectacles, credit cards, key rings, contact lenses. And she listened with bowed head while James outlined this to me, aware of my growing irritation. Once she dreamed about a lost wedding ring in the woods behind her family home in St Paul. Family and friends would lose their valuables and call her up, laugh about it, and sometimes – just sometimes – she dreamt them back.

If she tried too hard, it failed, James told me with mounting enthusiasm. She was quite unable to dream lottery numbers or Superbowl victors. It was just one of those things. But she seemed to take it more seriously than it was being presented to me. Her face shone mauve, and she tried to turn the whole thing into a joke, but the combination of the two cancelled each other out.

'Well, maybe you can dream me up another drink.' She irritated me unbearably. She seemed to patronize us both, as if she was God's chosen apostle of globalization. I took against the way her hair kept falling over her eyes. And I couldn't stand her mid-western twang and the peculiar way she told the time.

'It's a quarter of seven,' she said. 'How much were you intending to drink tonight? There's only so much in the cellar, isn't there James?'

'You've drunk it already, I suppose?' What was she doing? Was she flirting? Was she making common cause against me? Was she seriously worried about drinking too much? Or did this kind of thing really pass for humour where she came from? And really – of all the affectations you had to have – dreaming things really took the biscuit.

She wasn't unsophisticated. She had a round welcoming kind of face, perhaps a little on the plump side, and she seemed to smile all the time. I regarded her objectively as she chatted away to us, her arm reaching out like a piston towards the bowl of nachos on the kitchen table.

I twisted the tab off a can of Grolsch and smelt the grain, and heard about her English professor, and how he got drunk during the college dinners and made outrageous passes at all the American students. I heard about her parents and the deer that wandered into their garden in Minnesota. And most of all, I heard, shining out of almost every anecdote, her enormous optimism. She knew she would finish the thesis and get her PhD. She knew if she wanted to stay in England, she would find some way of doing so. She knew, clearly, that if she wanted James, she could have him. If she needed some nugget of Byron's life, then – even if scholars had failed to unearth it for two centuries – she would still succeed. The sheer effrontery of her optimism seemed to grate with the house, with all its modest English hopelessness and decline.

Or maybe it didn't grate; maybe it just melted a little. It just didn't melt me. Especially because, I realized, she was a major competitor for the missing poem.

'So this dreaming, then. How often do you do it?' I asked, when James was out of the room.

'Oh, I know it sounds dumb, and it *is* dumb and I wish he hadn't said anything. I just think it's worth a try, that's all.'

'You think what's worth a try?'

She was looking trustingly into my face, her fingers fiddling with her rings.

'Well, James didn't finish telling you. I dreamed about this old pile on Wednesday night.'

'You and me both. But what makes your dreams so much more exciting than mine?'

'I'm sure they're not, but you just went on about alcohol while James was going on about this. You see, I dreamed quite clearly I was in the house, and this strange weather-beaten little man, wearing leather and with this lascivious smile and this gnarled old face, came and woke me up.'

'It sounds like one of the long lost Weston family. James should be able to identify him.'

'No, I don't think he was a relative. He took me outside and showed me this strange dance around the house, like some kind of Celtic party, dancing faster and faster, their tongues hanging out and their teeth showing – it should have been a nightmare but it was actually rather sexy.'

'My God,' I said. 'A wet dream about Oberon House. You and James are clearly made for each other.'

She looked a little downcast for a second. Then she laughed at me. 'You're so cynical. I bet you're jealous. But wait. Let me tell you the end, then you'll be even more jealous. The little man took me back into the house, pointed next to the big old fireplace in the main room and there was a kind of wooden door there. And he tapped at it, and then he did something very strange. He licked the end of his finger, and he reached out and ran it down the side of my face. Then I woke up sweating.' Her eyes were glinting a little. I wondered for a second if she had made it up, but decided against.

'So let me guess. Because of this, James is going to take a pickaxe to the already crumbling masonry.'

'He has already.'

And indeed he had. Susie had seen a compartment in her dream and James had taken a pickaxe to the spot. I went out and looked at the sad little hole, with the dust still buzzing about like tiny flies wondering where to settle.

'So you're not ever so slightly embarrassed about this then?' I asked her as we looked at the rubble. 'It wouldn't take many more holes like that one before this place comes tumbling down. Can you lock your dreams away for a bit?'

Susie looked down again for a second. 'Yes, to be honest, of course I feel bad. It was my whim and I shouldn't have said anything.'

'Of course you should,' said James coming into the room behind us, and tripping against a large red brick. 'It was the most exciting half hour I've had for weeks.' His words seemed to echo in the lonely space. Behind him out of the window, the night was dead black with barely a moon.

Susie threw her head back and laughed the kind of unrestrained rattle you expect from cattle-ranchers, a real John Wayne rodeo laugh. I stared at her, annoyed that she hadn't blamed James and his over-enthusiasm for the pickaxe episode, as I had expected her to. It was the signal for us all to loosen up. The Bulgarian red wine flowed into the plastic cups, and the remains of our makeshift picnic – the old pizza wrappings, the packets of tortilla chips, the ice cream cartons – piled up around us in the sink. Susie described her period on Prozac and life in the sororities of North Carolina University, and I ranted on about the Underground, the hubris of Comic Relief and the imbecility of American foreign policy. James was silent, smiling and glowing a little. He hung on every sentence she weaved as if he was a spaniel watching her eat a chocolate biscuit. I watched for signs that they were sleeping together, and wondered at the way she brushed his forearm with her fingers.

Why did this enrage me? Something about their relationship had unravelled my pet view of the world, and of James – though he seemed to be behaving according to type. I tried to make myself feel better by drinking too much, and insulting American politics, American culture and the American inability to visit McDonalds without murdering everyone inside with automatic weapons. But as I hinted at the seducability of American women and the bribability of American men, Susie laughed all the more and capped each of my stories with even worse examples of her own. I even lost my temper when she claimed that British telephone boxes were impossible to use.

'Well, at least we don't have to lug whole sackfuls of coins into the phone box with us just to call the next state,' I shouted, but she just threw her head back again.

I pushed my chair back and stormed out, listening to her peals of laughter behind me and imagining her neck under her T-shirt and her hair against her skin.

In the main room, I stared at the hole in the wall, excavated with such youthful promise by James that he might have been excavating Susie, and I gave it an angry kick. The dust of centuries, the insides of bricks baked during the Wars of the Roses flew up in the air. But when I looked at it again, another small black hole seemed to have appeared in the corner, behind the chimney piece.

It was one of those moments when a million thoughts cascade through your mind at once – registering that other hole, and then one after the other, that this is unusual, that it could indeed be the compartment we have been looking for, that it might even mean James gets the money he needs, and it might even be that Susie has the power of dreaming lost things after all. Then there was the added frisson of disappointment that anyone else – whoever they were – might actually achieve their wildest dreams, as if the stock of available dreams to come true had been reduced again. But most of all there was the worry that Susie would get the poem instead of me. I just had to make sure I was around, that was all.

The hole gaped like an entry into the forbidden pleasures of hell. I felt a moment's temptation to cover it up just to avoid giving Susie the pleasure of having successfully dreamed anything. But I dismissed the idea, stroking my own cheek slowly and staring at the patterns in the old brick. The hole was only the size of a telephone directory, while the remains of the mane of some long-forgotten horse held the crumbling plasterwork together, but it was evident that there was a larger space behind it. I could even see what looked like the metal of a rusty tin box just to the side. This was not the kind of thing that could be hidden: it could, in fact, be the one thing we were all looking for.

The house seemed quieter than usual. The familiar creaks seemed to have stopped, the asthmatic lungs of the old building ceased their expanding and contracting, as if listening to what I would do. The night outside seemed still and shriller than usual. The old nut trees stopped scraping against the boarded-up windows, and for a moment I thought I heard music coming from outside, dull, rhythmic and unearthly. Music for the groin. Music that demands. I strained to hear for a moment at the window, then – with a mixture of chagrin and exhilaration – I called them both in.

XI

'Weep not, weep not my darling boy;
Hush altogether
And then Foul-Weather,
Thy day, will come
Tomorrow home,
Bringing a king's heart for thy joy
To play withall, a pretty toy.'

FROM A CORNISH FAIRY TALE IN KATHERINE BRIGGS'
A DICTIONARY OF FAIRIES

Oberon, November 1912

'IT'S ABSOLUTELY barbaric, this village dance. Pure paganism. It's as if the villagers are children, and as such we shouldn't pander to their childishness.'

Gerald was holding forth at dinner, dressed in an immaculate grey waistcoat in the colours of his reserve regiment. As he spoke, his forearm squeezed the thick silver knife handle that sat heavily in his bony hand. His gaunt white face seemed to stretch back on his forehead to the beginning of his carefully coiffured parting, which swept down towards his eyebrows like Tchaikovsky's dying swan.

'I don't know why the vicar encourages them in this foolery. They should grow up and join in the task of running the empire. Modernisation – that's what we need. Not these silly superstitions.'

His mother was not listening. Edward, looking more bluff and red-faced than usual, was examining his cigarette case. There was a variety of aunts and cousins, sporting their best jewellery and glancing around the room in the first minutes of sitting at an unfamiliar dinner table. Only Harry seemed to be concentrating on what his brother was saying, his head just above the big polished oak table, with its silver candlesticks, salt cellars, sauceboats and regimental mementoes.

It was Gerald's birthday, and the portraits behind him – mournful paintings of desert landscapes and Roman ruins – had been specially dusted for the occasion. It was the first time Harry had been allowed down to dinner. Normally he was given his high tea in the nursery by a bored maid, but his mother had insisted on including him. He smiled nervously at the servants in the shadows, bringing the dishes on to the hot plates, wondering what he should say to sound grown-up.

'You must say something, dear,' his mother had said, as she examined his red velvet jacket with approval. 'It doesn't matter very much what it is. It's polite, and you don't want people to think you're a baby.'

But he was aware, now that it came to the point, that his mother looked distracted and unlikely to take in anything he said. He watched the chandelier glinting in the candlelight, half aware of the awkward atmosphere, unsure whether this was how adult dinners were generally conducted, or whether the empty chair at the head of the table was a normal departure. Everybody seemed to be glancing at it, but nobody had mentioned the non-appearance of his father – who he thought had also seemed distracted over the weekend.

'We should serve, I think,' said his mother in a quiet voice to Gerald. 'I'm sure your father would have arrived by now if he could. No doubt the Charing Cross line has been difficult today.'

'Please go ahead and serve, Ted,' said Gerald in a loud and haughty voice, before continuing his detailed description of his dislike of village customs. 'They wouldn't dare do the dance, with those damn silly bells, if I was the squire around here.'

'Since you will be one day, they'd better start practising something else,' said Edward. 'What would you prefer them to do? Drill?'

'Well it would be more appropriate to the twentieth century and the age of the motor car than these pathetic fairy customs,' said Gerald after another sip of red wine. 'Ted, I did say go ahead and serve, so please do us the favour of going ahead and serving.'

Edward waved his white linen napkin in the air before putting it on his lap. 'I don't know,' he said with a twinkle in his eye. 'I think this fellow Barrie is onto something. I thought *Peter Pan* was one of the best adventure stories I've ever heard. It has everything, hasn't it – pirates, red Indians, crocodiles. You need a few fairies to leaven the loaf.'

'Yes,' said Harry, seizing the opportunity to say something he knew about. On his wall upstairs, he had Arthur Rackham's oak-framed pictures of fairies flitting across Kensington Gardens. They looked a little feminine for his taste. His heart beat fast, as the eyes of the table swivelled to look at him. It was as if they had noticed his presence for the first time. The child's first official word: 'Yes'.

'You've been listening to too many family stories,' said Gerald, who had his head screwed on so tightly it was hard for him to fully open his mouth. He was at Sandhurst and had a weak and carefully-chopped moustache and a particular interest in the battles of the Zulu wars. He spoke little, but the sound of his twelve-bore echoed round the estate. 'I remember, we whacked a boy at school for believing in fairies. Hulton, he was called. Soon changed his mind after that I can tell you.'

'Well, I don't have to change my mind,' said Harry definitely, feeling that some reply was expected from him and picking up his fork with studied nonchalance. 'I certainly don't believe in fairies. I thought *Peter Pan* was tosh.'

'You clapped your hands pretty hard for Tinkerbell, I seem to remember,' said Edward. 'I know. I was sitting next to you clapping hard myself to keep her alive. So don't desert me now.'

He smiled beatifically and everyone except Gerald laughed. Harry's face went the colour of the wine in the glasses round the table.

'In any case, we shouldn't doubt the existence of fairies here, should we?' said one of the faceless nameless chinless cousins. 'We all know what happened to Great-Aunt Emma.'

'Great-Great-Great-Aunt Emma, at least,' said Edward, licking his knife and pouring himself more wine at the same time. Harry's attention pricked up. Isn't it strange, he thought. You only have to hear something once and then suddenly the name pops up all the time.

'It doesn't matter how many greats she was. Emma never existed,' said Gerald irritably. 'I don't know why you persist in this fantasy. It's just a story. And rather an embarrassing one for the family at that. I'm surprised at you, Judith, for bringing it up in front of Harry.'

'Oh Harry's known the story for years,' retorted Edward. 'In fact, you know, Grandpapa mentioned it to him before he died, which is damned interesting, if you ask me. In any case, I rather like it.'

A red glow now appeared in Gerald's cheeks, but he said nothing. There was something about the illogical, the fantastical and the simply untidy that irritated Gerald. The world was hurtling towards confusion, he felt, and things must be kept in their proper place. The awkwardness of the world upset him, made him feel awkward himself and unsafe.

'What story?' said Harry. 'What story? Oh, please tell me.'

'You know,' said Edward, with a wink. 'You know the story about the mysterious disappearance of our relative? I couldn't possibly tell you that story. You're far, far too young.'

Harry kicked him under the table, but missed and hit one of the spaniels that lurked there at mealtimes.

'Oh, for goodness sake,' said Gerald, banging his fork on the table so that the tomato soup bounced in its bowl. 'I think we've managed to get a little further than that.' And the conversation degenerated into Gerald's views on military engineering, the great bridge over the Firth of Forth, the future of the White Star Line and the rational hope for the empire once sensible science had spread around the globe. It was Harry's first dinner conversation and he never forgot it. Not so much because of the disappearance of Great-Aunt Emma but because it was also the last of its kind. By the time they pushed their leather chairs back from the table, the family would never be the same again.

The empty chair was nothing new. There was often an empty chair for his father, with the indentation made by his bottom the last time he sat there desperately trying to conjure him back into existence. Usually it was a sign that John Weston was struggling away in the bank. But would he deliberately miss Gerald's birthday dinner? Harry's father was a stickler for punctuality when it mattered, expecting high standards of his tenant farmers and the foreman of the estate as much as from his family and his clerks. He kept card index records of his employees as well as his friends, with little notes about their birthdays and the occasions on which he'd had a need to reprimand them. A good half century later, Harry was still using them to write shopping lists on. He should have been there.

A kind of premonition gripped the company when Sophie the maid came in, very apologetically, and said there was a gentleman at the door. 'And he says he is from the *Daily Mail*.'

John Weston had rejected the idea of a telegram some hours before, but he wanted to do what was right. He realised the irony of this. If he could not face his family again, that seemed sin enough, but he hardly wanted to compound the evil by simply failing to turn up. He would write a letter, and give it with a substantial tip to the guard on the train past Oberon Station, to drop it off with the stationmaster. It was little enough, but it was the least he could do.

With this plan formulated in his mind, he stood at the tatty front door leading to Jenny's upstairs flat in Jermyn Street, looking only a fraction of the man he used to be, sure in his mind about what he had to do. He could barely look at her in the face, but she took his hands, then took his coat.

'Jenny,' he said. 'I seem to have ruined my bank, and I'm leaving on the boat train in an hour. I understand completely if you will not come, but I am here to ask if you will.'

Jenny flinched a little. The newspaper beside the door showed that she had at least guessed the reason for the crisis. In the most trusting moment of her life, she nodded her head and stared up into his face, wondering whether it was too tactless at the moment, too impolite, to ask just how much money he now had. As she packed her bags she kicked herself for not asking, wondering for how long she was likely to be away. She collected a few belongings – one dress, the photograph of her dead husband, his posthumous medal from the siege of Kimberley. John sat down to write the letter of his life.

'My darling wife,' it read:

By the time you read this letter, I will be on the other side of the Channel. My beloved, you will also no doubt have heard those things which I should have warned you against, as I should have warned many other people, days ago. You will know also what I should have told you myself, but was too ashamed to do – that we are all but ruined.

If I was more of a man, I would perhaps have ended it all here and now, were it not for the greater dishonour which would fall so unfairly upon you and the family. The disaster which has befallen us was not my fault, but it was my responsibility. Like a tragedy, it was only a small error of judgement – one that I will remember every waking moment for the rest of my life – which persuaded me to trust a man I should never have trusted. It was my mistake alone and by leaving now, at the moment I know when it must seem cruellest for you – I hope I shall impress on those investigators that it was I and I alone who takes responsibility.

You will wonder what my intentions are and I must keep those clouded, for fear that you will plan for me when I am unable to live up to your plans and expectations. You will also have to trust me when I say that, if it is in my power to do so, I will return and bring with me the means to undo this great wrong I have caused you today.

In my absence, please remember that I have cared for you and our children to the best of my ability until now, that your picture and thoughts of you will be with me always, and that you remain the sole guardian of my reputation in the family.

Oh, my dear, I am so ashamed of the pain I am causing you. It is better for us both that I should remove the cause of that pain from your life for a while.

Your devoted husband,
John Weston Esq.

He understood as he put down his pen and sealed the envelope, that dinner was probably being prepared at Oberon House. Although he meant every word of the letter, he knew he had not actually explained what some might consider to be the most important part. It occurred to him that when his family – and his wife in particular – discovered that he had fled the country with his mistress, they might feel that it cancelled out all the assurances he had given in the letter. But a wave of moral exhaustion overtook him. If that was what they felt, so be it. He had done what he could.

'You know what Charles of Anjou said when he realised his last battle as King of Sicily was lost?' he asked Jenny, as they heaved her luggage into the third-class compartment at Victoria Station, the smell of damp steam, egg sandwiches and cigarette smoke around them in a thick fug. 'He said: "Lord, since it pleases you to ruin my fortune, let me only descend by small steps".'

Jenny said nothing. She was looking out at the traffic and wondering what might have been.

'Small steps!' said John Weston suddenly and with self-pitying energy. 'I seem to have plummeted head first downstairs.' Then – thinking of his family at home – and realising he retained neither wealth nor reputation, and what remained of the latter he was about to fling away, he put his head in his hands. He stared at the criss-crossed string holding the luggage above their heads, then put his face in his hands.

'John? Are you unwell?' she said.

'No... no,' he said, struggling back to consciousness and determination. As the train heaved itself out of the station and the carriage wheels clicketty-clicked into a faster rhythm, a small part of Jenny's mind leapt in exaltation at a sudden realisation of her power, and a small part of his died. At that moment, the guard was stuffing his letter and tip into his waistcoat pocket.

Three hours later, with John and Jenny half way across the Channel, his letter was delivered to Oberon House by a junior member of the station staff. As he arrived at the door, the first newspaper reporter had just got there first. Oberon House had no telephone, and this was the first news that anyone had dared to bring to Mr Weston's family. As he handed it over at the door, two policemen in plain clothes arrived, having caught the same train down from London.

'Ma'am, two more gentlemen to receive you,' said Sophie to the table, which had still not got up, but had been exchanging nervous glances after the last bit of news a few moments before.

'Thank you, Sophie. What can they all want at this hour?' said John's abandoned wife, mentally fixing a face of calm to cover her worst fears as she left the room.

'I think perhaps we should accompany her,' said Gerald, white as a sheet. The two older brothers did so, followed by the aunts in embarrassed silence. Bemused and alone with the half-eaten meal, Harry looked first at the ceiling, glanced at the walls and pictures that had become so familiar to him, and then at the window. And then he started. He could have sworn two glinting eyes were shining through the glass in the dark.

They were not malevolent, nor even very interested, but they were aware and somehow intelligent, seeming somehow to represent the unspoken fear which had suddenly filled the house. Harry got up, stared back at them for a moment as they took in the scene dispassionately, the silver and plates and half eaten joint – when Sophie came in to clear away the plates.

'Look!' said Harry. 'Look in the window!' And he looked

back quickly but it was too late. All that remained from the eyes was a slight fogging of the glass from the other side.

'Look at what? Are you playing tricks on me again, Master Harry?' said Sophie. But she was shaking too much to keep her voice entirely steady, thinking about the implications of the visitors.

'No, no honestly, there was something there. Looking at me.'

'I expect he was looking at how much pudding you've been eating,' said Sophie briskly. 'What do you think those two policemen could want at a time like this?'

This was a rhetorical question that seemed to demand no answer. In any case, in those days it would not have been done for a servant to pry. But to express common bafflement and worry – that was somehow so much more polite. Sophie had stacked the plates and some of the glasses and cutlery on the tray. Harry watched her ample bottom, swathed in her black uniform, amble out through the door, with a faint ringing sound as glass rubbed against glass. That picture, more than the strange eyes, stayed with him, in later years. He remembered it as the last moment of security before his world, and the secure worlds of those around him, tumbled about him.

XII

'Lord Soulis he sat in Hermitage Castle,
And beside him Old Redcap sly; -
'Now tell me, thou sprite, who are meikle of might
The death that I must die?' –
JOHN LEYDEN

Letters found in old tin box in the panelling of Oberon House.

Oberon House,
24 Sept. 1811

My dear brother,

My heart goes out to you and I ask for your forgiveness, if only you can summon it up, knowing wt. I am about to do. I know I will be causing you more pain than your burned grain store near One Tree field this Autumn last; I know that you will call what I am about to do an elopement, yet elope I must – and I shudder just to use the fatal word. I know the strenuous & implacable anger with which you have opposed my deepening Friendship with Lord Byron. I know also that you have done so out of Deep and Fraternal love for me.

Let it not be said that I plunge the family's name and your happiness into the hands of the gossips through girlish ignorance or innocence of what I am doing. I am old enough to know my own Mind and to know the Difficulties I will cause, & yet I must still go.

Even so, I hope you will come through the seasons to understand, bearing in mind that your love for me rivals my own for you, that I must listen to the beating of my Heart and do what it commands. Yes, I know this will make the tongues in the village cluck, and old Aunt Hester's set in London will be sent into a gaggling frenzy, but I know also the Contempt in which you hold them. So I hope you will discover it in you, before too many moons have slipped by, to forgive your loving, if not entirely dutiful sister.

You and I have never agreed about these matters, I know. I remember so well, even when we were young, you would return to Oberon House with the sweat from the toil with the horses or sheep on your young forehead and dismiss my romantic prattle. Yet I must live in accordance with my own laws, and I am certain that I would not feel this clamouring in my own breast if it did not come partly from Heaven. Not perhaps from that dry old stick of a God which Parson Brightford preaches every Sunday, with those interminable sermons, but the God you and I know truly, of the wind through the woods at night and the Great Summer Moon.

You will realise from this letter that I have decided to go with him. By the time you read my poor scrawl, I will have slipped down the old passageway that you and I used to laugh about and in which we hid as children those winter evenings so long ago, and will be in the arms of my One True Love, and with him – God willing – we will play such Music that the very Angels will sing along with us. I leave it here for you to find. It comes with my devotion and love and contrition to you, my brother, with whom I have shared so much.

I hope your understanding of my decision will grow if I relate to you a strange occurrence of the past few days. For I believe I have seen the Little People. Once again, I know if I was to say this to you with your dear face in my sight, you would put back that great head of yours and laugh till the tears ran at what you call my foolishness, and pat my head and send me on my way. Yet the strangest occurrence must be reported to you, for it happened on your land, and may help you to understand what I am about to do.

You remember I have been asking you these past months about that man in your employ – I assume he is in your employ – with the leather jerkin who I see so often by the old barn, and seems to haunt my walks. His brazen stares, you will recall, I find discomfiting. All the more so because I do not remember seeing him around the village & have assumed that he must be a stranger – yet I have never seen him at work. Well, I have seen him again.

I was, I will admit to you, with my Love in the wooded path down by Tupenny Meadow, and the sun was low in the sky and the shadows long. If you were prepared to converse with him, he would confirm what I say. There was this strange man, who looks like a wizened pear, barring our way and smiling his toothless abominable smile. 'My good fellow, will you let us pass,' said my Lord. And the man stood aside with elaborate obsequiousness, keeping his eyes on me the whole time, and swept us by. As you know, I find his recent attentions worse than irksome.

I found myself gripping Byron's arm in fear as we walked over the stile, through that copse where you and I once played those games. But the first I realised that anything was amiss was a strange tinkling sound, like bells on the dancers at the Maytime festivities in the village, but so distant and so high-pitched that I which I could but imitate dear Portia, whose long brown ears could have recognised the sounds with ease. Byron heard them too and stopped and seemed to sniff about him. I was about to accuse him of behaving like Portia himself when we saw them. Dancing in a small ring, there seemed to be a whole crowd of the tiniest people. 'It is the Faeries,' said Byron with as much disbelief as I. 'I have seen the Faeries.'

I stood transfixed at the apparition and yet there seemed nothing ghoulish about them. Their shadows did not fall upon the grass as yours and mine do, and there was a strange atmosphere to them, like an awakening in the belly, an excitement which I blush to describe, as if they provided a portent of forbidden plenty. As if they wanted me in some way – some tempting way.

There were other strange things. I thought they had a greenish tinge, but as the thought formed in my mind, it became less clear. Was it green or red? I remain unsure, and discussing the matter with my Lord afterwards, he claimed that the colours were blue. And their clothes as well, seemed at first to be akin to that in which Robin Hood led his Merry Men, but at second glance I wondered if they were wearing clothes at all. They were, though, proportioned as to a man that we would recognise. These were no gnomes or goblins from a story book. They were little men & women and completely absorbed in their dance, occasionally smiling at me with a frightening hunger in their eyes.

My lord pulled out his haversack and said: 'We must leave them with some of our morsels. For I would fain see the Little People without leaving some token behind me. Let them not forget that as we have gazed on them, they have gazed on Lord Byron and his love.' He pulled out a plate, two slices of ham and a bottle of ale, which he opened, and set them down in front of us. And as he did so, the vision began to fade, like a cloud lifting and we seemed alone. I stared at the spot for what seemed like two strikes of the clock and so did he. We left the clearing and came straight home and said little to each other along the way. But as I glanced back, I could see that weather-beaten fellow still watching me across the field, as if he had somehow willed the whole event for his own amusement.

And oh! how my Heart was bursting to tell you as we came in the familiar front door of Oberon, with its old bell there on the slate & its familiar leather boots. How could I keep such a secret from my beloved Brother? But you would have been so angry had you discovered that I had ventured out against your will with Lord Byron alone in the woods – though I know him to be gentle and safe company for any lady, despite the unfair prattle of the London gossips, and despite his romantic and excitable nature.

I ached to tell you, Joseph – I ached! It hurt to keep the report inside, like an overfull belly after Sunday luncheon. But the story became yet stranger.

The following evening, I thought I saw a flash of green as I walked in the garden at the close of the day, but I dismissed it. Then I thought I caught sight of one of the little Men at the window. Odd little events took place, I remembered. I had found my petticoat neatly washed and pressed and folded at the end of my bed a couple of days later, yet was sure I had not put it out for Annie. Again, I could tell you nothing. Then just this morning, I was walking again – against your wishes – in the woods with my Love, putting together what I believe are the arrangements for our lives together, barely noticing the leaves and twigs around us. I confess, I had all but forgotten the strange dancing of a week ago, but when we reached the same spot, there was Byron's plate, and on it I was astonished to see a small number of tiny, fresh but beautifully iced cakes.

You know how little I can resist such delicacies. I believed we had stumbled upon one of the village family's Picnics, abandoned in the clearing, but the size and freshness of the cakes made me fancy that they were especially intended for me. I squeezed one between thumb and forefinger, and it was perfectly baked & succulent, like a timely parting gift from our little Friends. I went to lick my fingers, but Byron shouted at me.

I confess I was quite taken aback & dropped the cake, knowing that he had never before raised his voice to me. 'Do you not understand?' he said, 'that this is the food of the Faeries?'

'Well,' said I. 'I had wondered such.'

'Then do not let even a morsel pass your Lips. Have you not heard the tales of mortals who feed on the gifts of Faeries? Have you not heard the stories of men who feed at the Faery tables and wake up a century hence. How are you & I to be lovers if we fall into a deep sleep that lasts for a hundred years?'

'Oh fie, my Lord,' says I. 'I am but tasting it. There is no need for such a superstitious outburst. Especially over such old wives Follies.'

At this he became angry and I feared for our Love, having never before seen him rage & rant so at the idiocies of women, shouting that he would sooner eat the cakes himself, and how little he cared that our faerie Friends believed we shewed a want of gratitude. I know he is of Romantic disposition, and his moods swing so, but his rage frighted me sorely and I resolved to do what he wants. For if I give rise to such tumults in such a Man, then I must do his bidding.

I readily admit to you that, although I let the cakes fall back neatly on the plate and ran to his side, hoping to calm him, that I let a few crumbs remain on my fingers, so – when his back was turned – I was able to know the taste of faery Food. And sweet it was.

I know, my darling brother, that your good sense will make your cheeks puff out red in affront at these fripperies & dreams. I hope you will stay indignant at my silly tale & overlook my sudden tho' reluctant disappearance from our home. I remember how you & I played at Faeries many times when we were both but youths. I know that you looked hopefully towards the copse at Midsummer, expecting at least a glimpse of Puck himself. So how could I leave without telling you what I have seen & I believe, & though I am but a giddy girl – & more affected by love than I believed it possible to be – I know what I saw. Now having seen, I believe it was a sign that confirms what I must do.

Joseph, please pray for me while you do not forgive me, and then forgive me while you do not communicate with me, & then communicate with me while you still do not welcome me home. I must do this thing. I could not face my deathbed with the ghost of what I had not dared to do still haunting me. I go to have life more abundantly, but I go with you & Oberon House in my heart.

Your loving and devoted sister,

Emma Weston

St James' Street,
October 19th 1811

Sir,

I would be more than offended at your haughty & dismissive tone – did I not know how much it must distress you to write to me at all, – & did I not feel very personally your sense of loss. – I too have lost your sister. For I must tell you – in all honesty – & I shudder at the implications of this – that she is not with me, nor has she ever been with me since I was at Oberon House this past month enjoying your hospitality. I would of course say if she was – but she is not.

I wd understand your resentment of me if you believed I had perverted her affections, – as you say – and certainly if it had in truth been my intention to steal her away at dead of night, – but it was not, whatever you may have been informed. Nor is it my habit, – whatever you might hear – to abuse the hospitality of a gentleman by eloping with their sisters.

I will admit to you now that Miss Weston had some such fantasy. — You will have to take my word that this ws not my plan, & when I discovered it was hers I swiftly disabused her of it – which is how I came to leave Oberon House in such a hurry. I do not accept what you say about influencing her. Though I disdain the laws of Men and am half a machine-breaker myself, I did not discuss such things with her. – Nor what you say about our walks on your estate. Emma is her own woman & knows what she does.

As for your final outrageous sally — if she be not Intact, it was not of my authorship. I forbid you to repeat such scurrility.

I am – of course – deeply concerned about her whereabouts, given that I believed her with you, & broken to hear about her note to you, which would imply my betrayal. You must let me know what I can do to assist the search, but you must believe me clearly when I say that she is not with me. Would that she was.

I must end by assuring you of my continued regards. -

- I have the honour to be with continued respect, yr. most obedt. & obliged Servt.

Byron

XIII

'Taffy ap Sion stepped one evening into a fairy circle and danced, as he thought, for a few minutes, but when he stepped out everything was changed...'

WELSH FAIRY TALE IN KATHERINE BRIGGS'
A DICTIONARY OF FAIRIES

English Channel, November 1912

THERE was a little money left which the lawyers and liquidators were unable to touch. The days of unlimited personal liability for directors had gone, but John Weston and the other directors had allowed their personal wealth to be managed by the bank, so that had become entangled in the South American railway disaster as well. As his stomach heaved on the choppy cross-Channel steamer, where within less than two years his sons would follow on troopships towards the Western Front, he knew that only too well.

Every penny he had ever earned or inherited seemed to allocate itself one by one in his mind, and each one land with a sickening thump in his queasy stomach. As he gripped the handrail in the spray, he confronted the full shame of what had happened – the collapse of his somewhat smug and pompous existence, his family life, his dinners by candlelight, his faithful staff, the hopes and dreams of his wife and children, the warmth of their trust in him, an unknown number of centuries' habitation of Oberon House, stretching back into the fogs of the past. All gone, and in his brief tenure. Through his own small failings.

If only he had questioned Jordan more closely. If only he had spent a little less time with Jenny. Yet he also knew, as he fingered the broken varnish on the rail and watched the seagulls swooping into the surf, that without Jenny on the ship with him, he would have been unable to prevent himself from leaping over the side. He knew, in his saner moments, that this would have made the situation for those he loved all the more intolerable. But he also knew the fate that would befall him in the years to come. A pathetic, homeless, dependent family. The shame of living largely on Jenny's allowance, plus the small amount he had salted away in his Paris account for holidays. The unmentioned black sheep, the remittance man without a remittance, his photograph torn from the family albums, his name spoken in hushed tones and not in front of the children. His own family's very own Oscar Wilde.

He could smell the coal smoke belching from the ferry funnels, as if it came from the pits of hell. He felt as though God had sent an angel to swoop down and tear his intestines out before his very eyes. For a moment he saw himself as Job, buffeted by cruel fate, until he was overwhelmed afresh by his own culpability and slapped himself down for his pretensions. Then Jenny came up behind him in her long green dress and the fox fur he had given her, and gently stroked the skin over his stiff collar as he stared out to sea.

* * *

Harry often tried to recall the scene in the drawing room after the arrival of the reporter, the letter and the police in quick succession – his mother sitting red-eyed, his brothers standing, Gerald behind her chair, Edward staring out of the window as the occasional duck plummeted towards the pond, black against the sky. It seemed such an overwhelmingly fateful and unlucky moment. Not even the cruellest fairy could have brought together such a chapter of woes, even the one that stared through the window at him. In later life, Harry went through a period of despising his father, not so much for his mistake, but for involving him – tangentially, at least – in the arrogant and unholy obsessions of the City of London, where everything sacred could be transformed into money and counted on the exchanges. Where the centuries-old dust of Oberon and the fields and old Josiah could be melted down somehow into lucre.

Later he would rage to himself at the loss of his inheritance at the hands of a venal father. But something would happen to make him realize how easily ruined we humans are, and later still he honoured his father's memory with as much reverence as he set aside for Oberon House itself and its gigantic window on the world. But none of those things did he feel in the weeks that followed, as the implications began to unravel. There was the publicity. The arrest of John's colleagues and their eventual acquittal months later, and a warrant for John's own arrest delivered to the house and taken away again by detectives who had his disappearance explained patiently to them. There was the threatened bankruptcy, despite the small income that John had hoped to safeguard for his family by his disappearance: he had hoped that by deserting the family he could draw the debt-collectors away from them. He was wrong.

Harry's brother Gerald had to leave Sandhurst and take up work as a clerk in a firm of City solicitors, which made him miserable but no less pompous. Edward never hunted again across the Oberon hedgerows: he was shortly to be blown to pieces by a shell, with the words 'Love from the Ruhr' chalked on it in German. Gerald was to suffer a different fate immediately after the Armistice, at the hands of influenza.

Oberon House and the estate was handed over to the lawyers. Harry was taken away from school and sent somewhere very much less expensive – a small public school in Bath, with bizarre and unpleasant sado-masochistic traditions. It specialized in long homilies from the pulpit by the headmaster about the vileness of masturbation and the general filthiness of the world in general. John Weston set down roots in Dieppe. He settled down to a regular routine, waking later in the day – pottering around the town, eventually included in the games of *boules* – and going to bed at dusk, reading the novels of Thackeray over and over again, interspersed with Sherlock Holmes stories. Jenny, meanwhile, took in washing and sewing, and practised singing, while her lover grew prematurely old.

John's family was never able to discover what, if anything, he did for a living, though Jenny certainly gave music lessons. Even so, the occasional money order arrived through the post to his wife. At first, the letters he wrote to Harry were seized by the enraged aunts he was sent to stay with in the immediate aftermath of the family's collapse. Eventually a few of them managed to filter through, every six months or so, filled with strange admonitions and a kind of fantastical ignorance of life and reality. But Harry appreciated them and kept them until, years later, he threw them away in a sudden fit of rage.

Returning home from the aunts a month or so later, Harry found the house all but stripped of everything valuable. Sophie and most of the servants had gone and his mother spent most of the time in her bedroom. Almost alone in the house, Harry searched absent-mindedly through the books and found a dusty old photograph album in which all of the pictures of his father had been removed, leaving in one case just the top of his head. He closed it carefully, put it back on the bookshelf, walked into the woods and wept.

A few weeks later, there was little left. His mother had moved to a small cottage nearby. The furniture and silver had been sold, but a few sticks remained and the house had been all but repossessed by the bank, though in those more gentlemanly days, the new institution which seemed to own their lives was run by an old friend of Harry's father. In fact, Mr Wargrave was in thrall to Harry's mother. Both knew it; neither admitted it nor acted on it.

'Sad business,' he used to say in Harry's presence, more to himself than anybody else, when they met at the public sales in the drive of the house, watching his mother's beloved curtains, clothes and sideboards being knocked down to the highest bidder. Harry felt he should reply, but could never think quite what to say, so kept quiet.

Mr Wargrave sat through the rest of the proceedings impassively in his high collar, fighting the temptation to take Harry's mother's hand. The effort made him sweat profusely.

'My dear Mrs Weston, I probably shouldn't say this, but I am holding my fire on the sale of the actual house. I don't want to jump the gun. I feel sure John had something up his sleeve.'

'Mr Wargrave, isn't that terribly improper?' Eleanor Weston was wearily willing him to make no further declaration of his interest. One more favour, one more declaration, would be the straw that broke the proverbial camel's back, she said to herself – as their set of napkin rings went under the hammer.

'Mum's the word, eh? I don't want to turn you out on the street, if you don't mind me using the expression,' said Mr Wargrave, forgetting himself for a moment, and glistening in the afternoon sunshine.

'You have already,' said Harry, who was seething behind them. Harry could never bear bullies. From Mackintosh Major at school to the Kaiser, he pictured them all like Mr Wargrave.

'Harry, that's not fair at all. Mr Wargrave is doing the very best he can. Apologize to him at once, then go and do something useful.'

Harry did so, and as he did, the big oak table from the dining room was carried out of the house and heaved up onto the dais by two hefty balding men in overalls, its polished surface glinting in the sunlight. The auctioneer was beginning to look like Mr Wargrave as he moved in for the kill.

'Right, ladies, gentleman, this is a really beautiful piece.' There was a murmur of approval from the small crowd of people. 'I'd like you to pay special attention to the legs which reveal this as a genuinely sixteenth-century item and we know this one has been in the one family since it was made. Truly remarkable in this day and modern age, ladies and gentlemen …'

Harry glanced up at his mother and saw her white-faced and biting her lip.

'Mother, do we have to be here? Do we have to listen?'

'Hush dear,' she said, patting his arm, but not taking her eyes off the auctioneer. 'Remember, they're doing this for us. It seems that your father hasn't managed after all. I've scoured the house from top to bottom for his special investments for a rainy day. There's no sign at all. We need the money.'

There was a murmur of excitement around them, and a man in a bowler hat and tight-fitting suit bobbed up.

'Sold to Mr Rowbottom thank you, sir,' said the auctioneer without breathing between the words, searching for his handkerchief at the same time. Harry fled.

The news that his mother had been searching the house fired Harry with new energy and hope. As the afternoon wore on, and listening to the occasional ripple of greedy applause from outside the front of the house, Harry peered into cupboards, felt around the inside of doorframes, poked around in chimneys, the dust settling happily onto his tweed suit. He trawled through the empty house, past the gaps left by the chandeliers, the dark patches where the hunting pictures had once been, glancing into the remaining bowls and out-of-place teacups, and feeling in the cobwebs behind the empty glass cases.

There was something about Oberon House that prompted people to start combing through it. Harry's mother was not the first, nor the last, to imagine that the house somehow held the key to dreams or rescue hidden away in its wainscots. It was even said that you could hear the echoes of centuries of long-dead people carrying on their searches in the house, night after night, or people who still needed finding long after the end of their natural life – at least one maid had walked out complaining of ghostly children crying in the dark – but Harry had never heard anything of the kind. As a hunt, Harry's search was successful. He found old marbles, yellowing sheets of paper with news about Mafeking and Kimberley, piles of old pennies, a couple of rubber bands and a whole menagerie of spiders and earwigs, living a separate existence in the house.

Then there was the parlour, into which he had barely set foot since his grandparents had died. As he pushed through the green baize door he could see, silhouetted in the afternoon light, the familiar old high-backed chairs, which had escaped the attention of the teams of valuers that had stormed through the house. He stroked the worn arms, almost shiny from their years of occupation, and felt the woodworm holes winking back at him. He sat in the chair belonging to his grandmother and watched the serious-looking men with papers, passing and re-passing the windows that looked out on the gardens. He felt a terrible mixture of sadness and rage, but no immediately deserving object of hate sprang to mind; nobody he could really blame. Even his father seemed a pathetic figure, the victim of tragic circumstances rather than the monster who had brought despair and disrepute down on his family. Instead, Harry focused his anger on the smug bloated figure of Mr Wargrave and his patronising 'support'. The way his red throat squeezed itself over his collar; the way he fiddled with the shiny end of his nose as if tempted to pick it; the way he patted Harry infuriatingly on the head.

The shadows were beginning to lengthen in the garden as he sat down on the chair, and the long shadow of the old oak tree – the one which took the place of the tree which had provided wood for the chair – crept along the rhododendrons. Harry rocked back on the legs a couple of times, keeping it balanced on his toes. Suddenly there was a small crunch as the chair descended an inch or two to the left. It was the last straw: the right leg had splintered at the back.

With that combination of rage and shame, there was only one place he could go. To the cellar under the stables, where he had barely ever ventured, except with Edward. There was nobody interested enough to watch where he went, and he headed off to the familiar corner. There were no bales of hay obscuring the entrance in the floor, because the horses were long gone, and so were the stable hands. The entrance was under a stone with a large rusty ring in it. It was extremely heavy to lift, but Harry had watched Edward use a crowbar to heave it open in the past, and it was still there. Harry could barely lift the crowbar, let alone the stone, but by pulling it down with his whole weight, it suddenly lifted and jerked out of place.

Down these narrow dark steps, along the passage to the chamber with the well at the bottom, the cavaliers in hiding had spent months during the Civil War, and the Protestant clerics, clutching their printed bibles in English and their copies of Cranmer's prayer book, had cowered during the reign of Queen Mary. For more than a hundred years, its entrance had been hidden by hay. Its existence in the centuries that followed was continually forgotten and then rediscovered by children and lovers, so that the great stone lid on the stairs had become progressively easier to shift. There was another set of stairs leading from the chamber which evidently went up to the house, and ended in a brick wall, and another locked door which led, evidently, to the legendary passage.

In the weeks that passed on his increasingly rare visits to Oberon House, when nobody seemed concerned about where he was for whole afternoons at a stretch, Harry made the cellar his own. He took down books and candles and sandwiches provided by the caretaker Mr Moony – with his bizarre and old-fashioned side-whiskers and his collection of medals from the Zulu Wars – the only servant left in the family's employ.

But on this visit down the dark damp stone steps, all by himself, Harry found himself driven by the picture of Mr Wargrave helping his mother lasciviously up from her chair at the end of the auction. The men in leather aprons and the day-trippers in bowler hats and the women in crinolines began to disperse, and the shadows once again engulfed the house. Harry had brought with him a few mementoes of their previous life. He had an old letter of his father's from before his disappearance, a piece of headed paper from Granite & Partners, and – torn carefully from the photo album – all that remained of the top of his father's head.

In the corner by the well, there was a small alcove and

waist level. He put them all there, together with a couple of candles he found in the scullery, and some rose petals from the garden. Whenever he escaped down the passageway, he would light the candle at this makeshift shrine, hoping that if he did so – and if he thought clearly and positively about his father – he could somehow conjure him back, recapture the house and heal the dolorous blow. When he left, he blew it out carefully, but the thought of the candle burning away in the darkness next to him made him feel there was some kind of magic he was creating that would eventually put things right. In his more pessimistic moments, it just seemed a little like himself – a small flame, staying alight by the skin of its teeth, in the immensity of the world.

XIV

'From Oberon, in Fairyland,
The king of ghosts and shadows there,
Mad Robin, I at his command,
Am sent to view the night-sports here.'
BEN JONSON, *ROBIN GOODFELLOW*

Oberon House, June 1998

'OF COURSE we're going to have to find out where this passage goes,' I said. 'But are you sure it isn't some kind of a hoax. I can take UFOs, even angels. But fairies? Come on, James!'

We held the two letters in our hands, crisp to the point of crumbling into their constituent chemicals, as if the flimsy paper was held together by the ink alone. We had unwrapped these dust-covered missives from the cheesecloth in which they had laid for a century at least. They had not actually come out of the hole, but from a rusty black box, with no lock, hidden between the bricks and the old wood panelling. It was unclear when this had been hidden or by whom, but it fell out on James' arm as he removed more of the bricks.

The why was pretty obscure as well. Why not just destroy the letters from Byron and Emma, especially since they may have cast an embarrassing glow on the family's past? And why hide them here?

'Oh, I don't know,' said James vaguely, staring at the black quill scratchings, almost green with age, nearly unreadable in their obscurity. We were both, I think, a little disappointed that these were not the missing poems.

It was the morning after we had come upon the hole and we had taken the box and the letters upstairs to the great window in order to read them again by the light, and to watch the extraordinary patterns the wind was making with the clouds. One by one, we read through the two letters – the long one from Emma and the short note by Byron himself – James with a look of triumph on his face, his nose at a jaunty successful angle, me with incredulity, Susie in smiling silence.

I have almost nothing that belonged to my parents. I have no keepsakes, no bracelets, no hair clips even. I have almost no photographs to explain to myself where I came from. Susie's traditional American rootlessness had taken her many thousands of miles from Minnesota and everything she called her own in a permanent sense. Yet here was James apparently rebuilding his genetic make-up, wire by wire like an electrical circuit. I felt insubstantial in the house, as if I didn't quite exist, and angry at his luck.

I could understand the triumphant expression as well. There may have been no poem in the box – nobody finds exactly what they seek as easily as that. But the mere fact that there had been a box at all seemed to point towards the possibility of other treasures, holding their breath waiting to be found. If only we knew which wooden panels to demolish. The contents of the ancient letters – assuming they were genuine – also implied the existence of some kind of passageway and of the reality of the old story about Byron, Emma and her disappearance. There seemed to be no resolution to the mystery in the box, no key, no forwarding address, but there was at least evidence of something rather bizarre, some unrecorded byway in the life of the great poet. I wondered to myself whether it had anything to do with the noises in the night.

But fairies? They seemed to take the story to such a fantastical level that it threw everything into doubt.

'No mention of Father Christmas, I see,' I said, looking out at the clouds. 'Disappointing.' They ignored me.

'Oh, I don't know,' said James again. He was at his most dishevelled, his hair almost individually tangled – as if each strand is reacting differently to what he had been reading – his teeth unbrushed, his face unshaven. Yet despite this, he seemed to be growing in authority, and had been ever since he arrived at Oberon House. It irritated me all the more.

'Don't you think that if people believe something for millennia, that – in itself – might make them real? Don't you think we might be able to personify the forces of nature which guide evolution and make the trees grow and the rocks wear away? Do you really think that what we can touch and see are the only things that are real? Don't you think that nature has a special power, like music, all of its own?' James was animated in a way I had never seen him before. He dropped his cutlery on the floor suddenly, and the clang echoed around the old rafters like a trumpet sound for his dogmatism.

Rather to my consternation, I found myself exchange glances with Susie. I had certainly not intended sharing even this much with her, but she gave me a look that was amused and knowing – the kind of look one outsider gives another, the sort of glance pale English couples give each other at customs checkpoints in Europe.

'When she or I lost something, my mother used to tell me that the fairies had moved it,' said Susie, still smiling. 'To this day, I'm not sure they hadn't.'

'Same here,' said James. 'Maybe your mother was right. All those little things that go wrong – lost glasses, empty petrol tanks, dropped spoons, those little tricks that nature plays on us. Of course it's fairies. It's trickery. It's the Great Trickster at work. Is there a better explanation?'

'Tiredness, incompetence, subconscious desires?' I said, world-weary.

'But why do they happen sometimes rather than others? Why risk it? Keep on the right side of the fairies. I'm going to.'

We laughed at him, my pig-headed, hopeless friend. It

broke the mood and there was a moment's silence. The house seemed to be listening to us. It breathed more easily than it used to, as if we had cleared an asthmatic obstruction to its windpipe. I could almost feel its breaths creaking in and out. In fact, something about the intricate search we were making seemed to relieve the house. I had been woken by no children in the night, no searching mothers since we started.

Or was it something to do with Susie? She seemed to be having a miraculous effect on James. He was more confident, more certain of himself. She had been the handsome prince to his Sleeping Beauty. But a part of me, and I certainly didn't acknowledge it at the time, made me wonder whether it was her that was calming the house, not us. There was something about her that drew the house round her as she walked through it, like an old eiderdown. It was as if the old bricks and mortar, and maybe the mysterious mother's voice too, had been waiting for her. Now she had arrived, they seemed to be content just to watch. She was very ordinary in most ways. Probably her assurance and her laugh had as much to do with an American high school education, with all its dating and cheer-leaders, as anything else. But by laughing so much, she seemed to calm those around her. Even me.

I knew one of us would have to test out the passageway, if indeed that was where the hole in the wall led to. We had spent so long looking for the Byron poem that it made no sense to stop now. Susie had her own reasons for wanting to find it. The story of the disappearing dog un-nerved me, but I could see James was determined. As if the elusive poem might somehow contain in it the alchemy that would keep Susie there with him happily, in his house, in his life and – I gathered from the way he touched her – in the general direction of his bed. As if it contained the power to transform his life completely. I hardly need say that I still wanted that poem, too.

The proper way to explore a secret passage is to hire some engineers, or some experienced cavers at least, who could know what to do if the roof suddenly collapsed on top of them. But there was no money and James was too impatient – and reluctant to be embarrassed if nothing was uncovered.

'You have deeply ventured,' said Susie unexpectedly and for no obvious reason, except that Byron said it first. 'But all must do so who would greatly win.'

'I don't think *all*. There's no way I'm going down that hole,' I said.

'That's fine. We need someone to be here in case for some reason we don't come out.'

Susie was quoting some little known poem by Byron that could have described a passageway under the bowels of a great house, and the dream-like mythical creatures he encountered down there. It sounded like an opium trip to me. Maybe he and Emma went down there and blew their minds on poppy seeds. Still the letters implied she went down there to elope, though she equally clearly never managed it.

'Hey,' said Susie suddenly, putting into words something that must have been at the back of our minds all the time. 'Maybe she's still down there.' A small chill scampered down the back of my neck.

'Then persuade her to come up, will you. She could be drawing her pension by now.'

* * *

I thought about Emma as I drove up from London in the early hours of the morning the following weekend, ready for the great exploration. I listened to the bleak tunes Radio 4 broadcasts to start their transmissions, hours before the first glint of sunshine. It was quite possible that Emma had shared the fate of the dog described by Canon Micklethwaite – the spaniel that had disappeared into thin air. Emma had escaped down the passage, clutching her trousseau, and had fallen into a pit, and James and Susie would either trip over her skeleton or disappear themselves.

I knew that James would not be able to resist some exploration before I arrived. They would be down that bloody hole as sure as eggs is eggs, but I felt pretty sure they wouldn't go too far down without some back-up and I was glad to provide it.

There was little traffic on the roads at that hour and I was shivering in the pre-dawn chill, a little apprehensive. The last thing I wanted to do was to plunge down the black hole in response to their cries for help, but a peculiar fantasy seemed to keep coming back – and it involved rescuing Susie. Just the thought of it gave a tinge to the most un-erotic period of the day. It was embarrassing. I tried to suppress it. I carried with me two torches, a couple of things to read and a baby monitor in the shape of a squat indolent-looking Bugs Bunny. I had thought of this at the last minute, wondering how we could communicate once they entered the passage, and I'd had gone round to borrow it from one of the few ex-girlfriends with children with whom I was still on speaking terms.

There was no sign of James when I got to Oberon House. With the first rays of sunshine, the mist was just rising from the overgrown lawn.

'I think you'll come down with us,' said Susie. She smelled like toasted muffins and the sunlight seemed to snatch at her hair. 'You won't be able to resist it.'

'I absolutely assure you. Nothing would induce me to go anywhere small and dark. Somebody needs to be responsible and it's going to be me. Who's going to look after you?'

'Oh, I can look after myself, I reckon,' she said, with a knowing smile.

'Come on, Susie. I don't want you buried alive before I've had the chance to sleep with you.'

The moment the words were out of my mouth, I realised they were true. I really wanted her. This was a shocking discovery. I could see the surprise in her widening eyes and the faintly heightened colour on her cheeks before she laughed. As I said it, I also realised there was something about the way she put her head on one side, like a thoughtful sparrow, which made me wanted to feel my lower lip against her upper lip. There was something about the way she blinked – as if in innocent surprise – that made me want to stroke her bobbed hair.

Something in her enthusiasm for living and her rampant optimism that made me want to sink into her. Suddenly I could imagine her brushing back her hair with a flick, the precise way her back muscles would move as she did so, and the tiny point of sweat in the small of her back.

People like me have to believe our own feelings. When we feel something powerful about someone, that sense is mirrored across the great ocean of division that separates individuals. We have to follow our instincts: the propagation of the species depends on it. It isn't always the same feeling we share, yet I swear I could see that behind her surprise, she too was searching her own feelings to see what was there.

Can it really have been such a Damascus Road experience? My aggressive throwaway joke seemed to have woken in me something I had known all along, and with it all the jealousy and self-doubt that goes along with it. All these things shot through my head in the seconds after I had uttered the words. And yet I did not regret them.

I was already feeling that Susie was both the only thing I wanted in the world, and that I was too brutal and ignorant for her. I also felt a growing resentment that she was about to disappear down a dodgy tunnel alone with James.

I had slept with James' girlfriends before. More than once, actually. I justified it on the grounds that a particular relationship was going nowhere or that it had been at the instigation of the girlfriends – I've never been very good at saying no. Only afterwards would I discover he was agonising about their sudden elusiveness or, if they left, their memory. It was always tempting to say: 'She wasn't worth it – she slept with me, too'. But I knew it would probably just make him hanker the more. This time there seemed to be no real decision to take. Sometimes you just have to take what turns out to be yours.

'That's pretty improper,' said Susie. I wondered whether I could detect a flicker of interest or flirtation behind it. 'I think you're getting a little ahead of yourself,' she laughed. 'But we need someone on the surface who can do something about it if we don't come back.'

'What do I do? Raid the larder?'

It was a miserable morning outside. The drizzle was being lashed by the breeze, but Bugs Bunny seemed to raise the atmosphere a little, as James appeared in his old track suit bottoms, a small camera strapped to his waist, looking like a kind of yuppie miner. He switched on his powerful torch. I felt claustrophobic just looking at them, though even my childhood fear of small dark spaces was being soundly challenged by my newly discovered lust.

'Be good,' said Susie, as she followed James into the hole. I settled down into a chair, set down my cup of tea and turned on Bugs Bunny.

'Just don't take any risks, OK?'

As well as piecing together what was happening, as they progressed through the passage, I would have the benefit of a full description later. The hole went downwards, via a set of worn stone steps that met another set at a small platform.

'They must go up towards the stable,' I could hear James say; the reception seemed clear. They described an ancient bench sitting against the wall. Underneath it was an old pewter mug, covered in cobwebs.

'Look at that!' said James, swinging his torch up to the brick ceiling, to a small stalactite wrapped around a cobweb of such complexity that it looked like a piece of skin hanging down from the roof. The torch cast bizarre shadows across the walls. An almost empty rack of wines covered one wall. James reached over for one of the bottles, and pushed the cobwebs off the label. It said 1901.

'OK, now where's the passage? Is it down?'

'Put the torch over here,' she said. 'What's this? Some kind of sluice?' The lamps picked out at old brick arch, but it was barely above ankle-height. It looked like there might have been room to squeeze underneath, and there was definitely space beyond – James shone his torch into it – but it would be a tight and unpleasant fit. Something that looked like a pile of centuries-old mouse droppings seemed to be heaped up just where they would have to put their hands. But next to it, encrusted with age and barely recognizable, was what appeared to be an iron ring. James pushed the end of his stick through it and heaved. There was a sort of snapping sound of popping air and the stone moved backwards suddenly and easily, as if on hinges, revealing another small flight of stairs under the arch. Something small and black raced out of the gaping hole and into the shadows.

Unlike the medieval stone steps you find in places like Canterbury Cathedral and Westminster Abbey, these ancient steps seemed not to have been worn at all. It was as if they were discovering the Antarctic for the first time. Or the secret back stairs to the Centre of the Earth. 'This is it,' said James. 'Who's going to go first?'

'You can. They're your steps. And I want you to meet the creepy-crawlies before I do.'

The steps ran down about 20 feet. They were uneven and covered with cobwebs so deep that it felt like wading through a swamp. As they made their way gingerly downwards by torchlight, clutching the rabbit monitor, the camera, a compass and an old plastic bag, the smell became danker – like a long forgotten larder, years after the food had rotted away, or a pharaoh's tomb after the last seed had withered. It was as if nothing live had existed there for centuries. The air seemed completely still.

'We should have brought a canary down with us,' said James sounding through the rabbit like he was trying to break the disturbing atmosphere.

'A canary? Why?' asked Susie. 'Why not a boa constrictor? Can canaries swallow rats?'

'Can boa constrictors smell marsh gas?'

Moving slowly and checking the low roof of the passageway as they went, James' compass showed they had moved slightly south, and must now be under what had once been the edge of the lawn, about 10 yards from the house. Then the tunnel seemed to shrink.

'Am I growing or is the roof getting lower?' I heard Susie say over Bugs Bunny.

"It's alright. It opens out." He had been down, the sneaky bastard.

Both had to turn on their sides to get through. And then the passage suddenly widened out into a stone chamber and the air seemed suddenly rich with moisture. Green foliage seemed to have grown like moss into the walls, and ahead of them was the reason. At waist height in the middle of the chamber was a well, and – though they shone their torches down it – there was no answering glint from the water.

'Whhooooo!' Susie shouted down it.

'Shh! Don't do that! You'll dislodge something. Hang on! What's this?'

James' feet had touched something propped up at the edge of the well. It was a book, and it was covered in cobwebs like everything else. Both shone their torches at the cover. It wasn't as old as they thought: *With Custer in the American West*, by G. A. Henty, said the book cover. And, barely legible on the inside, was the name Harry Weston and an inscription: 'HARRY, ON YOUR BIRTHDAY, FROM YOUR LOVING FATHER, MAY 1910'.

So Harry had known about the passageway, but why had he never said anything about it? And how long had he spent down here? James remembered his grandfather, frail and doubled up with smoker's hacking cough, choking away between reminiscences, many of them about Oberon House – the tennis parties, the farmyard, the great pond, the history, but nothing about a passageway. Maybe it made him feel too nostalgic? Maybe he had forgotten about it.

His life had evolved into so many other things, his theatre reviewing, his work in Germany with the Allied Control Commission, his post-war efforts with the Red Cross – maybe he had dismissed the tunnel in the end as faulty imagination. Whatever the reason, he never said.

Then, in an alcove on the wall, they found a strange collection of paper torn up by bugs and other creatures, part letters, part newspaper, as far as I could make out. Next to papers was a pile of congealed wax, another old candle burned right down to the stub, some rose petals and what looked by the light of the torch like an ancient photograph of the crown of someone's head.

'What's this?' said Susie. 'Has somebody been burning papers? There's something a bit pathetic about it, isn't there.'

At least the tunnel's use was now obvious. It had provided a safe water supply for the house in difficult times. There was nothing very mysterious about that. James felt divided as he looked at their discovery. Part of him was relieved to have banished the mystery; part of him felt disappointed. It was like reading a great psychic adventure story and discovering at the end that it had all been a dream. The bits of paper and the candles were odd, but no odder than the existence of the passage in the first place. There was another passage leading up to the chamber, and a quick examination made it clear that this also led to the surface somewhere near the stables.

Meanwhile, Susie was scouring the walls of the chamber looking for an opening or secret cupboard that might contain the missing poem – if it had survived the damp and the mice.

'I feel like Alice in Wonderland down here,' she said, with her usual giggle. 'I shouldn't have tried that bottle that said 'drink me'.'

Nothing. James absent-mindedly threw a small piece of masonry into the well and waited for the splash. There wasn't one. Disturbed, he shone the light down into the bowels of the earth. He tried again. Still nothing.

'I hate this,' he said. 'It must be really deep. What else can we throw?'

They needed the torches, his stick was too flimsy, and it seemed a pity to throw the book. Susie waved Bugs Bunny with an interrogative look.

'Let's take the batteries out first, otherwise it'll sound like we've fallen in.'

They took them out and dispatched the rabbit over the edge, counting one elephant, two elephant ... At nine elephant, James thought he could hear a very distant plop.

'I wish we hadn't done that,' he said.

They had told me they were just coming back up, but I

hated being cut off like that. They sent one last sweep of the torch round the chamber, but this time there was indeed something to see. There was a small wooden door in the wall. James and Susie did a double-take.

'How did we miss that?'

The door was only about three feet high, and its wooden slats seemed as old as time itself. The edges were encrusted with moss and the door handle was missing. Even the keyhole had silted up with the detritus of history. But most inexplicable of all, there was a nail on the front, and on the nail hung a garland of ivy, a foot across, neatly entwined with blue cornflowers. Neither of them spoke the obvious question: the cornflowers looked as if they had only just been picked, yet – as far as they knew – nobody had been down there since the beginning of the century.

James felt around the outside of the door with his penknife, trying to get behind it. He pushed the end of his tick into the keyhole and pulled. Some of the wood splintered, but the door didn't budge at all.

'Maybe it's just ornamental,' he said.

'Why does an ornament have an ornament on it?'

It was no use. James' backbone felt mushy and they were both disturbed and keen to leave.

'We'll come back with better tools. The torch batteries are running low. We'd better get back.' Susie picked up the garland and, with a backward glance, they made their way back along the passage.

XV

'Round and round the tree of gold,
Round and round dance we.
So doth the great world spin from of old
Summer and winter, and fire and cold,
Song that is sung and tale that is told,
Even as we dance, that fold and unfold
Round the stem of the fairy tree.'
ANDREW LANG, *THE TERRIBLE HEAD*

London, September 1913

PERHAPS it wasn't so surprising that Harry became an auxiliary air raid warden in later life, after a career between the wars as a hack theatre critic on provincial papers, desperately trying to impose order on recalcitrant directors, actors and lighting designers. The business of checking black-outs, sounding air raid sirens and herding people into air raid shelters suited the same instincts. So did his next job, as a press attaché to the Allied Control Commission in occupied Germany, helping in the seemingly never-ending work of reuniting scattered and traumatized families. In the face of rising chaos, whether it was the chaos of occupation, poor direction or the Luftwaffe, Harry would fall back on books of rules and agreed processes. Despite his charm and sense of humour, some people dismissed him as 'hidebound'.

Harry was so hidebound when it came to chaos, he was almost sclerotic. The more disorder, the more rigidly he imposed the regulations. For Harry, the world had been descending into chaos since the arrival of the plainclothes policemen at Oberon House on Gerald's birthday. And from then on – via the death of the Austrian Archduke in Sarajevo – it was downhill all the way. He rigidly imposed the rules of theatre production – as he saw them – in the gossamer comedies of the 1920s and the gritty realism of the 1930s, just as he had volunteered as an auxiliary bus driver to head off the expected chaos of the General Strike. He rigidly imposed the rules about the precise measure of light allowed through the blackout curtains, and he urged on Neville Chamberlain in his efforts to appease the dictators to ward off the menace from the chaotic Bolsheviks in the East. You might think from this that Harry was an unimaginative man, but that was untrue. Or an intolerant man, which he never was either – except of people's constant moral failings. Nor was he rigid or dry company. Harry was unfailingly friendly, as delighted to be waved at driving his strike-breaking bus as he was to play with his children before they went to bed. It was just that he disapproved of systems and people that did not work, for whatever reason, and was particularly horrified at modern art. He was frightened of it, and anything else which threatened muddle.

From the moment his father stepped onto the boat train at Victoria, Harry's life seemed to have unravelled. Within six short years of disorder and war, he would find himself on the cross-Channel troopship on his way to his brief service on the Western Front. On the way there, he looked back at the loss of Oberon House and most of its contents, the deaths of most of his closest family, and his mother's poverty – not to mention the great hum of mourning you could feel from one side of the country to the other – and assumed he would not return from Flanders either.

He did. By luck, his unit only spent a few rather dull weeks in the trenches, during which he took part in only two uneventful patrols, and many more even duller months behind the lines training for an operation that never took place. Almost exactly twenty years later, after the Munich agreement in 1938, he made his way through the children crowded for evacuation at the railway station to try to join up again. He was pronounced unfit. So he spent his evenings of the next few years in the ARP, and his days in a small office just off Fleet Street – filling in for the jobs of younger men – then walking down to Bank station to take the Underground home. Then he would walk the rest of the way, along the black-and-white painted kerb-stones and the advertisements for Bovril, to the ordered safety of his small flat in Clapham and his wife and children, one of which would later be James' father.

There was another divided aspect of his life, and not just during the war – though it affected him as the disruption of the Blitz and the long absences from home took hold. He was charming company at work and in the bars of the Aldwych in the evenings, and could bear only three months of his children's evacuation in Shropshire, despite his best efforts not to love them too much. He was shy and self-deprecating and would usually defer to other people's opinions if they were held strongly enough, but he just could not tolerate human frailty. He railed against the missing cues and incompetence during productions of *Hay Fever* and *Macbeth*, and most of all he reserved his horror for divorce.

When his colleagues left their wives – it usually was that way around – and tripped off to Brighton for evidence of their own infidelity required by the divorce courts, he just could not bear to talk to them or catch their eye. If the long wartime hours in mixed company got too much for his friends, they could expect no support from Harry. It was not considered quite proper to express outright disapproval – and Harry never believed in doing anything improper – and he never cared about his friends any the less, but he just could never bring himself to condone the end of their marriages. The sheer destruction of divorce appalled him. It was, in its way, a small Blitz of its own. Worse than an army of Nazi storm-troopers laying waste a whole civilization, and whole language of way of understanding. It was as tragic in its way as the fall of Rome.

When his closest friend Geoffrey Draine left his wife, gallantly agreeing to pay for her private detective to track him to Brighton, Harry could not bring himself to speak to him for three months.

'Come off it, old man,' said Geoffrey. 'You know as well as I do that she was shagging that dreadful old bounder Gerry Clark.'

'I know that, Geoffrey,' Harry would say. 'You just have to be patient with me.'

But inside, the sheer pain of the world unravelling dug deeper into his ribs. For Harry, marriage was forever, with or without the full commitment of everlasting love. Even till death us do part seemed to smack of compromise with the forces of chaos. He took extra precautions to protect his own marriage. He made sure he was never alone with another woman, not in a restaurant, not even in a Lyon's Corner House. He had no private meetings with any of the women running his newspaper or with theatre publicists. For Harry, there were no innocent cups of tea or glasses of wine *á deux*. If he found himself in a compromising position, he made polite excuses and slipped away. It was all very discrete, as he slipped charmingly through people's fingers, but very determined. Very little made him doubt that he was right to behave so fastidiously, but in Germany, something would happen to make him think again.

In 1919, all that was in the future. Then he came back to London. Out of the army, visiting his mother in her flat in Clapham, he surveyed the future with as much alarm as he remembered the past. He dreamed of Oberon House most nights. He thought about it in the day, while he was wandering round the newspaper offices looking for reviewing work. Most of all, he thought of the tunnel and the strange chamber underneath the lawn at Oberon.

He had left his book and candle there the last time he had been down, and he had left his shrine to his father, too, when he had finally given up the search. Not for the first time in his family's history, it had occurred to a Weston that there was something about the house that seemed to inspire people to search it. And – although his mother's explorations had been undertaken in the vain hope that she would uncover her husband's secret stash of wealth – for Harry it had been more complicated, something less defined. If he was ever to admit it, even to himself, Harry had been searching for a kind of magic, a kind of Holy Grail, which would heal the damage done to his family by a greedy bank clerk. It was partly in search of this, and partly to escape the endless procession of lawyers, estate agents, furniture removers and auctioneers that arrived during his school holidays, that he carried on escaping through the old stables. There he went, day after day, down the old stone stairs, along the old passage and into the chamber – his heart in his mouth and his hand shaking as he held the torch.

Harry also found a little wooden door, and in the weeks that followed, he had tested out as many keys in its lock as he could possibly find, culled from the great bunches in what had once been the housekeeper's pantry. When they failed to open the doors, he would sometimes fling the whole bunch down the well behind him, and listen without success for the answering splash.

English houses were cold in those days, especially in the so-called landed classes from which Harry's family was rapidly exiting. Shortage of money had reduced his mother to keeping just one room warm, and this was where she spent all day with her knitting and romantic novels, still faithfully practising her facial exercises in front of her mirror. The rest of the house was abandoned to the Arctic drafts. As the winter approached, icicles began appearing on the windows in leaky wainscoting. The lawn began to grow a foot, then two foot and the brambles started to appear on the driveway. When Harry was not away at school, where the mornings were equally cold, and the icicles hung above the bathroom in the morning, he used to escape to the stone chamber. There he would read adventure stories by candlelight to avoid wandering around the frozen empty house above, and slowly getting used to what had originally seemed a dank and eerie passage. There, his bottom hard against the ageless cold stones, he would read about the exploits of Nelson and Drake and the peculiar tale of *Puck of Pook's Hill* that his father had sent him from exile.

His father remained in Dieppe, and his father's colleagues had been tried and acquitted on charges of fraud and false accounting by the time the final posse of men with ill-fitting suits and measuring tapes invaded Oberon House. As he read Henty's old book in the underground chamber below, Harry happened to glance up at the little wooden door. He had paid little attention to it since exhausting the housekeeper's keys. This time he looked at it absent-mindedly and saw, to his astonishment, a little ivy circle like a wreath, entwined with tiny blue cornflowers.

He got up and looked at it closer. The flowers and foliage smelled so fresh they could have been picked within the hour. It was just a small wreath and it seemed to be welcoming; and the implications of its appearance took a few minutes to sink in. By the time he had thought about it, his heart was already racing. Where had it come from? Who had brought it when only he, his mother and an occasional visiting maid lived in the house? When even Josiah Goodbody seemed to have disappeared? In a moment's panic, Harry dropped the book, abandoned the candle and fled up the passageway, banging the old stone flag back into place behind him in the stable, pausing just long enough to make sure the coast was clear before he emerged blinking into the light.

'Harry, I've been looking for you everywhere,' said his mother in her long gown, advancing towards him across the courtyard. 'We must get packed. The bank has asked us to leave at last, and I want to go by twelve o'clock.' Harry shrank from her as he looked up into her white face, which seemed to be struggling to keep itself ordered. When your world caves in around you at the age of 12, you need your mother to be strong. So he fled again to his cold bedroom, and piled his most important possessions into a small box – *Puck of Pook's Hill*, a small pile of lead redcoats and a Dreadnought made out of matchsticks. Most of his clothes had already been sold or packed: his mother had expected this moment for months.

She stared straight ahead in the cart as they left Oberon. He stared backwards at the old house as they made their way slowly past the black drainpipes, along the drive until all he could see was the gigantic window above the front door glinting at him through the bushes. At the end of the road, a car containing two official-looking men in bowler hats was waiting. They patiently raised their hats. Harry's mother looked the other way. He could see the tears rolling down her cheeks as they clattered away from the house forever.

'You're very brave,' said his mother, touching his hand for a second. 'Very brave indeed.'

As the train clicked its way through the Surrey countryside towards London, he imagined the candle he had left behind, still burning brightly down in the secret passage until it burned itself away and was extinguished. For years afterwards, Harry imagined that it had never gone out – that it was still burning there, like the eternal flame in St Peter's in Rome – as a kind of token that things do not have to end. Didn't he love the old house? Didn't love last forever? All the evidence around him cast doubt on it. Yet if love didn't last, what was the point in it? Deep down, some part of him decided that – unless he could possibly avoid it – he would not love again.

As the next few years passed, his mother seemed, in her small flat, rapidly to be losing her health. There was a little money from her own family trusts, so there was coal for the grate and enough for someone to come and cook and clean, but Harry could see her cheekbones appear through her increasingly pale skin. He noticed she no longer spent hours on her facial exercises. In the long hours of gaslight, he found her writing page after page. Harry guessed these pages were to his father.

'Has the newspaper arrived?' she would ask Harry every morning. Then she pored over the personal columns and the property announcements. Only a chance remark by Edward made him realise what she had been looking for.

'I see the sale still hasn't been advertised. Two years or

more and no sale. What are they doing? They profess to care so much for their blessed clients who are out of pocket because of our family, but they drag their heels doing anything about it. They were pretty damn enthusiastic about us moving out.'

'What sale?'

'Oh catch up, Harry! The sale of Oberon House. The bank must sell it to repay some of the money. It's been years now and the whole long-drawn out saga is absolutely crucifying Mother.'

'Do they absolutely have to sell it?' asked Harry. Homes may be bricks and mortar to banks, and if your ancestors have lived there for generations, that is not how it seems at all. You can't just inject that into a bank account. 'Can't we buy it back or something?'

'Afraid not, old chap. I'd like to wallop them for their slowness, but the execution is inevitable in the end. Nothing short of Armageddon is going to stop them sooner or later.'

But Armageddon did come, and only a few months later. Fearing a collapse of property prices, the bank decided not to sell the property on the Weston's behalf, but to sell a long lease on it. Theoretically at least, it would eventually revert to the family. But for Harry it might as well have been sold; none of them honestly believed they would ever see it again, not even at the end of the 99-year lease. Soon Armageddon was occupying more of their minds than the house, as Edward marched off with the British Expeditionary Force and the lamps went out all over Europe. But whenever he thought about the old house, Harry imagined his candle still burning away underground, waiting for his return.

He thought of it through the Great Depression, too, and on a wintry day at the crematorium, at his mother's funeral, with the trams criss-crossing through the leafless trees. He felt very alone. He thought of it at his wedding, keeping his fingers crossed as he stood by the altar, promising himself not to love his wife too much. And he thought of it again as the air raid sirens went at the end of Neville Chamberlain's speech announcing the declaration of war, and when he wandered through the heart-breaking ruins of Hamburg a few years later.

His only other contact with Oberon House was the few bits and pieces kept by his mother, which she left behind after her death. Her favourite earrings, in emerald and silver, and the great family bible. There was Emma's name in the inside page of it. 'Emma Weston, bapt. Sept. 7th 1792, Oberon Parish Church. Godpts. Jeremiah Hurst Esq., Miss Jane Weston and Mrs Arabella Philpot'. There was the family laid out for him to see, their baptisms and their deaths, and the sad deaths of so many of them, so young, including all but one of Emma's nieces and nephews, the children of Harry's beloved Grandpapa and Grandmama. The bible had ink stains on many of the pages. In the Sermon on the Mount, grubby fingers had worn away part of the page from rubbing along under the line. Centuries of reading the same bible stories had almost eroded the words. At the foot of the list of names inside the cover, somebody had written the lines from Thomas Gray: 'And leaves the world to darkness and to me'.

The bible became Harry's most precious possession. So precious that, at the outbreak of war, he took it down to an obscure branch of Martin's Bank in Taunton – safe from the blitz – and put it, along with his mother's earrings, in a safe deposit box in the vault. He went back there a year later, certain of invasion, and wrote a little note on them in German, asking for them to be given to his son in the event of his death. By then, he had replaced his old boyhood altar to his father with a mental shrine to his long-lost ancestor Emma. He collected everything he could about her and her disappearance.

There were the written reminiscences of elderly relatives who could testify at least to the subject being a closed one throughout their lives. There were the books about Byron, none of which mentioned her at all. And there were a few ancient guidebooks to Surrey which mentioned the story in passing. He spent his days off in Somerset House, checking through the death records from the 1830s for an Emma Weston – there were hundreds of them. He spent his weekends researching the places she might have gone in the high summer of 1811. The continent would have been closed to her because of war. Did she escape to Bath, or did she – as he feared in those early days of research – end up dying in poverty, hunger and degradation like her namesake Lady Hamilton, in the fatal disease-ridden back streets of Seven Dials or Blackfriars.

What memorabilia he found he collected in one bookcase of his home. Sometimes he lit a candle beside them. It was a distant memory of his youth, a fitting successor to the shrine underground, and a kind of patient watch for her return – figuratively at least – after more than a century. He became obsessed with Emma, as if she held the clue to the restoration of everything else. But as he buried himself in history books and public records, events were conspiring to release a fiercer kind of chaos than any history had conjured up before.

At the height of the V-weapon assault on London, the destruction of Bank Station by a doodlebug had a profound effect on him. He had watched the flying bomb zip down the stairway from his post on the roof of a bank – by coincidence next door to his father's disastrous business premises. The bomb slipped in down the steps he had walked up only that morning. It did so neatly, as if it was designed to. He spent hours that evening helping to dig out the bodies. With dust soaking through his uniform like water, he crawled home that evening in a daze. It had been so mechanical: the bomb had been blasted into the air from near Antwerp, had travelled across Kent and Surrey – maybe over Oberon House – and popped down the stairs. Was that chaos or design?

'I just don't know,' he said to his wife, putting down his peeling black helmet on the dresser. 'I just don't know.'

There seemed to be nothing to cling to. Harry felt his world swaying with no axis. All he could think of was the small flame of hope, still burning underground by the well, and the little door and the strange wreath of ivy that had come from nowhere, as if it had been summoned up by emotion to bring a tiny hint of order in a chaotic world.

XVI

'Would'st know what tricks, by pale moonlight,
Are play'd by me, the merry Sprite,
Who wing through air from the camp to the court,
From king to clown, and of all make sport...'
THOMAS MOORE, *THE LEGEND OF PUCK THE FAIRY*

Oberon House, July 1998

WHEN HE arrived to live in Venice in 1816, Byron soon became a well-known figure – as only outsiders can – by flinging himself into the masked balls, the lewd gambling parties, watching the local beheadings, and enjoying the company of the city's 20,000 prostitutes, one fifth of the local population. Even by starting an affair with his landlord's twenty-two-year-old wife.

'There's a whore on my right/For I rhyme best at night,' he wrote happily. You have to throw yourself in at the deep end.

Presumably by throwing herself into the genteel life of Oberon village, Susie already seemed to have become a well-known local fixture. I noticed that people waved to her as she walked down to the George and Dragon pub, which also doubled as the village shop, post office, vintners and parish council office. Even Mr and Mrs Baldwin crossed the road to say hello. I watched them eyeing her up and down as she walked away. She seemed to attract people with her smile and – in her ineffable mid-western way – that hint of formality that led her to call everyone by their proper title. I didn't even know their real names, but there was Susie deferring to them, as 'Mr and Mrs Baldwin' followed by 'How's it going?'

I discovered later that Susie's charm was not the only reason for this local fame. She had used her services to find the Baldwins' scrawny missing cat Simon. She did not ring their tasteless doorbell chimes and claim to have dreamed it into the car park of the garden centre, on the other side of the bypass, but she just suggested she might have seen it there. And there it was.

'We are so grateful,' said Mrs Baldwin. 'Do pop in sometime and have a glass of something. Where did you say you were from?'

But her most potent success had been in solving a serious problem that had beset Jess some months before – the loss of the only remaining key capable of letting air out of the church's ancient black radiators, which looked as if they had been installed by James Watt himself. Again, I believe she avoided telling Jess that she had dreamed it into a forgotten cupboard in the Rectory, under an ancient version of the bible, covered in dust after two decades of disapproval from the Church authorities. But she led him there nonetheless.

Jess was showing an unhealthy interest in Susie. When she was in Oberon, which seemed to be most of the time, he would unexpectedly drop into the house to persuade her to take on some role in the fertility ritual he was planning for Harvest Festival.

'But that's month's away!' I heard James complain.

I kept out of the way of Susie, but became increasingly attached to the house. I came down in the dark of night at weekends, avoiding her eyes as I slipped in through the back door in the early hours of the morning, to find her still up – preparing to dry her hair, with a green towel around her head. Every week that went by, I felt a little more usurped by her presence in the house – undermining the only roots I had – yet I also found I had been dreaming about her.

Maybe there was some kind of link here, like an electrical circuit, that could connect my dreams to hers. But there seemed to be little sign of any meeting of minds or spirits. She still treated me with the same wry amusement; I treated her with the same bantering condescension. My own inability to find what was lost showed no obvious sign of improvement. I just found myself watching her: the way her shoulders curved up to her neck, the way her calf muscle bulged out from the knee, the way her breasts nuzzled away under her shirt.

'What are you all about?' I asked her one morning. 'Is it your research? You know I'd also like to find this poem? Do you want to stay in England? Are you in love with James – and if so, why aren't you sleeping with him?'

'How do you know I'm not?' she answered, side-stepping the question. 'Have you been peering through the keyhole?'

But I did know. If I had been listening at the keyhole, I would have had to wait some time. The heightened tension in the house, James' frenetic energy and close attention to her – they gave it all away. The days were getting hotter and stickier as we hurtled towards midsummer, and the calmness she brought at the outset of her visit had begun to give way to something quite different. Susie was like a small sun with serious sunspot activity. Her presence in the house got bigger and redder and lower in the sky, day by day, as she moved in her orbit, from the kitchen to the great window upstairs, staring down at the tangled jungle beneath. Every time her laugh echoed down the crumbling corridors, it seemed to get hotter.

Normally I would have chatted to James about it. I would have urged him to bring matters to a head. I would have waggled my sexual experience in front of his hungry eyes and laughed at his slowness. But I didn't: I was afraid I would betray myself, revealing that there was something about Susie that had wrong-footed us both. The last thing I wanted was a conversation that would demonstrate our sexual equality. What we talked about instead was the passage, those two letters and the doorway.

At the very least something would have to be done about

them. One of us – if not all – would have to make a renewed assault on the door to make sure it was the 'decoration' it appeared to be. I confess I hoped it would be James, leaving the two of us upstairs, sharing a common experience with the run of the house. Or despite my claustrophobia, we could leave him upstairs and go down the passage together.

Was I ashamed of thinking about my friend and host in this way? You might well say I should have been – but I wasn't. I worked out that James *owed* me: for years of free dinners, bail-outs, friendship at extremely inconvenient moments. For taking him up when we first met as children and nobody else would touch him. I felt after all that, he owed me this one thing I could hardly ask for and seemed unable to achieve for myself: a night at least with Susie. Preferably more.

In the meantime, Jess's bible had given her an idea.

'Didn't you have some kind of bible?' she asked James. 'I thought you old families all had some kind of family tome with the history all written out.' James looked a little confused. He called his father via his answerphone in Bremen, who did not call back. He asked his ancient cousin who had, for years, been Harry's closest relative, and – looking out from under her green eye shade on the terrace of an old folks home in Worthing, she pointed us all in the right direction.

'Of course there's a family bible. I'm surprised you don't have it in the house with you. Oh no, Harry put it in the bank during the war. It's probably still there. Now, I remember Harry in the Blitz. Did I ever tell you the story of my sister Jane and the doodlebug? Well, let me tell it you again.'

'Cousin Judith, which bank was it? Can you remember?'

'Bank? What bank? What are you talking about?'

But she did know, somewhere in the recesses of her memory, and upon looking through her few remaining belongings, James discovered a battered letter from Harry providing her with authority to retrieve a safe deposit box in the event of his death. It was dated September 1945.

'Just before he went to Germany,' she explained.

Getting into a safe deposit box is no simple matter. There

are old executors to contact, bank managers to harangue, more letters of authority to draft. Even Harry's death certificate to extract – the cause of death was set down as bronchial pneumonia. It took three weeks, but with Susie in charge, the pieces seemed to fall neatly into place.

'You should be a lawyer,' James told her.

'Or a great literary critic at Harvard,' she said. 'Or how about a great sex symbol?'

'Or a professional dreamer,' I said. 'It's a pity you can't dream things on demand. We could bypass this safe deposit box altogether if you could just find us this poem.'

She looked a bit embarrassed. 'She can't dream things she *wants* to find, isn't that right Susie?' said James in her defence.

'Don't you think I'd have dreamed some jackpot winners by now if I could. Wow, I could have dreamed myself rich by now.'

She and James went to Taunton by train. The bank had long since disappeared, they told me when they got back. The address was now a wholefood café, and the safe deposit boxes had clearly been updated and centralized into the regional branch of NatWest. But there it was, and they brought the entire contents back with them. I found these later, laid out under the light from the great windows, curling at the edges like long-forgotten reports in a dusty Whitehall cupboard.

There was little enough there; some letters that had obviously been important to Harry: his appointment from the War Office sending him to Germany after the war, as press attaché to one of the myriad of Displaced Persons Sections of the Allied Control Commission. There were a couple of letters from his wife, and one from her lawyers during their divorce in 1948. There was one letter from someone signing herself Renata. There were some much older letters, yellowing with age. And there was, right at the bottom of the pile, what looked like the last letter he ever received from his father. It was written in strong black ink and was dated March 1915.

'My dear Harry,' it read:

You will understand how much the circumstances which have prevented me from writing to you more than I have has pained me. It is no less painful to me to have to write at such a momentous time for us all. You may not know that the German army's advance has forced me from the house I had set my heart on moving to outside Dunkerque, so I remain here at Dieppe, where all the men of the town have been joining up. I realize that, to look them straight in the eye, I must do the same.

I thought at first they would never accept an elderly gent like me, but I find I was wrong. I have no military experience and I feel strange joining the army of a country which is not my own. But for reasons your mother has no doubt explained, I am unable to return to England – though it goes without saying that I have been thinking of you and putting my mind to your future.

It is difficult being absent to know how to admonish or encourage a son. I know my absence may have damaged or even irrevocably undermined my paternal authority, such as it was. But though I am far away, and though the months ahead may mean I shall not be able to write to you again for some time, let me assure you that there is not a moment in the day when you are absent from my thoughts – from the moment I wash in my little porcelain basin, staring out over the woods, to the moment I damp the fire down for the night.

I have made many mistakes in my life – it is part of being a man. But any father is consoled by the hope that their son might avoid them and live the life they always thought was possible for themselves, and I feel the same for you. I watched you grow up with tremendous pride and I know it was not misplaced. I hope you will accept this from a father who has, in many ways, failed to discharge his duties. I hope also that you will pay special attention to your mother in these difficult times, when you are the only child who remains safe in England, and when she will need comfort more than ever.

I remain, my son, your affectionate father,
John Weston

The letter was flattened, but again had shown signs of having been screwed up at some time or another. Some of its corners were also a little burned. I could imagine the young Harry ignoring the love that shone through it, taking violent exception to his preaching after such an absence – and to his father's irritating assumption that Harry should comfort his mother when that was exactly what his father had failed to do. It was a poignant letter, given that I knew he had been killed in the trenches at Verdun – shot by a sniper as he strolled nonchalantly along in the way he believed Englishmen were supposed to do. There was a short letter of condolence from Jenny, apparently back in England during the war, and post-marked Paddington, and there were even telegrams providing what must have then been the devastating news about Edward: 'THE WAR OFFICE REGRETS THAT 1ST LT E A WESTON, 4TH BATTALION ROYAL WEST KENT REGIMENT, IS MISSING IN ACTION'.

'But look at this one,' said James, handing me some more yellowing fragments. The paper was obviously intended as an *aide memoire* for Grandpapa Jo – written by him for fear that he would become forgetful or senile, though it could also have been written for future generations. I could have been written for James.

This is set down this day, 18th September, this year of Our Lord 1858, while I am of sound mind. My will is writ and shall suffice, but in honour of my sister Emma, and the love I still bear her, I pen this memento in the hope that she will return to her home before I die. In case she does not, I have left her last letter to me in the house, safe from the prying hands of damn lawyers.

There then followed some hieroglyphics that I couldn't follow and the same line from the poem: 'And leave the world to darkness and to me'.

'It's a reminder of where he put Emma's letter,' said James. 'Look, that's the staircase, that's the nut tree outside the window, and that's the fireplace.'

Taken together, the lines and the import of the notes were

extremely melancholic. I made myself some more tea and stared out of the great window at the sun beginning to frazzle up the overgrown lawn. Again it seemed lower in the sky and bigger than the day before. It reminded me of Susie. Then I turned my attention to the family bible.

As Susie had predicted, it had a long list of births and deaths back to the Restoration, petering out during the last century. Emma and her brother Jo were the only entries without any notes about their death – Jo presumably because he had died so late: his birth date had also been scrubbed out. Perhaps modesty had overtaken him as he got older; perhaps he just preferred to keep his age mysterious. But there was no RIP by Emma's name either.

'Look at that,' said Susie as we pored over the details. 'Emma's brother – the one who lived so long, right? – had six children, but only one of them grew to adulthood. This guy Jack. And there's no birth date for him either, just this baptism in 1812. Strange.'

'Oh I don't know. Think of all the diseases they had then. Ricketts, TB, cholera. It's surprising any of them survived to have children.'

But it was strange, that lack of dates. Emma's fate clearly remained a mystery, and such an enticing one. Where did she end up? One of the nameless poor on the streets of Covent Garden, huddled in doorways giving comfort to drunken clients. Maybe she lived long enough to die in one of the new workhouses two decades later. Maybe she met a rich cotton planter and went overseas, or lived out her days on the tobacco plantations of Jamaica. Or maybe, like Emma Hamilton, she made it in the end to Napoleonic France. I wished there was some way of knowing. She seemed the one cosmopolitan light in the polite provincial darkness of the Weston family. I felt I was on her side.

'Have you seen this?' said Susie, pulling out a battered old envelope with black funereal edges. Inside was a small miniature in a brass frame, and a portrait of an attractive flirtatious young woman with black ringlets. She seemed to share, unfortunately for her, something of the Weston family's nose. But her black ringlets and low cut Imperial dress made her look every inch the bold Jane Austen heroine. She seemed to be looking out of the picture over my right shoulder, as if she saw something there, aware of her sexuality, confident of the future. It was a moving picture somehow, one that leapt out of the past.

'Is it her?' I asked. 'Is it Emma?' There was no indication. I turned over the miniature in my hand, and on the back was a label written in blue ink – much more recently, I imagined – with one word on it. It just said: 'Magnificat'.

XVII

'Up the airy mountain,
Down the rushy glen
We daren't go a-hunting
For fear of little men...'
WILLIAM ALLINGHAM, *THE FAIRIES*

Hamburg, December 1945

SHE SEEMED to have come from nowhere, he thought afterwards, and he replayed the moment afterwards again and again in his mind for the rest of his life. Wherever she came from, the encounter in the bombed-out ruins of a German abbey turned Harry's tidy life on its head. The whole situation had something peculiar about it, as if some force of coincidence had conspired to create it.

It was peculiar enough suddenly to find himself in uniform just as everyone else was talking about being demobbed. It broke all the official rules, but his old divorced friend Geoffrey Draine made good on a five-year-old promise. Geoffrey had gone happily off to war in the honorary rank of major as press liaison officer, and had managed to avoid the enemy throughout – though he had faced a near squeak after the retreat from Tobruk. He had promised to wangle Harry a place after his application to join up had been turned down, and now – when it was all over – he suddenly asked for him by name. Nobody else would do for the sensitive post better than Harry Weston. The whole business was agreed and dusted down and Harry designated with an honorary rank of captain within a week.

There was little in the way of uniform – press liaison for the Allied Control Commission was barely in the army anyway – but there was a khaki tunic and a shoulder epaulette and reams of standing orders, and instructions about how to behave to the civilian population. It was not even as if Harry spoke German. He did speak a little French, and the army bureaucracy seemed satisfied by this completely inadequate state of affairs. He was a linguist. French, German, Italian – it was all the same to the military mind.

For Harry, the military meant order: it gave him a sense of mission as he crossed the English Channel, proud that he was doing his bit to impose it, but he had never in his worst nightmares imagined such chaos. His battlefront was intended to be a small part of the gigantic task of re-uniting stricken families. There were million upon million of them, divided by the final Allied push towards Berlin, divided again by the intransigence of the Soviet authorities, the sheer weight of numbers, the breakdown of all authority, and the beginnings of the long process of de-Nazification. There were the children left behind on railway platforms, their dolls still clutched tightly under their arms, their black eyes staring out hopelessly. There were the mothers separated from their families and driven insane by the incessant bombing, the fathers and grandfathers who somehow escaped the almost universal call-up. It was a revolution, and thousands more starving children arrived in reception centres day after day.

Often they were starving from lack of food, but that was not Harry's department. They were also starving from a loss of love, from having their home or the people they belonged to blown to smithereens, from having their mothers and sisters raped by enemy troops in front of them. That was not Harry's department either. Somebody else was dealing with the problem of the approaching winter with no firewood, of the eight million 'displaced persons' and the threat of mass epidemics.

Somebody else was dealing with the reception of the orphans roped together with notes pinned to their ragged clothes, just as they were dealing with the shooting of seventeen-year-old looters. Someone else had the job of dealing with the groups of youthful vagabonds who roamed the streets, nearly all of them believed to have VD. No, it was Harry's job to go from UNRRA camp to local newspaper office, organising the photos of missing and found children onto posters or newsprint, and hoping for the best.

He had wandered into the ruins of the abbey that afternoon partly on a whim to see the charred and blackened crucifix above the altar while he enjoyed a brief cigarette, but partly for a break. He had been working with a newly appointed but morose non-Nazi editor of a local newspaper, filling the pages with his stacks of photographs – hoping that somebody out there might be searching for their faces. It was an exhausting, distressing business, knowing that most orphans would probably remain so, knowing that the next day's trains would bring hundreds more.

Normally Harry could relax at the Atlantic Club, formerly the Hamburg Yacht Club and now reserved for British officers, the lights of which blazed out night after night across the battered and impoverished city. But that day he simply could not face the patronizing glances he received from youthful battle-hardened veterans, who made it through the war in uniform and made him feel even more fraudulent than usual. Most of all, he could not bear one sneaking suspicion, as he regarded the sheer arrogance of his fellow victors. Some of them seemed to demonstrate that beating the Nazis had meant just a little of the enemy had rubbed off onto them.

He had written all these things to his wife and family, but he had left out the blank hopeless faces of the children, the desperate selfishness with which the ragged population scavenged for food and the rain-soaked posters of missing kids staring out in their hundreds from the station platforms. He had also left out the BEWARE OF WOLVES signs that had begun appearing on the distant outskirts. It was easy to say that the joy he felt at one child re-united could outweigh all the pain. He knew he was supposed to subscribe to such sentiments, but he could not do so. The whole experience was unremittingly painful. It seemed to feed on his worst fears of impermanence. Better Hitler than this, he thought to himself, then realized he didn't think that either.

Looking at what had once been a beautiful city, a centre of the old Hanseatic League, from where the great voyagers had once set sail for Africa and the Indies, he bled for the past. He could not imagine what strategic benefit the Allies had gained from devastating memory and history along with bricks and mortar. As he kicked one of the bricks on the abbey ruins, he uncovered the blackened remains of an ancient hymnbook, in gothic text screaming out in the bright modernist air. He thought of the destruction of the past, and inevitably of Emma and Byron and all that remained of them. He barely stopped thinking of them.

Then there she was, walking towards him gracefully, though the rubble lay around them where the seating and graves and great vaulted ceiling had once been. She was dirty. She had a great tear in her blue-striped dress and her dark hair was falling over her eyes, yet she walked with calm and dignity across the dirt and rubble. The only part of her which displayed any sign of desperation were her hands, which seemed outside her control, large and alternately ringing and gesticulating like great useless white diggers. Her cheekbones stood out in hunger.

She told him later that she had lost her entire family in the raids. One bomb, lovingly manufactured near Walsall and loaded onto an RAF Lancaster near Luton, dropped at suppertime, had flattened her parents' home and suffocated her relatives hiding in the cellar. She had been on night shift at the time. She now had nothing of her past left, but when Harry saw her stumbling towards him across what had once been the nave, she still carried herself with dignity.

'Excuse me,' she said. 'I wonder if you could lend me a couple of cigarettes?'

'You speak extremely good English,' said Harry, amazed to be addressed at all. Something about her reminded him of his mother. Maybe it was the complete lack of make-up. Maybe it was the fortitude in the face of homelessness and a widening emotional abyss.

'I spent some time in England before the war,' she said. 'I studied English literature. Not all of us are stupid, whatever you might think.' Harry had never seen anybody look less like a bluestocking, but she walked a little like one and something else too – like someone born to have her books carried for her. There was an attractive arrogance about her that seemed to have been hidden or beaten out of so many of her compatriots. Harry reached into his pocket and began to remove a couple of cigarettes, the new currency in these impermanent times. Then he thought better of it, and handed her the whole packet. She smiled suddenly from one side of her face to the other.

'Thank you, sir,' she said, adding shyly. 'I don't actually smoke myself, you understand. They're for my friends.' She went a little red as if she had given herself away a little, and revealed a feminine defensiveness: for some reason, she hadn't wanted him to think she smoked.

'You don't have to call me "sir". Do you have family?' Even then, with the war barely with its stake in the heart, conversation about it was difficult. And rare. Harry was unused to passing the time of day with any of the locals.

'My family is gone,' she said, looking down. 'But I live with a kind of family now.'

Harry suddenly realized he was smiling and frowning in sympathy. Her name was Renata. She was 27, but looked older. Her father had been mayor of a small town south of Hamburg, she told him. She had been engaged to a U-boat captain, with a white jersey, sea boots and an unshaven smile, but he had failed to return from patrol in 1944. He noticed she had big brown eyes and realized he was already fascinated by her.

Every day that went by, Harry found himself admiring the German civilians more, with their quiet dignity and care about their appearance in the most difficult circumstances. You could describe them as blank and emotionless – the newspaper reports back home describing their day-to-day world amid the ruined streets did just that – but you could equally well see them as proud and determined. Defiant even, in their refusal to succumb to cold, hunger and poverty. Renata summed up that feeling as he talked to her. Then it transpired that she had something specific to say to him, and she had engineered the meeting. Yet he warmed to her all the more, as if she had picked him out from thousands.

'You see I live with friends, with my family in way. It is not so luxurious, I'm afraid, but I must take you there. We need to talk to a British officer. It is very serious. Please do not mind that I am asking you.'

'Don't be too ready to listen to stories from attractive women,' said the introductory pamphlet he had been given on arrival in the British Zone of Occupation. 'They may be acting under orders.' Yet something about Renata made him oblivious to the obvious risk. He wanted to go with her.

'Shouldn't you just go to the police? Or the Control Commission office if you have a problem? I shouldn't come with you. I'm not even a proper soldier. I'm not sure I can help at all – I just deal with missing people.'

'Quite so,' she said. 'I apologize for being so firm with you – but that is why we need to talk. Please help us.'

'Talk about what? At least tell me what it's about, and then maybe I'll come.'

'I fear I cannot,' said Renata. 'Herr Gruber will tell you. Not me.'

Knowing that he was breaking regulations and flying in the face of common sense, Harry went with her. And as they flew together down the back streets, Harry wondered what on earth he was doing. As a very traditional gentleman, he felt impelled to ignore the advice of his superiors and go to the assistance of a lady. No matter how gruff his old grandfather had been, he had learned that from him above all else. But there was something else as well. A kind of glow, a magic about Renata and her long thin neck. Something that made the ruins around them seem fuzzy and unreal and compelled him to follow, like the Pied Piper, into the forbidden hillside.

Despite this, their conversation about pre-war London seemed relaxed and civilized as they walked along. Yet as he looked up the alley to the right, Harry suddenly caught sight of an altercation and a flash of knives, then – as the antagonists saw them – a flurry as they dashed away into the shadows. A beggar lay in rags on the corner. Harry gave him four cigarettes.

'You see, we are afraid of the snatchers,' said Renata eventually. 'I can say no more than that.'

'The snatchers? Oh, you don't believe all that Sweeney Todd stuff, do you? It's all been thoroughly investigated.'

'Believe? But we know. We have already lost Ingrid. Not my friend exactly, but one of our family. But I must say no more. Herr Gruber will explain.'

The street was deserted as he followed her through a rickety door and ducked down to waist height to get under a small opening, which looked as though it had once been used for delivering beer. Above him were the ruins of another church, a tarpaulin covering part of the nave to show that it was back in use for workshop and maybe shelter.

His eyes adjusted to the light and Harry realized that, although it looked as though he might have stumbled on the cellar of a junk shop in Notting Hill Gate, he was also in a kind of underground village. Across the crypt, spaces for families had been staked out with blankets between them. There were makeshift beds and a few pieces of furniture and many old boxes. Possessions were occasionally in heaps, and sometimes arranged tastefully as if there were walls and roofs. An old wireless set. A favourite plate. Some carefully folded bedding.

'How many people live here?' Harry asked.

'About 60. We don't usually venture out in daylight. We take it in turns then to go through the rubbish. We get by. We sell things. But it's not very good.'

'I'm sure it's not,' said Harry. 'It's amazing what you've got down here.' He looked at the cinders of a couple of fires from the previous evening, with a strange contraption held up with string to direct the smoke out to the surface. There were pans for cooking and a strong smell of elderly cabbage and human bodies. Some had gathered round them a bizarre mixture of the basic necessities and whatever they valued most in the world. A picture or a photo in pride of place, many of them of wedding days. The really valuable stuff, if there was any, would presumably be hidden away. There was a handful of mountainous elderly women under piles of jerseys. A couple of children playing with a wire mesh in the corner, and all around, the sleeping shapes of exhausted and defeated adults.

'Come!' said Renata. 'I will show you to Herr Gruber.' As she did so, she touched the skin between his hand and his khaki tunic and a charge like electricity shot through him. It shocked them both and they stood looking at each other for a moment. Then she beckoned and led him past a towel hanging up on the stairs and into a darkened room.'

'Herr Gruber, *darf ich Ihnen Herr Weston vorstellen.*'

'Delighted, delighted,' said a stout elderly man in pinz nez and a shawl, with twinkling eyes and a double chin. His white eyebrows looked like a small forest under his forehead, and he was not so stout that he couldn't haul himself up from the picnic chair he sat on to greet Harry. 'My dear sir, I am grateful to you for coming. Please be seated.' He picked up one of a number of piles of open books off a bench so that Harry could sit down. The remains of old candles were perched all over the room, together with enormous numbers of dirty plates. He noticed Renata treated the old man with some reverence.

'The truth is, my dear sir, we are besieged. We have been able to find enough to feed and clothe ourselves, but I fear for the winter, I really do. But there is something very specific we would ask of you.' Harry looked expectantly at his own hands and resisted the temptation to bite his nails.

'You must realize I have no authority. I'm not even a proper soldier.'

'We know who you are, Captain Weston. We have watched you at work at the station. We know you are a man we can trust. We must trust. We dare not do otherwise or go elsewhere.'

Harry looked at him in astonishment. He really did seem to have been enticed into this bizarre underground hovel. He swiveled to catch Renata's eye, only to find she had disappeared.

'We know, of course, of your expertise with the missing. We have too a problem with the missing. Our friend, a member of our family, Ingrid Strauss, has disappeared these two weeks ago. These are brutal times, of course, and we are tempted to think she may have travelled home to Bavaria without telling us. But we fear she has not. I must tell you that I fear an organized snatching.'

Harry made a dismissive gesture. 'We hear stories, of course. But nothing has ever been proved. I can't see how I can help, I'm afraid.'

'But Captain Weston, you must. Because we have proof – we just dare not take it to the authorities ourselves, for fear that they would look unkindly on our family here.'

'Why? You're not doing anything wrong. There are many other people like you in this city, I can tell you.'

The old man smiled patiently. 'Ah!' he said. 'I fear your colleagues of the British Sector do not take kindly to gatherings of Germans, even hungry ones. Particularly hungry ones, in fact. We will have to trust you, but you must trust me about this.'

Harry looked confused and stole a glance at his watch.

'Here, let me tell you what I mean,' said Mr Gruber, beckoning him closer as if he was about to impart a dreadful secret – which, in a way, he was.

'Young Adolf – did you see him as you came in – about thirteen years old? On Monday, he was accosted by a middle-aged woman near the station. She looked tall and exhausted, he told me – grey hair. She told him: "I am lost. I must get this message to my friends, but I have no time and must catch a train. If you take it, I will give you this dollar bill. Can you do that for me?" And Adolf, helpful boy – he took the envelope and the dollar and went to the address she had written down for him. Down by the docks it was.'

Harry sat fascinated as Gruber spun his tale. There was the air of something very ancient about it.

'But half way there, Adolf thought there was something strange about the woman. She was well-dressed. And why did she not offer occupation marks? She looked odd, he said, so he did not go.' Gruber reached a kind of story-telling crescendo.

'So he's all right then?' He ignored Harry and was searching next to himself on the cluttered shelf by his desk. With a flourish, he pulled out an envelope, his eyes flashing.

'Ah yes, he's alright. But this is the envelope he was given.'

Harry took it, saw that it had been opened and pulled out the letter inside. Scrawled across the sheet of paper in bold untidy capitals, were the words: '*DIES IST DIE DER ICH IHNEN HEUTE SCHICKEN WERDE*'.

He knew enough German to get the gist, but it took a few moments for the implications to sink in. 'It says: 'This is the last one I shall send you today'.'

'I can see. Can it be true?' asked Harry. The letter wanted to make him retch.

'True!' said the old man with triumph. 'But we cannot report it – it would bring the British snooping down here. And yet it must be investigated. It's only 48 hours ago. What we want you to do is report this horror to the army. I fear … I fear … I hardly know what to fear.'

'It could be innocent, of course,' said Harry, and as he said it, the possibilities ran through his mind. What would they have done to the boy if he had arrived with the letter? Prostitution? White slavery? Even in this dismal food shortage, there were ugly rumours about cannibalism. 'And what will I say? I can't say it happened to me.'

'Captain Weston, you are an intelligent sensitive man. I know you will do your best. I know you will because like us, you fear there are monsters in the city.'

Nodding and accepting the terrible letter with its tell-tale address, Harry shook his hand and pushed past the towel in the doorway. The darkness outside was beginning to fall. The eyes of the cellar people watched him square his shoulders and walk out into the late afternoon. When he reached the street, Renata was waiting for him.

'Come back soon,' she said.

XVIII

'If ye will with Mab find grace,
Set each Platter in his place:
Rake the Fier up, and get
Water in, ere Sun be set.
Wash your Pailes and clense your Dairies;
Sluts are loathsome to the Fairies.
Sweep your house: Who doth not so,
Mab will pinch her by the toe.'
ROBERT HERRICK, *THE FAIRIES*

Oberon House, August 1998

SOMEBODY once told me to be careful of what I wish for, because it would surely happen. It is quite true, of course. It just tends not to happen at the most appropriate moment – like when you want it most. But then, I wished for Susie. I lay awake imagining I could stretch out my hand across the bed and pull her towards me. I imagined contorted erotic positions of power and vulnerability in which we might spend the night. Wafts of her reached me even at work, in the driest meetings I would suddenly find myself thinking about the small of her back, and the way she put her hair behind her ears.

We tend to get what we crave, God help us, and late one night there was a knock on my front door and there she was. We eyed each other carefully for a moment. Her fringe fell over her left eye. She looked upset and dishevelled. I tried not to reveal any emotion at all, afraid that my look of triumph and excitement might drive her away.

'Come in,' I said, glancing down the deserted street for companions waiting under the yellow street lamps. 'Have you had a disagreement with James?'

She said nothing and I watched as she took her coat off and collapsed on the chair.

'You're the only one I can talk to – you're the only one who knows him.' The light in her eyes that used to thrill me so much had seeped away. I poured her some whiskey and put the kettle on, and the light began to seep back again. I could hear a siren dashing by in the main road outside.

'I don't think James and I are quite the same,' she said, tossing the hair out of her eyes.

'Tell me about it!' It was the wrong thing to say. I had awakened her vigilant loyalty to him.

'Ah well,' she tailed off, taking a long swig from the glass. Longer than she meant to. She caught her breath. I found it hard to see how I could help or explain anything, or what she might want from me, but then maybe she simply wanted to talk about him.

She suddenly started chatting, about the hours he would spend drawing diagrams for the architect he couldn't afford to employ, the weeks he would spend studying the same document, the weeks he might take to write one letter. I could understand her frustration: James had never held down a proper job. Time management was unnatural to him. But the poem, she went on – well, it was a bit of a joke, wasn't it? And now the joke had got out of hand.

'It's not as if we're *really* going to save the house that way, are we?' she said with animation, and I had to agree. 'So why do we spend so long looking for it?'

I could see this was partly frustration with herself. She had found the neighbour's cat, found Jess's key, but she had failed to find the one thing we had all searched for. She was also absolutely right. She had said as much to James and he had descended into a black mood for 48 hours before she snapped, left and took the train to London.

'How do you know there's nothing there?' James had shouted. 'Why are you being like this?'

'Are you serious?' she had shouted back, she told me, ignoring the second question altogether. 'With that well underneath the house, and goodness knows what else, the damp would have destroyed anything hidden centuries ago.'

I suppose it was partly the betrayal of his ideals and hopes that James had reacted against, but most of all it would have been the pent up frustration and disappointment about the sex. Why had she not been sleeping with him? Perhaps he had never suggested it. Perhaps the erotic spirit moved over the house and settled on me instead of her. Perhaps it had been unsure in all that disorder where to land. No, if she had wanted him, she would have arranged it. This time I decided not to ask about it.

'You see, I always felt I was supposed to come to Oberon,' she said. 'I know you don't really believe all that stuff, but I did. I kind of think there was some connection between me and the place – I don't know what it could be. My family have been in and around Minnesota or the Midwest for getting on for two centuries. But I knew when I studied Byron, and found this connection, that I was somehow supposed to come here. Then when I met James in the library, and he was looking for the very same bit of the very same book, it seemed to be inevitable. It's strange, isn't it? You never know quite how life is going to throw you into the midst of what you wanted, do you. I don't know what I expected when I talked to him, but I certainly didn't find him attractive or anything. I was just following what seemed to me to be the clues about where to find myself. And now ... well, I don't know.'

'You mean, now you've decided you do fancy him,' I said irritably.

She drew herself up on the sofa. 'Tell me this,' she said, with intensity. 'Why is it that English men shy away from the light?'

I knew immediately what she meant, about James and about all of us. He had wanted her brilliance and fire and the way she embraced life with such enthusiasm. He had wanted her because he lacked that fire and certainty himself. He wanted her like a butterfly collector wants the brightest variety pinned under glass to his wall. But what would he have done with all that life if he had been given it? What did it mean for the real passion in his life, for his home? Maybe all English men are Taureans at heart. And Susie saw herself trapped in this emotional treacle, with a man who averted his eyes just a tiny bit when she walked past, and averted his emotions, too.

I had no idea how to answer her directly but I listened and she grew more honest as she talked. It is a peculiar phenomenon that I've noticed before, that the more you listen to someone, the more they trust you. When she trusted me, we looked at each other for a moment.

'I tell you what,' I said calmly. 'Not all Englishmen shy away from the light.' Then I kissed her boldly on the lips and stared into her eyes. I had never seen her look very surprised and she did not look surprised then, though she seemed to hiccup inside to herself and I felt her slowly open her mouth.

In my experience it is a rare thing, vouchsafed to few of us bachelors, to act out our most thrilling fantasy with the one person in the world we have been dreaming of. I slowly undid the buttons on her shirt, I ran my fingers over the spot on her back I'd been imagining, I tugged at her hair with my fist and she urged me on with her unfathomable Mona Lisa smile – or so it seemed at the time.

Some hours later, I leapt out of bed to make her breakfast, as if the weight of London had been lifted from my mind, but she was already up, looking as close to flustered as I had ever seen her.

'I must go,' she said. 'It's been good to see you, but I must go. I must go back.'

'Oh come on, we've only just begun.'

'No, we haven't begun anything. We just had an aberration.'

'Rather a wonderful aberration, don't you think?'

'If you say so.'

'Oh I do, don't you? And what do you mean by back? Not back to the old house, surely. Stay here, for goodness sake.'

'Yes, I do mean back to the old house. James will be quite distraught. He'll probably go down to the well chamber again and it isn't safe to do that alone. So I've got to go back. I've *got* to.'

'And you don't know what he might find, do you?' I said, sensing her fear that she might miss out on finding the poem after all that she'd said. She ignored me and carried on packing herself together.

'Yes, but that's not the most important thing, is it. I mean how would I feel – how would you feel – if we discovered James had died under a heap of medieval rubble while we were having it away up here? I'd never forgive myself and I'd never forgive you. So thank you, but I'm going to go.'

I pulled my jumper over my head and picked up my car keys. 'Well if you're going to go, I'm going with you.'

'Are you kidding? After this? No way am I going to go in there with you. "Oh yes, James, I just laid your friend too." Sure. He's really going to love that.'

I agreed but we compromised. I drove her down to Surrey, past Box Hill and along the A24, past the old hill fort with the birds gathering on the branches as if they could see autumn somewhere on the horizon. I dropped her at the end of the drive and watched her denim bottom disappearing round the corner of the brambles. Afraid it might be for the last time, I sat in front of the steering wheel fighting an overwhelming urge to follow her down the gravel and drag her back. Then I wound up the window, shutting off the sharp cold tang of the morning, and drove away. Five miles later, I thought of Susie and James reunited in their hunt for Byron's damn missive, and I turned round again.

Susie was at the back door when I arrived, and seemed lost, distracted and unsurprised to see me.

'The door's open, but I can't find him,' she said, peering on tiptoes over the distant stone wall and across the fields. I had visions of James suddenly – my old friend – driven mad by Susie's disappearance, picking up our betrayal of him somehow by osmosis. As if he had borrowed some of Susie's unusual skill and dreamed it.

'Have you looked up in the roof?' I asked. We scampered through the house.

'James!' she shouted guiltily from door to door. I stayed silent. Either way, there was no reply.

'What about the well?' We both stopped. Susie dashed to the kitchen to find the torches. She was back in a moment. 'The best one's gone; he must have taken it. But I found this.' She shone it in her face. It looked pathetically weak in the morning light. 'Hold on here. I'll go down and find him.'

It was a disturbing moment. The thought of going down into the dark passage with one weak torch appalled me. I felt a rising nausea in the stomach, but there was no way I was letting her reunite with James in that moment of guilt and self-abasement.

'There's no way I'm letting you go down there by yourself.'

'I thought you hated dark holes. You're already looking queasy.' She was climbing into the hole in the wall. I saw her switch on the beam inside as she looked for the steps.

'Wait!' I shouted, taking a deep breath. 'I'm coming with you.'

As we trod gingerly down the stone steps, mopping the cobwebs out of our faces, with the dusty brick roof and stalactites moving downwards, I regretted it bitterly. I tried to concentrate on the beam from her torch and to put the darkness behind me out of my mind. It was much as they had described it, with the mouse droppings like marbles under foot, the occasional damp down the walls and finally the well chamber itself – bigger than I expected. I peered towards the well, trying to make out James' dark shape.

'Shit!' said Susie suddenly. I froze. She pointed the torch at the ground, and a wreath of blue cornflowers. 'How can it still be fresh?' And then a second later we were both staring at a hole in the wall. The ancient door was wedged open with a squash racket, which I recognized as mine. We both stared in silence. Susie went to the door and shouted 'James!' down into the blackness. The name echoed back at her.

'He must have gone in.'

I suppose that was inevitable. As I walked through the door behind Susie's dancing light, and I tasted the damp cold air on my tongue, I felt it was the bravest thing I had ever done. I dared not even speak. Then I thought of the story of the dog.

'Keep the torch pointed at the ground. We don't want to just disappear.'

Susie took no notice. 'I knew that door wasn't just decoration. This must be the way Emma ran away. Watch out!' She ducked below a dripping stalactite, and indeed we did seem to have entered a cave. The bricks had gone. There seemed nothing man-made about this passage. Soon I could hear nothing but our panting breaths, stumbling over the occasional boulder. The walls began to look green.

'We must be beyond the lawn and under the fields towards the copse by now. How far have we been walking? A couple of hundred miles? A quarter of a mile?'

I could not bring myself to reply. My heart was in my mouth. Somehow being in this confined space had brought my half-forgotten limp back.

'Or maybe we're going in the direction of the village. I can't work it out.'

Then we came to a fork. Susie carefully took off her scarf and laid it pointing the way back. At the second fork, she took off her belt.

'I hope there aren't too many of these. It's getting like strip poker.' I could still say nothing.

The cavern seemed to be opening out, and there was sand under our feet, and then a strange thing began to happen. It seemed to be getting lighter. After a few minutes more, I could see the back of Susie's head. A few minutes later and she turned off the torch. But it was a peculiar light, greenish and dreamy.

'I think we're getting there,' she said.

'But where?' There was indeed light flooding into the cave in front of us. Soon we could see the sky, through some bushes. It looked streaky mauve and green, of the kind you see at dawn, rather than the mid-morning light we had left behind upstairs. But the bushes were real enough as they scraped their faces, still wet with dew, and so were the primroses under our feet. There was a cool spring-like feel in the air and a rustling of leaves. As we reached the mouth, leaning on a thorn tree in his decorating trousers, looking elated and proud, was James.

'Where on earth are we?'

'I've no idea,' he said. 'But wherever it is, it's exciting.'

I felt much braver now that we were out of the confined space, but it was clear that something unique had happened to us. Wherever we were, these were certainly not the surroundings of modern Oberon. There was no traffic and apparently no people. It was lush, in the height of summer. And the green speckled light flickered over everything, dappled through the leaves. It almost hummed. In the distance, great vertical pillars of rock, like islands in the middle of the plain with lost worlds at their summits, poked over the landscape like fingers.

We walked along the unkempt path in front of us like Dorothy arriving in Oz, barely speaking, our hearts beating considerably faster than usual, thoughts of the night temporarily gone from my mind. We walked through the first clump of trees and found ourselves in an abandoned village, with the roofs of the huts fallen in and a medieval church beside a great oak tree. As we walked down the street, with the doors of the barn hanging off their hinges, the sounds seemed muffled and the images swum before me – as if we were walking down the main street of a sunken city, Port Royal, Atlantis – with the echoing noise of the church bell banging against itself in the current.

'It's Oberon,' said James. 'Or it was.' He gestured towards a decayed and crumbing wooden contraption that looked like a long-abandoned stocks, in the midst of a forest of brambles.

Before we had time to reply, we heard the music, and we

all three stopped still and listened. It was a speckled sunny kind of music, green like the light, and so quiet that it might also have been the breeze or the current in the branches or even the beating of our pulses. Soon it was obvious and infectious, like all the jigs and dances you ever heard, rolled together in an insistent beat. Nor was it quite clear where it was coming from, except that it was somehow nearer, like hooves beating towards us. I was dizzy and disorientated as it flickered around us, and just conscious enough to be scared. I tried to catch Susie's eye to reassure her – though, as usual, she looked quite assured without me – and I saw her slip her hand into James's, as if it was completely natural for her to do so. They didn't look at each other. Infuriated, I turned away and lost the ability to think at all.

It was as if the sun was beating down on us, and the music around us reached a crescendo of love and death and all the fierce power of the natural world, beating out the memory of battles long ago. It was a dreamlike moment, and like so many dreams, impossible to grasp the elements separate from each other and pin them down. It was also difficult to know how much time was passing in my light-headed befuddled and irritated state, except that the tune and beat were coming from all sides. Through my confusion, it was just possible to glimpse – out of the corner of the eye, rather than face to face – a sense of people leaping in a circle around us. Not human people, either, but some smaller prehistoric version of us – smooth, ancient and filled with a kind of amoral and angry joy.

We found ourselves drawing near to an enormous, gnarled oak tree, its branches like exhausted tentacles stretching across the field. I found myself thinking that it was some kind of turning point. Furious as I was with James and Susie, whatever was happening to us was outside anything I had experienced before. I was unsure whether we would ever break the dream, but somehow certain that if we did, nothing would ever be quite the same. These dreamy fantasy creatures were certainly not fairies. These were no gossamer creatures with wings, and they exuded a brutal kind of power, like piranha fish or the other hidden beasts of the forest. The beat seemed to defeat comparisons, but through it all danced the sheer implacable charge of sex. The dream merged with a kind of half-awake fug and the memory of Susie's limbs intertwined. Occasionally I was aware again of the rhythm, and of hundreds of tiny feet, stepping so lightly that they left barely an imprint on the grass or dandelions.

'This really is no place on earth,' said James. 'How did we get here?'

I felt increasingly drowsy – we probably all did – but we all three plunged on towards the tree. I grasped Susie round the waist, and took her chin in mine and bent her face towards me. Her eyes were half closed, and I would have torn her shirt off there and then, but I felt so exhausted. We all three lay on the ground under the branches and panted, whether from desire or tiredness or fear I could not be absolutely sure. A moment later I wondered if I had actually touched her at all.

And then I was asleep – one of those cloudy summer dreams you have on beaches or cricket fields. It was a dream of Christmas. I dreamed I was on the roof of my flat in Clapham. I could feel the cold air sharply on my face, and my overcoat skittering about in the wind. Just below me, one of the block's massive chimneys was pumping smoke. It was not my Clapham as it was as I knew it, but the days of James grandfather – 50 or 60 years before. I could see the Underground station, and the red lights around the Italian cafe across the street. Then in the distance, I could see the windows and roof of Arding and Hobbs and beyond them the common, and beyond that there seemed to be line upon line of houses, brightly lit, with plane trees swaying across the lighted windows, and Christmas still going on inside.

I could see the lovers holding hands by the garden gates, and the drunken husbands sulkily slamming the front doors behind them, and the disappointed children, afraid of the long wait until the next Christmas, and the abandoned mothers with the washing up, and the elderly ladies dreaming of long dead gentlemen, and the taxi drivers swearing and pulling on long woollen gloves as they sipped their tomato soup in the street outside. Beyond that the railways, the engines pumping clouds of steam – bringing the cheques and the postal orders – and the tired prostitutes, and the washerwomen, and the jobless men in caps and mufflers too ashamed to go home, and the beaten weeping children, and all over London – an endless monumental Dickensian novel – laid out before me in the smoky post-Christmas haze.

The light was rising faster and faster, ending with the milkmen, as if it was the day just gone, then sinking into dark again. Then the alternations between dark and light seemed to be gathering pace. Soon I was in a sky which was flashing on and off like a child with the bathroom light. I floated over Clapham Junction in the alternating light and dark, as if it was a movie that had been accelerated so fast that months – years even – went by before me. Whole towns and villages exploded, and spread out across the countryside, and black ribbons covered with cars spilled over the landscape below, and in the far distance a series of tornadoes uprooted trees and benches and cottages and farms and tossed me down towards a disintegrating village, which I knew to be Oberon ....

It could have been hours before I was aware of voices. There was nobody there. I seemed to have been abandoned by both of them. I leapt up, brushed the vegetation angrily from my clothes and looked around. The plain still stretched forever in the green light. I wondered with horror if it was going to be my fate to wander and die there just walking into the fog. But then I could see them, a couple of hundred yards away, under another tree. They seemed to be talking to somebody and they looked up as I approached. Neither of them gave any looks of recognition or welcome. But an unusual looking man hailed me.

'How do, Sir,' he said, wiping his warty nose with the back of his hand. He seemed only about five foot tall, wore a battered and ancient leather jerkin, and smelled seriously in need of a bath. He could have been as old as the tree, with skin as weather-beaten as his clothes. In my confused state, he barely seemed unusual at all. I think it must have been clear to all of us – though we had barely spoken since the start of the adventure – that we had stumbled somehow into a nether world, maybe part of our imaginations, maybe real in some other way. As my head cleared it became an increasingly worrying thought. I could see by the way that Susie was stroking her own shoulders that she was concerned, too.

'I welcome you – another visitor – we're honoured!' said the man without getting up, in a jovial and yet slightly menacing tone. He spoke from the back of his throat, as if retching. The flies buzzed around him, but seemed to wilt in his breath. He picked his nose as he looked us over again. 'No, as I was saying to your friends here – you came of your own free will so you can return of your own free will when you choose. And you can take back my best wishes to the world above, God bless it – and God does bless it, doesn't he!' The man seemed pleased with his little joke.

'But how?'

'How, my fine fellow? Well you came here as easy as a russet apple, did you not? Just follow your nose back the way you came. Past those trees over yonder then straight on till evening stretches your shadows and shows you the way. But that ain't it, is it? You're searching.'

'Searching? We're not searching. I'm not searching,' said James impatiently.

'And I'm not searching either.' I wondered whether I should repeat Susie's incantation as if it was some kind of form we all had to fill in, but the man was talking again.

'Oh, you're not searching, I know my lass. I know what you're thinking. I know very well.' He poked towards her with his stick and Susie reddened. I saw her glance at James with a worried look. 'You make the cobbles of these lads tingle don't you. But *he's* searching. And I know what he's searching for.'

Of course James was searching. He had been searching in a kind of half-hearted way ever since we had met as a nine-year-old. But I thought that, in Oberon House, he had actually found something of what he was searching for, and in Susie he might have found the missing bit of the jigsaw, though I admit I was doing my best to extract her.

'And you're not searching, I suppose,' said Susie suddenly, looking irritated. The man checked himself for a moment and stared at her. Then he laughed with an unpleasant gurgling sound. It made his leather coat chafe against his belt, and the trinkets around his waist began to rattle.

'You're a pretty one and no mistake. I've seen you searching and all. Night after night – searching for keys and dogs and spectacles and whatnot. Fair scouring the dark like a widow woman you do. I knew you when I saw you, I did. So, yes, I'm a searcher of a kind. You and I recognize each other, don't we, from those corners of the night you sweep clean, from those spaces between the minutes where no one else sees. But your man here – if he is your man and not this fair wretch who's in such a whirl – your man's looking for something special. And I know where she is.'

We looked at him, astonished. It was an unnerving speech, as if he was making some kind of common cause with her. As if, like a lascivious old uncle from the depths of her childhood, he suddenly knew more about her than she did herself. She stared at her shoes. I stared at her. I had assumed, since we were in this dreamworld, that he had meant James' endless search for the missing poem.

'Who?' said James. 'Who do you mean – she?'

The man looked more saturnine than ever. He examined his dirty and broken fingernails and whistled a little.

'Ah now, that would be telling, wouldn't it,' he said, gripping James by the wrist. 'Aren't you the young man who was searching for love that lasts forever, or was that somebody else? My mind forgets itself through the years.'

'Does anything last forever?' I suppose I was trying to lighten the atmosphere a little. The green light seemed to be growing deeper and the trees and vegetation seemed to be gathering themselves together for some kind of dusk. I had hardly meant it as a momentous question, and yet the silence that followed seemed to make it so. Even the old man seemed to have gone suddenly dreamy.

'Down here maybe; up above maybe. But where you come from, nothing. Nothing. It dies, it rots, it bears fruit again. How could anything last forever in the world. T'isn't natural. That's what we do. We keep the old world turning away. We keep it dancing. And when something dies we turn it into mulch. But when something came from our world, when it's just a block of wood, without a soul quickening its pulses, when it's a changeling – why then it doesn't really die, because it never really lived.'

At this point Susie suddenly lost her temper. I had never seen her do so before, but I've noticed that Americans start off awed into silence in foreign places and then they lose their cool.

'Oh for goodness sake stop playing around with us. Just tell us where we are and what we do about it and then scram.'

The jerkin was shaking his head in a patronizing way and maybe he was thinking what I was thinking. I wondered if it was this talk of changelings without souls that had annoyed her. But in a flash, I realized she was jealous of this 'she'. Some fear had gripped Susie about poor dull James – about whom she had been so certain. She would normally have been so calm and charming, but the strange state and predicament in which we found ourselves had unsteadied her. She ranted on at him and his eyes gleamed all the more. He seemed unreachable, implacable and completely amoral, and enjoying it, too.

'Answer me his riddle and I'll bring her to you and you can take her home.'

'Oh for goodness sake.'

It was irritating me as well. It may have been a crass thing to do, but I offered him money. It has been known to oil such encounters, but not this time. Jerkin burst out laughing, throwing his head back until tears ran down his cheeks and he had to wipe them away with a leather arm. Then he did a little jig, like Rumplestiltskin or maybe Hitler after the fall of France. Then he went straight on with the riddle.

'Shall I ask you this one – "What was the drink I drank

yesterday, which was neither spring water, nor wine, nor mead, nor ale?" Know it? It's the dew of heaven. "What dead lungs did I see blowing to war?" Know it – of course you do – it's a blacksmith's bellows making a sword. "What animal is four-footed in the morning, two-footed at noon, and three-footed in the evening?" No, no, I'll ask you this ...' The man seemed to have puffed himself out with his exertion and stopped for a moment before drawing himself up to his full five foot two:

'What is greater than a mouse, you find a-wandering through the house? What is the land that we can see, that lies far deeper than the sea?'

There was a short silence at the end of this.

'Well?' I said to Susie. She ignored me.

'Don't ask me,' said James.

'You don't get it, do you?' said the jerkin, chuckling away. 'You don't get it, but you've still got time. So come with me and get thinking, my clever friends.'

With that he set off at a great pace in the direction he had originally indicated, striding ahead like an angry gnome, with us hurrying along behind. As he went, he told a story which sounded a little like this.

XIX

'I have had a dream, past the wit of man
to say what dream it was...'
WILLIAM SHAKESPEARE, *A MIDSUMMER NIGHT'S DREAM*

Josiah's story

ONCE THERE *was a kingdom, not far from here, where the corn always grew as high as the night owls and the badgers spent the dark hours weaving delicate clothes of starlight. It was a happy kingdom, where the country people sang in the daylight and the city people sang at night. The farmers were happy, the king was happy and his family, musicians, knights, magicians and servants were happy, too. Only small problems ever furrowed their brows, but they would think deeply and the answers would pop almost unbidden into their heads.*

But despite all this wisdom and happiness, they lived the shortest lives. By the time they were twenty, they were almost middle-aged. By the time they were thirty, they were old. The generations passed by quickly and smilingly into the dust. But they knew no different and filled the years they had with joy and music and hunting.

Only one person in the whole kingdom had a problem which seemed beyond resolution, and he hugged it to himself, searching for an answer. That was the prince, the eldest son and heir to the throne. He lived in great finery, with tapestries of exotic beasts hanging from the walls of his room, and daily breakfasts of quails' eggs and baths of the best warm wine. Yet one small flaw in his character kept him awake night after night. He kept losing things.

They were insignificant things at first. He lost the key to the great trunk where he kept his most beautiful robes. Though his servants scoured the palace from top to bottom on his behalf, there was absolutely no sign of it and the trunk had to be forced open with a metal bar. He lost his favourite dagger, with pearls and rubies on the hilt and a kiss from the most beautiful princess in the world planted firmly on the blade. He had it with him only the night before. It was extraordinary how his things just disappeared. He even lost his favourite horse. He just stopped for a nap by the road during a long ride back from the outlying provinces, and when he had woken up, it was gone. Though he called its name until his throat was sore, though he led a hundred followers calling through the forest, all they ever found was a silver horseshoe and some tell-tale prints in the mud.

It was not the most serious problem in the world, but it kept the prince worrying into the small hours. It was all very well losing things when he was just a prince. He had access to untold wealth, so there was no difficulty replacing trunks, daggers and horses. But what about when he was king – which could only be soon now that his father was well into his thirties? He could hardly go around losing things then. He might lose a province or two if he was careless. Worse, he might lose a battle. What could he do?

On his fifteenth birthday – when the young people of that kingdom came of age – the presents and letters flooded into the palace from cities of which he had never even heard. There were tapestries woven by badgers. There were ceremonial quails and translucent daggers, their blades kissed by the most fertile women. There were pictures and goblets and princesses and advice. And at the end of the day of celebration and feasting, he was preparing himself for bed, and there was a knock at the door.

It was his old nurse and he threw his arms around her neck. She told him that, now he was fifteen, it was time for her to leave the palace and go back to her family in one of the most distant provinces, where the trees grew directly upwards and it was always night.

'But before I leave I have a special present for you, which I have kept secret all these years, and which I am sure was made to solve your difficulties,' she said. She took him in slippers and on tiptoe through the quiet back corridors of the sleeping palace, to a door the prince had never seen before. It had a tapestry in front of it which hid it from view and great iron rivets to hold it in place.

'What is in this room?' said the prince, intrigued by the secret.

'I will show you,' said his nurse, knocking three times on the topmost rivet and turning the handle. Inside was a gigantic window, and through it in the fading light, the prince could still make out the shapes of trees, castles and houses and in the distance, glinting in the new moon, the sails of great ships waiting in the harbour.

'But this is not the view from my palace. Where am I looking?' he asked.

'That is the kingdom of the lost,' said the nurse, with a stern authority he had never heard from her before. 'Everything anybody has ever lost is there. So this is my gift to you, my beautiful boy,' she said. 'If you have lost something you value, come secretly to this room, open the window and call to it across the roofs and you will see it coming to you. Only be very careful. You must use this gift sparingly and only for unimportant things. Sometimes what we lose must be lost, and you must know when this is. If it is an important thing, you must leave it in its proper place.'

'I do not understand you,' said the prince, his initial delight turning to irritation. 'If they are not important, why should I want them back?'

The nurse guffawed. 'Come now! Have I not seen you call-

ing and cursing about unimportant things like keys and daggers and horses? Here – open the window and call your missing horse and see what happens.'

So the prince opened the window, felt the night breeze on his face and saw the people moving slowing around the town below. Drawing a deep breath, he shouted 'Galahad!' There was a flutter of wings as the crows nesting on the palace roof took flight, and a moment's silence through the city of the lost below. Then unmistakably, he could hear the clip-clop of a horse making its way down the road to the palace, and there was his missing Galahad, whinnying to itself outside the gates.

'I can hardly believe it! What an extraordinary gift! It is by far the greatest gift I have ever been given!'

'Yes, my child, but do not whatever you do forget my warning …' But the prince was already outside and making for the palace gates to welcome his horse. By the time he came back, the door with the rivets was firmly shut and his old nurse was gone, but in the years that followed, he heeded her advice. He was careful to use the magical room and its extraordinary window only rarely. He used it to find a ring with a topaz from the furthest East which he had lost somewhere in the palace gardens, but when he lost some books in the town, he shrugged his shoulders. He used it to recover a bag of gold belonging to one of his sisters, which he lost on the way to the market, but when he lost his favourite necktie he just let it go – and bought another one twice as good. When the most beautiful princess in the whole world rejected his offer of marriage and slipped through his fingers and rode off to her own distant province beyond the mountains, he longed for her. He spent almost a week without sleep wondering whether to tiptoe to the room and call to her and hear her trotting back to him. But he knew it was just too important – and anyway, maybe she would come back of her own accord. He congratulated himself on his strength of will and on keeping his nurse's condition.

Then one day his father, the old king, died at the grand old age of thirty-eight. The whole city wore black for a month, and a thousand lambs were slaughtered for the funeral feast. The prince escaped to his quarters, and barred the door – until his mother, his sisters and the king's council came hammering on it, demanding that he should come out.

The prince knew he must. Sheepishly, he unbarred the door and was led away to his ritual washing, his ritual dressing and his coronation. As they walked slowly down the main corridor, the King's Council badgered him with questions.

'I know this is a difficult time for you, Sire. But it is most important that we take a decision on the south east frontier where the tribes are behaving in a most disturbing way.'

'I wonder if you might quickly turn your attention to the case of Tom the Cobbler whose plea for clemency must be decided by midnight tonight …'

'We have the menus for the Coronation Banquet here for you, Sire. I wonder, though, if we should be seating the Earl of the North Desert quite so close to the Bishop of the Long Forgotten Isles. I fear that would be asking for trouble …'

The prince nodded nervously and shook his head, and his courtiers and advisers seemed to be satisfied and scuttled away to carry out what they clearly believed were his instructions. But inside, his stomach was turning to quicksand. He missed his father enormously for his comforting words, his thoughtful advice, and he simply could not understand the questions he was being asked. He had never even heard of the South East Frontier. They could have seated Tom the Cobbler next to the Earl of the North Desert for all he cared. Yet he had to care. He would make some disastrous mistake and the bishop would raise an army and the kingdom would be ruined. Or worse. Any number of appalling possibilities passed through his mind. He simply could not do it.

What a time to lose his father! It was important, but it really was vital for the kingdom that his father should be found. Could the magic room and the magic window put right such fundamental losses? It was too important, probably, for his nurse's warnings – but it simply had to be tried. The future of the kingdom depended on it.

So it was that, on the night before his coronation, he tip-

toed in his stockings down the corridors and up the spiral stairs, knocked three times on the rivets and slipped into the room. He unclasped the window and felt the warm grassy air of the summer night. Then with all his might, he called for his father.

The word echoed over the rooftops. He froze to hear if anyone in the household had been disturbed. Then unmistakably, he could hear footsteps approaching the drawbridge below, and the clink of his father's armour and the sound of his familiar cough, then his voice, then he could almost feel him pounding on the great oak doors to the palace. His heart in his mouth, the prince dashed downstairs, not pausing to refasten the door, and ordering the guards to open the gates – and flung his arms around his father's neck.

But his father seemed unmoved by the meeting. In fact, he seemed to be in a terrible rage. When the palace awoke the next morning and, to their astonishment and fear, found the old king as healthy as ever and sitting on the throne, the plans for the coronation were quietly abandoned amid much whispering.

So life returned to normal. Nobody mentioned to the old king that they had thought him dead. The prince returned to his lessons. The coronation robes and crown jewels were put silently away – only now life seemed strangely different. The prince found that he now lost nothing at all. Many of the things he had thought lost now turned up in their proper place, including the missing princess – which was inconvenient because he was now admiring a different one. Even the things he discarded were back the next morning. Old clothes, old dishcloths, old handkerchiefs appeared back on the shelf. Within a week or so, his shelves and cupboards were growing under the weight.

Worse, his mind seemed to be seizing up – not because he kept forgetting things as usual, but because he forgot nothing. His memory was cluttering up with the most irrelevant facts and overheard conversations – and embarrassing moments that he desperately wanted to forget all hammered away inside his head. He soon noticed that something similar was happening to everyone in the palace. Nothing could be discarded. The slops and rubbish put out each night were back the next morning. Soon they cramped the kitchen and passageways and a sour human smell wafted down the corridors. Everyone seemed furious all the time.

As the weeks went by, he could also hear them complaining about the king.

'He's stale,' they said. 'We need something new. Fresh ideas. Youth. He's a great man, of course, but he's stuck in the past. The prince should have his turn.'

But they were all stuck mysteriously in the past, though nobody spoke of it. And the prince could see as well that, down in the city, the piles of rubbish and the angry constipated faces showed that the problem had spread there, too. Nothing could be lost and life was grinding to a halt. The weather stopped. The seasons stopped. Dead patriarchs dropped back for unexpected visits. Colds stayed put. Moods stayed put. Nobody changed their minds. Nobody changed at all – yet because they did not change, they also changed all too much.

In desperation, the prince escaped to the magic room, knocked on the rivets, opened the window – only to find that, this time, the view was the old familiar one of his own palace and his own city below. He ordered the door bricked up, ordered his horse and set off for the far province where it was always night. Days later, he knew he had reached it because of the chilly wind and the dawn that did not arrive. Asking at every house he came too, he was finally directed to a small cottage with a tartan door and there was his old nurse, just as she always had been. He flung himself on his knees in front of her, sobbing and begging her to forgive his stupidity and rescue the kingdom.

'Tsk tsk,' she said. 'I blame myself. The temptation was just too much. But I hope this has been a lesson to you. There are some things you just have to lose. That is all there is to it.' Then she went out into the back garden, and called to the badgers and night owls in a strange language the prince had

never heard before. Then the wind got up and swirled through the hedges in the dark, buffeting them and making them twist. There was a flash of light, a bang and a strange noise, like cracking ice, a trickle of water and then a gushing torrent.

'Well, that is that,' said the nurse. 'You must now go home.'

As he approached his own city, he could see people sweeping their front doorsteps, and the streets clean and sparkling in the morning sunlight. The piles of stinking rubbish had completely gone.

'We really must arrange your coronation,' said his chamberlain back in the palace, as if in mid-conversation.

As the years of his reign went by, and he rapidly grew in age and wisdom, he still lost his socks, his money, his ornamental badgers and occasionally his way. So he was sometimes tempted to look for the little room with the enormous window where he could find the things he lost. But every time he searched the strange corridor, feeling his way along the brickwork for the door, he simply could not find it.

XX

'We must not look at goblin men,
We must not buy their fruits;
Who knows upon what soil they fed,
Their hungry thirsty roots?'
CHRISTINA ROSSETTI, *'GOBLIN MARKET'*

Oberon House, August 1998

THAT WAS the story as I remember it, although I've embellished here and there because it was a good tale. As it ended, we had arrived in a familiar looking orchard, with more than its usual share of bees. There was an oak tree, with the branches reaching down like welcoming arms to the ground and a mass of twisted undergrowth. There was an entrance in the rocks ahead of us that looked very like the cave from which we had emerged – days ago, it seemed. Weeks ago. The buzz in the air was as strong as ever, like an august afternoon in midsummer. I felt exhausted, confused and hungry. Through the apple trees, I saw – or I believed I saw – a gargantuan feast sprawled out on some wooden tables. As we got a little closer, I could smell the scent of bacon cooking and of oranges and pomegranates wafting on the breeze. Even the tables were beautiful, with their strong intricately turned legs, like spider's webs holding up the weight of the food.

'Wait!' said James sharply, as I moved towards it purposely. 'If we're caught in a dream about fairies, we should keep to the old rules. You don't eat in Fairyland.'

'Rubbish,' I said, picking up a chicken drumstick and deliberately licking it. James' peremptory tone of voice was almost the last straw as far as I was concerned. Had I not always shown him what to do at parties? Had I not lent him money and given him detailed instructions for the scrapes he got into at work and with women? And now here he was pushing me around. I was fed up with him taking the lead, as if this was his damn dream. The chicken looked juicy and succulent beyond the best barbecued meat I had ever tasted. 'If it's a dream it isn't real, right? If it is real then these kind of things don't happen.'

James made an irritated gesture. Susie ignored me, and I saw she was looking further down to the next table but one. I put down the drumstick unbitten. There, partially obscured by the branches bowed down by fruit, was a young woman. No ordinary young woman. A number of peculiar possibilities leapt into my mind. She was dressed simply, with a low-cut white dress with no waist, like a Jane Austen heroine. Her black, curled hair was piled on her head and held there with a small red bow. There was a far away look in her eyes, as if she was vaguely aware of us but tired beyond imagination – like a bored millionairess trapped in a loveless marriage. Her eyes were dark-rimmed with exhaustion.

I wondered for a second why she looked so familiar and considered whether it was the similarity between her and James – I think it was the large and distinctive nose they shared. Then it struck me: she looked exactly like the girl in the miniature. This thought had clearly already struck James, who stood rooted to the spot. He tried to move towards her, but could get no more than a few yards. I glanced at the man with the leather jerkin and he was already scoffing the food, bits of ham and lettuce failing out of his mouth as he ate. He was also watching us all in an amused kind of way.

'It's simple,' he said. 'Simple. Answer me the riddle and you can take her back home – and your greedy friend.'

James was taking no notice. I could see his mind working, his face contorting with mental effort as he stood in front of us, staring at the woman.

'Emma?' he said quietly. 'Emma?'

She barely moved. But just when I thought she would reply, she suddenly stretched out her arms to him, and said slowly and hopelessly, in the most exhausted and defeated voice you have ever heard: 'Take ... me ... to ... my ... child'.

My heart was thumping. There seemed to be in that voice a sadness and distance I had never heard before. Though I did not entirely believe the experience I was having, I still rather wished that I hadn't licked the chicken. I felt the kind of sense of foreboding that you feel when you've eaten prawns and fear they may have been bad. I also felt angrier with what I saw as Susie's defection with every minute that went by. I had no idea what to make of the story, the food or the ghost – if that was what she was. But through all that confusion, the woman's simple plea sounded like one strong, pure distant note echoing around the orchard in a minor key.

'And if we answer the riddle, we can all four go home?' asked James, with the same new note of confidence in his voice.

'If you answer it correctly, then with my blessing, my fine gentleman. Or leave them behind, my fine gentleman. Leave them here to take part in the great Dance.'

'The answer is the soul in the underworld.' Susie had broken the silence, an almost mystical look on her face. 'That's right, isn't it?' The jerkin stood there chewing with no facial expression whatever. You could hear the bees in the silence between us.

'Hah!' he exclaimed when he finished his mouthful. 'Hah! You don't have it, my fine young lady. You haven't guessed it right. You haven't seen through the maze. Now you must stay and sing.'

But before I could register the disappointment on her face, James suddenly began to sing. I did a double-take, as he added a further twist to what had started dreamlike and now seemed to be verging on the ludicrous. For a moment I simply couldn't believe he was dealing with this cross between Bottom and Puck by singing him 'My Funny Valentine'.

'*Sweet funny Valentine, you make me smile with your heart* ...' he sang, and I could hear Susie humming along, too. I realized it was from his favourite Chet Baker album, one of the pile of execrable CDs he gathered around him of best-forgotten music from between the wars – anything from 'Cheek to Cheek' to 'Chattanooga Choo-Choo'. It was about the last song I was thinking of at the time, and yet it seemed to be moving the old man. He stood transfixed, an apple half-way to his mouth.

'... *Stay little Valentine, stay. Each day is Valentine's Day,*'

I looked at the Jerkin as they finished, and they burst out laughing at each other as they did so, and a single tear was rolling down his face. Of all the things I had seen in this dream, their dream probably rather than mine, this was the bit I refused to believe.

There was an awkward silence.

'Now listen,' said James in a commanding tone I had never heard from him before. 'Listen to me. We are all four going back. All three of us and this ... woman ... who I take to be ... Miss Weston, my relative. So if you're not going to help us, then get out of the way.'

The Jerkin was laughing uproariously by now. I had never seen anybody actually slap his thighs with mirth, but he did – first bending down to do it, then lifting each leg in turn at waist height. It was a repulsive sight.

'Hold on, hold your horses, hold on,' said the Jerkin when he had calmed himself a little. 'You don't need to take that tone with old Josiah. Your music has a kind of magic of its own. She is yours, Sir, and welcome.' I glanced over at the forlorn-looking woman and she seemed not to understand the proceedings at all, and like me had been totally unmoved by the song, even as its final notes echoed through the leaves. I suppose I breathed a small sigh of relief and headed for the mouth of the cave. James hung back.

'No, young sir,' said the Jerkin, who could see what he was thinking. 'You are still in my world. You cannot speak long with her until you are back in the land above. And let me give you this warning. You must trust. You must trust completely. She will come, but if you turn around and make certain she is following, then you will undo the magic. Take the path by which you came, but keep your eyes fixed ahead. Don't look back. Whatever you do, don't look back.'

'That's a condition, is it? You never mentioned conditions when you set the riddle.'

'Condition? What am I – one of your shyster pen-pushing lawyers? No, this is just the lore. It is just the way. People who have stumbled into the world below, the world of the little people, do not normally return. They get a shock if they do, because time slides past down here like an old fox. So there are ways. There are traditions to keep. There are rituals to respect. It is not my rule – it is simply the way.'

'Very well then,' said James and pushed past me towards the cavern mouth. As he did so, in the distance beyond the trees, the strange music began again, dreamy and insistent and evocative and this time rather more menacing, as if the chorus of Blackbeard's pirates were ambling along the lane. As the music got closer, we stood there watching a frightening transformation overtake the young woman. At the first note, she had started like a frightened rabbit. She began to shake and, as the sounds became nearer, she began frantically rubbing at her arms as if they were hopelessly and irredeemably dirty. She seemed to be muttering under her breath, '*No, no, no*'.

Susie and James both advanced towards her but could get no closer than the nearest trees, and stood looking helpless. The glint of green light from the direction of the music grew bigger and nearer, and – I have to admit – I could sense, rather than see, the small green figures dancing implacably round and round. The ground beneath us seemed to be heaving with life. I could almost feel its heartbeat through the earth and see the sap rising in the plants, as if all the fertility rituals ever practiced had been rolled into one. Tears were now streaming down the woman's face. Her fists were clenched.

There was a peal of laughter and, as the music died away, I thought I could hear a light joyful voice, playful in the sunlight.

'We gave you our child,' it said. 'And we took him to the world above.'

'What can we do?' said Susie. 'We've got to take her if we can.'

'We're going to take you to my home,' said James in a loud voice. 'To Oberon House'.

She replied with the voice of one disappointed in love with the wound as fresh as ever.

'That is my home too, Sir. It is strange that I do not know you. And I cannot go without my child.'

'Your child is ... has been ... cared for above,' said James haltingly. 'But the world has moved on.'

'Many years have past,' said Susie. 'This is your closest relative. Do you understand what I'm saying?' A tear ran down the woman's face and dissolved in her muslin dress. But she ignored the question.

'You know no power on earth or under it shall take me from this place unless it is the power of iron. Josiah will confirm that. You shall be my iron key to the door of this underworld, if you will, Sir. Give me iron and I will follow behind and we will tiptoe away from the little people while they dance elsewhere. Only take care to heed Josiah's advice. Do not look behind for me, because your vigilance will alert them. They can sense it, and since I have partaken of their food and drink, I am theirs. I am beholden to them. And they took my child also, and although you say he was taken above, they may still keep him here in the undergrowth and feed the babe on grubs and seeds.'

'Is this a good idea?' said James. 'We're playing with something we barely understand.'

Susie ignored him. 'Do we have anything made of iron? Yes, of course we do.' And she reached into James' pocket and pulled out the old keys to Oberon House, inches long and rusty. She pulled one off the ring and gave it to me. The rust came off on my hands. And she laid the other on the ground as close to the woman as she could. 'This is made of iron. Can you pick it up?'

She did so and concealed it in her palm like Harry Houdini. As we turned around, with a final glance at the smiling man in the jerkin, and walked away, her quiet voice followed us through the bushes: 'Remember what I say. Pluck me from your minds. You must now pay me no attention as you walk through the passage. You must make your minds empty and, above all, not look round. My escape depends on it. The little people can hear your thoughts.'

'And,' she said, as we went out of earshot, 'beware of the Trickster.'

I had no idea what this meant. As we walked down the cave and switched on the pale torch, I imagine that the three of us were thinking very similar things. We were all wondering I expect, as I was, what kind of experience we had just been through, and if it was real, what would happen in the world above. Whether the woman would disappear, or if she was really Emma and nearly 200 years old, whether she would crumble into dust and bones. Or whether she simply would carry on her missing life. I expect we were all wondering whether Susie's belt and scarf would still show us the way back, and whether we would actually get back to the ordinary world of parking tickets, mortgages and the nine o'clock news, or whether we might be locked into this fantastical ancient place we had unwittingly discovered. I expect we were all also realizing that thinking about Emma at all risked losing her entirely.

But I probably had two thoughts not shared by James and Susie. I was once again terrified of the narrowing cave in the dark, and the dripping walls and stalactites. I was also looking at what I could see of Susie's back-view striding on ahead, noticing how quiet she was, and how her body language had excluded me – and whether this was guilt about what we had done or whether she had really decided that James was her future and not me.

She stooped down, pointing her torch at the ground, and saw a wild blue flower growing there, almost out of the light. I watched her snap it off and put it in her pocket. It was at this point that the temptation to look back to see if the woman was following became almost overwhelming. Perhaps she had gone altogether. Perhaps she had tripped and needed help. Perhaps she had lost sight of us and had failed to find the scarf and the belt that pointed the way. Perhaps she was being held down by a raucous band of captors. I could feel my head being pulled involuntarily to the right, before remembering that I must not even entertain the thought.

As the cave gave way to ancient brickwork, I emptied my mind by trying to imagine what the others were thinking. I imagined Susie thinking of driving down the New Jersey Turnpike, or Christmas at home in Minnesota with every house lit by coloured Santas and leaping reindeer. I suppose I hoped that, in the middle of it all, she was thinking of me above her and the whiskey bottle on the floor of my flat. James was probably thinking of money and the lack of it.

We were climbing stairs, with the torchlight bouncing off the walls ahead of us, when we first heard noises from behind. As we passed the small wooden door in the well chamber, we heard the woman's voice unmistakably, as if whispering in our ears.

'You are home now. You can turn round.'

But we were still in a place where nothing was quite what it seemed. Susie gripped James' arm.

'Don't. That isn't her. It's the Trickster making one last minute appeal. Ignore it until we're in the house. Don't look round.'

But the voice began to whimper a little. Tears were rolling down Susie's face with the strain as we desperately cleared our minds over and over again, like frustrated mediators. Every time we closed our minds to her, she seeped back in.

Even so, I don't know why James glanced round. Had the suspense become unbearable? Had he simply forgotten? Or was it, as he said later, his certainty of victory and his absolute determination to remake his life and rebuild the house? Either way, all he caught was a look of horror on the woman's face, then resignation, and then a fog and wind seemed to sweep us off our feet as it swept passed us down the passage. I clutched at Susie just in time as the force of the storm caught us. There was a scream from behind us and as the tumult swirled around us and small distant voice shouting something I could not hear. It was the last I ever saw of her.

When the wind stopped, we picked ourselves up and found the small wooden door was shut behind us and there was no way back.

XXI

'Her eyes the glow-worm lend thee,
The shooting-stars attend thee;
And the elves also,
Whose little eyes glow,
Like the sparks of fire befriend thee.'
ROBERT HERRICK, *'THE NIGHT-PIECE, TO JULIA'*

Hamburg, March 1946

WHEN Harry's wife heard about his affair with Renata, she left him. He never discovered who had written to her about it, but somebody had. Nor did he understand quite how he had become so passionately involved, despite all his careful precautions. His letters had talked about the freezing winter, the refugees, the desperate shortage of firewood – even about the 'body-snatchers'. He never mentioned anything about smuggling Renata into his quarters in the dark, or the nights he spent with his legs entangled in hers, with only a blanket separating them from the next door family of underground exiles. It was extraordinary the privacy that an old candle and some blanket partitions could give you. Yet his wife had heard.

Harry never forgot the peculiar sense of intimacy without privacy. He remembered it as a mixture of Renata's strong smell and the odour of candle wax. Despite the cold, despite the muffled coughs from other parts of the cellar or the grunts of people turning over and talking in their sleep, his stolen nights in the crypt were among the most romantic of his life. In those hours in the underworld, not quite real – a million miles from the food queues and the heart-rending photographs in the world above – Harry and Renata got to know each other. He remembered the way her hair fanned out on the dirty old blanket under her head and the way she shielded her breasts from him as he got undressed.

Harry had taken the letter to the British major in charge of policing in that part of the city. The major offered him a cigarette and put his feet up on the desk as they talked.

'You know, I'm not saying this kind of horror stuff doesn't happen, but we have never actually found hard evidence of it,' he said. 'You do understand that?'

'Of course, but isn't this hard evidence?'

'Well, maybe, maybe not. I mean what does it actually refer to? It says "*this is the last one I will send you today*", right? What does that mean? Fish? Cigarette packets? Piles of firewood? It could be anything. We'll check it out of course, and I'm glad you brought it to me – don't get me wrong – but I don't think it's exactly the promised land.'

Harry handed over the address and they kept it under surveillance for a week. Nobody came. The place was deserted. Months later, he even went there himself. Raindrops fell from the windowsill and a dusty plaster Madonna stood in the window.

With some embarrassment he retraced his steps to the crypt he had been taken to, and told the old man they had made no progress.

'Lord, what fools these English are!' he said with irritation, exclaiming at the ceiling, and them immediately regretted it. 'I apologize, Sir. I am very grateful to you. We just have to be vigilant, that's all.' As Harry slipped away again, he felt a hand in his pocket. He gripped it and found himself holding onto Renata.

They met increasingly often in the ruins of the old church where she had first approached him. She watched for him through the broken remains of an old medieval fan window.

He brought her sausages, bread and cigarettes and later anything he could spare. He never knew how much her love was based on these vital material comforts, but also knew that it hardly mattered – because he was passionately in love with her himself. He loved the way her nose wrinkled when she laughed, her affection for everyone – from old women hobbling along the ice to stray cats. He imagined life together in bombed-out London after he went home, but it was not to be. When he went home the following year, they agreed between them was that she would follow him as soon as he could find somewhere to live, but she never did. Back in London, Harry found himself estranged from his own family, too. He sat alone in his one-roomed apartment, astonished that somebody so fearful of divorce – of chaos of any kind – should have reaped such a chaotic whirlwind.

He and Renata exchanged copious letters, but every letter demonstrated just how involved she was becoming in the politics of the new West Germany and the rebuilding of the city. The old man Harry had met had become a leading intellectual in the new Social Democratic Party. But Harry was patient – he knew if he became impatient, she would never come. He never became impatient – that was not his nature – but she never came anyway.

He missed her with a continuing pain that felt like a knife around his heart. Every morning when he woke, he imagined her next to him in a cosy, leisurely beginning to the day – something they had never managed when he was a reluctant acolyte of the Allied Control Commission, with his uniform folded beside her old mattress and the candle lit for the morning. He missed his wife and children, too, but she was in the process of marrying again – to a wealthy landowner in Cumberland with his own lake and woods. Harry's guilt made it difficult to contact her often. He tried not to invade her chance of renewed happiness, and he had to run the gauntlet of her rage and contempt every time he did so. He also felt the new husband could probably give his children a better upbringing than he ever could.

Instead, he flung himself into his new job organizing public relations for a department store in Sloane Square, about twenty minutes brisk icy walk from his flat along the bombed, neglected and impoverished Kings Road. He wrote press releases about the New Look, organized Father Christmas every year at Christmas time, juggled photographs for the summer fashions. In his spare time, he helped the Red Cross trace some of the thousands of missing relatives divided by the war. It was a slow process, writing letters across Europe, waiting often months for the reply, comparing answers with their banks of dog-eared record cards across one wall of the office. Often the relatives turned out to be dead – victims of blitz, concentration camp or battle. Often they turned out to be looking for each other.

There was something special about the reunions for Harry. As if he was doing something small but significant to remake the world and hold back chaos – which loomed ever closer with the Cold War and the prospect of atomic annihilation. But for someone who despaired of change, it was a dispiriting time to live in London. The constant talk of austerity. The fuel and food rationing. The drab black window frames and respectable disintegration. The overgrown bombsites. The disgusting food, the prefabs, the constant shortage of money. It was as if London had resigned itself to drizzle. Looking back over his life, it seemed that his worst fears had come to pass – a father and two brothers dead in war, his ancestral home stolen away, his wife and family betrayed by himself, his lover drifting away. Nothing lasts, he told himself. Nothing lasts – and unless you can accept that brutal fact, it only makes it worse.

To escape from the depressing conclusion, Harry spent his weekends wondering again about Emma. He recovered some of the detritus of his pre-war investigations: long lists of people with the same name in registers around southern England, lists of passengers emigrating to America – and a trail to what is now Minnesota – tiny detailed notes of conversations with elderly relatives. They stayed piled in one corner, all that remained of his little shrine to her memory when he was a boy.

He also researched the history of the house.

He was inspired to do so by a chance discovery in one of the many second-hand bookshops in the Kings Road, where he used to spend his lunch hours. It was a book called *The Forgotten Houses of Surrey*. It was published in 1925, and somebody in the intervening years had clearly used it as a place mat – coffee, tea and wine stains ringed the cover and the index pages were missing. But there was a whole section on Oberon House. Harry gratefully parted with 1/6d and drank it all in.

'We now pass through the little village of Oberon,' read the book, 'where the rustic splendour of Oberon House, now sadly in a state of some disrepair, deserves a brief pause.' It described the old church and the Weston family tombs in it and their inscriptions: 'ONCE I LIVED NOW HERE I LYE/TO LIVE WITH CHRIST ETERNALLIE'. It described the house in detail with its impressive window, which Harry still remembered glinting in the sunlight, and all the stories were there. Even as he glanced through the entry with the cold draught in the shop snapping round his ankles, so much of it came flooding back. The dog in the tunnel, the Domesday Oak, the disappearing daughter – and one story he had never heard: the baby on the back doorstep.

It was just another story, with no name or dates – just a hint that it referred to the early nineteenth century. It described how a newborn baby had been discovered early one morning in a tiny basket, woven out of duck feathers, and that the astonished Weston family had taken it in and brought it up as one of its own. The story rang a bell in Harry's head, though he had no conscious memory of hearing it before. It inspired him to make a long-planned visit to see his father's old mistress, living in a freezing basement in Paddington.

As he arrived there, the coal men were dusting themselves down after delivering the contents of their black bags through her coalhole in the paving stones. Jenny was well into her seventies and had no telephone, but he had written to her and received a welcoming reply. The dark room she lived in was full of antimacassars, photos of long dead gentlemen in military dress and the all-pervading smell of cats.

She handed him his tea in a cracked china cup and wrapped herself more tightly in her shawl. Harry had met Jenny before, but not since long before the war; he was moved by her welcome and stared at her fine perfectly white hair. He edged furtively round the subject of his own family, not knowing whether she had been informed that he no longer lived with his wife. As he told her about his work, he noticed the photo of his own father smiling down from the mantelpiece, in a stiff Edwardian suit. It seemed incredible that this frail old lady had so captured his father's heart. Her legs seemed to painfully thin, even in her thick stockings and woollen socks. Yet she still seemed to love life.

'Yes, I remember many of the stories your father used to tell about the old house, and I certainly remember that one. The baby on the doorstep. I know he believed it was true – in fact I seem to remember he wondered whether he was actually descended from the baby on the doorstep himself. I suppose that would mean you were, too.'

'Really?' said Harry. 'What made him think that?'

'Oh, I'm afraid I can't remember that. It's all a long time ago now. I fear your father would not have approved of life today, would he? Now, have you been to visit this new Festival of Britain people are talking about? You wouldn't catch me dead in it ...'

As Harry moved towards the front door, taking in the china bowls of unfinished cat food on the floor and the ancient pages of the *Daily Express* underneath them, she called him back.

'There's something I wanted you to have,' she said. 'I nearly forgot.' Harry's heart sank. He was afraid she might have bought him something she could ill afford. Worse – she might have bought something for his children.

Hurrying out, she pressed into his hand an old envelope. Inside was a metal frame. It was a miniature of a beautiful young lady with a muslin dress and a red bow in her black curly hair. She seemed to possess all the optimism of youth, with a dash of sensuality as well – like a miniature of Emma Hamilton. Harry was captivated.

'Your father gave me this, but I'm sure he would have wanted you to have it. You were very special to him, you know. And this is a picture of one of your own family, after all. Your father believed it was the young lady who disappeared.'

The miniature focused Harry's hobby. He became fascinated by Emma and a close reading of the notes in the front of the family bible convinced him that his father had been right. If there really had been a baby on the back doorstep, it was probably Jack – the elfin wanderer, who would return with strange tales of Red Indians, buffalo and mermaids. Jack was his own great grandfather. None of Jack's siblings, the children of Harry's long-lived great-great-grandfather Old Jo Weston, had survived into adulthood. Alone on the list, there was no recorded birthday for Jack.

Did that mean that Harry was probably not even a Weston after all? Even this underpinning of his identity seemed to wobble. Unless of course – a great leap of wishful thinking – Jack had appeared in his feathered basket shortly after Emma's disappearance. *Unless Jack had actually been Emma's child.* Soon he had completely convinced himself of it. That was why Old Jo and his wife had brought up the child as their own. They had known or guessed it was their nephew. They believed Emma would return at some point and reclaim the child, and probably had some reason to do so, but she never had.

But if Emma was the mother, who was the father? The obvious contender was Byron himself, but a search through Byron's papers and letters made this seem unlikely. He never mentioned her to anyone, and although he mentioned his brief visit to Oberon House – though not by name – there was attraction but no hint of love. If Emma had thought him in love with her, he was probably only playing.

The other scenarios became more vivid for Harry. That Emma had another secret lover who she had actually eloped with, but who had died of consumption – coughing and spluttering in their love garret – forcing her to give up the child.

That she had run away with the intention of joining Byron but had been taken captive by a band of vagabonds or highwaymen who had raped her and she had died in childbirth. That she had died a pauper in the London of Oliver Twist. That she had escaped down the secret passageway and ended – where?

Harry relaunched his search for her name in the parish records and in the register of deaths twenty years later, and again turned up many Emma Westons, but there was no reason to believe any of them was her. He tried to remember more of his childish conversations with his Grandpapa and Grandmama at their great ages: they would have known the answer, or at least guessed it. If only he could have asked them. The truth was, they had been so old they had probably forgotten – and yet some dim memory kept them going. It was almost as if sheer determination to wait for his sister had kept Grandpapa Weston alive those 130 years. Harry could remember the lines of Gray's *Elegy* he had particularly repeated. It was not as if either of them had been 'resigned' – as if they had '*left the warm precincts of the cheerful day,/Nor cast one longing lingering look behind*'. They had clung on until she came back.

'Remember this, young man,' his Grandpapa had said, as far as he could remember, he was talking about the American colonies. 'If once you lose something important to you, never rest until you have it back safe. That is what Our Lord said and that was how England was made.'

Then there was the secret passageway. There was indeed something mysterious about Oberon House, he felt. As Harry found himself hurtling towards retirement, and a new bearded, beaded, colourful generation had invaded the Kings Road, his mind went back to it increasingly. He remembered the frightening last time he had ventured down into the well chamber. He remembered the Dance, his strange conversations with Josiah Goodbody, even the strange implacable eyes at the window the night the news came through that his father had gone. It was as if the house had stood at some kind of intersection between two worlds.

But then that was the magic of childhood, wasn't it? He took his own grandchildren to see *Peter Pan* the year he retired, and felt almost bowed down by lost magic amid the drab motor fumes and Formica of 1960s London. He spent weekends visiting Oberon by Green Line bus – he never owned a car – but recognized nobody. It was the first time he had been back since 1912, after all, but he knew the names on the First World War memorial, including those of his two brothers. The new estates of glass and concrete were going up around the village. Cars lined the streets and queued sometimes through the main road. The hay carts and most of the farmers had disappeared, though there were some pick-your-own fields. The field where he used to talk to Josiah was now a caravan park. He even found himself standing at the end of the deserted driveway to Oberon House, but could never quite bear to fight his way in.

There seemed to be almost no controversy about the destruction of the Domesday Oak for the Gatwick Airport link road, and on one of his visits he found it had gone. It came as no surprise to anyone who had written futile protest letters, as Harry had, to preserve the Euston Arch. He wrote again and complained to the county council and was told that 'you can't stand in the way of progress'. A funny kind of progress, if you ask me, thought Harry.

He still wrote to Renata every Christmas, although it was almost two decades since he had seen her. She was married to the mayor of Hamburg, so his letters were reserved and matter of fact and betrayed no hint that he remembered his nights with her in the cellar as the moments he had felt most alive in his entire life. Nor did he tell her of his conviction – based on little more than fancy – that his ancestor Emma, of whom he had talked, had fallen victim to an intersection between worlds, maybe in a similar way that her old colleague Ingrid had done in 1946. He corresponded regularly with the only surviving relative of his generation, his cousin Agatha, but he could not tell her either. Centuries ago, people were said to have been stolen away by the fairies, kidnapped by the little people, and were never seen again. In the dim recesses of folk memory, they complained that their children had been substituted with lumps of soulless wood in the shape of children. That was what he came to believe had happened to Emma, and maybe to Jack.

It reminded him of Hamburg and that chilling note he had been given when he first met Renata. But there was something even more chilling: though Emma's captors had not been human, they had made her pregnant and she had given birth.

There was no way of testing the theory. But with every investigation he still carried on, tracing people for the Red Cross, every successful response he received, every record card ticked off, the thought of his stolen ancestor lay behind it. Every victory for him was a victory against chaos, change and those supernatural tricksters that interfere in human affairs. Does love last forever? No – but there are things I can do to make it last longer, he said to himself.

Of course, there was no way of proving that Emma had been stolen away, but he wanted to guide future generations if they were ever interested in what had happened. Simply to say so would mean he would be dismissed as a fantasist. Nobody would believe him and they certainly would never take the trouble to look any further. No, this was one family story he was not going to repeat to his grandchildren – not even to James, who seemed more interested than the rest. What he would do would be to leave the merest hint behind. It would be a clue to anyone working along the same lines – a small confirmation, perhaps. It would be no more than a pointer that the baby on the back doorstep had been hers and that it had not been conceived in the normal human way, but by some supernatural process which he dared not understand and preferred not to dwell on. A small hint to show that Emma had done nothing wrong. She was like Mary, he thought to himself: a virgin had conceived and born a son.

So before he sent the miniature for safe-keeping to the deposit box in Taunton, he wrote a little note on the back – a hint for investigators after him towards the truth as he saw it. It said simply 'Magnificat'.

XXII

'These Bodies be so plyable through the subtlety of the spirits that agitate them, that they can make them appear or disappear at pleasure.'

REV. ROBERT KIRK, *SECRET COMMONWEALTH, AND ESSAY OF THE NATURE AND ACTIONS OF THE SUBTERRANEAN (AND, FOR THE MOST PART) INVISIBLE PEOPLE, HERETOFOR GOING UNDER THE NAME OF ELVES, FAUNES AND FAIRIES, OR THE LYKE, AMONG THE LOW-COUNTRY SCOTS AS THEY ARE DESCRIBED BY THOSE WHO HAVE SECOND SIGHT, 1691.*

Oberon House, August 1998

IT WAS LATE evening when we got upstairs to Oberon House. The sunset was flooding through into the kitchen. We sat drinking whiskey in the gallery, watching the last glows of the day through the great window and staring ahead of us. There seemed to be nothing to say.

I suppose we were all physically and emotionally exhausted. When we had picked ourselves up off the floor of the well chamber, sniffed the smell of rotting vegetation and found the little wooden door shut to us, I took it in turns with James to wield an axe he had found in the kitchen. But when we had hacked away the old wood, the blows echoing around the ancient passage, all we found was the hard black rock behind it. There really was no way back – nor any evidence that we had ever been through.

I suppose it was also a relief to find our belongings strewn around the kitchen – my old sleeping bag, James' lists, Susie's books. At least we had not returned like Shon ap Shenkin or Rip van Winkle to find ourselves a century in the future and everyone we had ever known dead and buried.

'Well, you have to laugh don't you?' said Susie with a grin. 'I mean, can you imagine anyone you could tell that story to – let alone anyone who'd believe it. That's what comes of having fairies at the bottom of your garden.'

'Don't joke about it,' said James. And we all remembered the agonizing sound of the woman's scream as the wind had blown her back to where she had come from. If she existed at all, of course. If we hadn't just taken part in some common dream. It had been a supernatural experience of some kind: how much of it had been real?

'Do you know,' said James, anxious to clear the air, 'the most frightening aspect of today was that dance. That's what will forever stay in my mind. I don't know if I'll ever be able to sleep again.'

'I know what you mean,' said Susie. 'The way their eyes flickered.'

'And the way they smiled! Ugh.'

'It was terrifying, but I don't know – kind of exciting at the same time. I felt we were seeing things nobody has seen before, and under this house. And I'll never forget how dignified they were, for all that carousing.'

'Hang on!' I said. 'What are you talking about?' I hadn't seen any dance. I may have sensed it, I may not have done, but I hadn't actually *seen* any little people. Yet here I was sitting with two people I assumed had seen what I'd seen, talking about flickering eyes. Were they pretending just to annoy me? Or had they really seen little people tugging at each other and slapping their thighs as they danced round and round us. I certainly hadn't. I don't think we saw anything.

Susie and James looked at me as if I had become slightly unhinged. 'You know what all this means,' he said, changing the subject.

'Of course not.'

'It means that the child listed in the family bible with no birth date but a baptism in 1812 – Jack Weston – wasn't the son of old Jo Weston at all. He was Emma's son, Emma's son after some kind of bizarre liaison in the underworld, after some kind of magic. That's what it means.'

'You mean magic rape,' said Susie.

'Why couldn't he be Byron's son, conceived before she ran away?'

'I don't think so,' said Susie. 'It could be, but he denied it pretty strongly in the letter. I think he would have taken more notice if the relationship had got that far. Of course he wasn't to be trusted, but that letter carried some conviction. No, if James is right, that makes Jack Weston some kind of changeling. And changelings have no soul, right?'

'Hang on a minute.' I consulted my mental dictionary of Oberon stories from all my years involved with James. 'You're descended from Jack yourself. Does that mean you have no soul?'

James looked distracted for a moment.

'I think people can grow their own souls,' said Susie. 'They can certainly suffocate their souls, so I'm sure they can grow them too if they want to.'

As she spoke, I found my irritation with the two of them growing again. As if any defence of James by her was some kind of betrayal of me. So what if James had no soul? I stormed off to fetch the whiskey bottle, furious that they could collude together in this tale of dancers to humiliate me.

When I got back, James had slipped away to bed and Susie was preparing to go, too. I caught her staring out of the window across Harvest Hill, under which we must have confronted our fantasy that day. I could see the headlights from the nearest road snaking in the distance, and a small buzzing light where the tennis courts had once been.

'What's that?'

'I don't know. Firefly? Will o' the wisp?' We stared at it

standing next to each other for a minute. The old house creaked like an arthritic cow as the night air cooled.

'Susie, what are we going to do?' She flinched but said nothing. 'Don't say anything for a moment. Let me tell you what I want. I want us to leave all this behind – preferably tonight – all this fairy stuff, this creepy underworld stuff, and start looking to the future for a change. You and me, I mean. We could have a future that's really magic, not this kind of foetid ancient stuff. I want you to come and live with me now, tonight. OK, I know I haven't been very good or reliable about love so far, but I really believe you're the person who can change that for me – change me maybe. I've never told anyone that they're just wonderful before, but ...'

'Stop, stop. I can't let you go on like this.' Susie was red in the face and emotional. 'Look, I was so wrong to come and see you last week – last night – whenever it was – I shouldn't have even knocked on the door. I was so confused then, and after today I'm even more so. It was wrong of me, and wrong of us both to lose control like that. I owe something to James – and so do you – and there's something about this place I can't abandon. So can we leave the subject just now and go to sleep? It's not that I don't appreciate what you say. I promise I'll decide what to do and I'll talk to you properly – after I've talked it through with James.'

'You're surely not going to tell him?'

'Don't you think it would be worse just to go? I've got to. Just let me do whatever I do in my own way, OK?'

It was late. I was exhausted, too. I watched her pad along the corridor, her hair bobbing behind her as she went and I realized I had lost her. And if I hadn't lost her then, I would the moment she confessed everything to James. I was too tired to leave, but as I climbed into my sleeping bag in the kitchen I felt angrier and angrier. I was powerless to prevent her throwing herself away on someone as hopeless as James and his great pile of crumbling masonry and half-forgotten stories. I had witnessed the intimacy between them during an extraordinary day. It was absolutely hopeless, and deep down I couldn't help feeling it was something to do with my leg.

I barely slept. The events of the day jumbled themselves in my head. The dark tunnel, the wind, the tragic helpless woman, the insistent erotic beat. I kept turning over to relax enough to sleep as the night wore on, and found myself going over in intricate detail the strange story told by the man in the leather jerkin – the missing horse, the magical nurse and the great window that finds what's been lost. A window like Susie's dreams. I wished I had the same kind of ability.

As I lay there on the hard floor in the dark, listening to the creaking of the house, something crucial suddenly fell into place in my head. I knew where the poem was.

XXIII

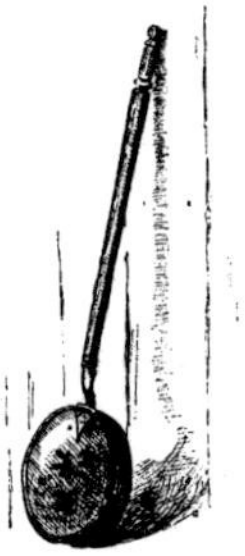

'The iron tongue of midnight hath told twelve;
Lovers, to bed; 'tis almost fairy time.'
WILLIAM SHAKESPEARE, *A MIDSUMMER NIGHT'S DREAM*

Chelsea, London, February 1978

'I QUITE agree that he can feed himself and get dressed well enough. He still does all his own shopping and can get in and out of the bath. And he seems healthy enough. No, it's his mental state which concerns me.' Harry's caseworker was flicking through his file at the local department of social services.

'Really? I always believed he was pretty sane and happy enough.'

'Oh, I agree, quite happy enough. Only a number of times now I've heard him mention fairies. He says he's studying the subject.'

'Fairies? In this day and age? Surely not.'

'No, really. I questioned him about it. I said: "Mr Weston, how interesting – and do you ever see them?" He just said he hadn't but he believed he might have done once, a very long time ago. He didn't laugh or anything.'

'I see what you mean. That does put rather a new complexion on things. What is he now? 78? 79?'

'He's 78, I believe. Let me just make sure ... yes, 78.'

'Well, it might be possible to arrange a place for him in the Pinner home. He can be kept under pretty close observation there. I mean, it's not as if he's been violent, is it.'

'I realize he's not going to be very happy about this – giving up his independence and so on – but I think there is a clear duty of care issue here. And after all, Pinner will be able to take a few of his books and a couple of favourite possessions – though perhaps we ought to quietly censor the fairy studies.'

'Have you been in touch with the family? That flat he's in must be worth a bob or two – just off the Kings Road.'

'Rented, I'm afraid. His children are abroad, but I'll obviously write to inform them. He has grandchildren. I believe one is at university and visits him quite often. We don't have the address, but we can get it I'm sure.'

'Could you do that? We'll arrange a case conference in a week or so, but I think we have sketched out the correct course of action. It's all about catching danger signs early, isn't it. Thanks for keeping your ear to the ground.'

XXIV

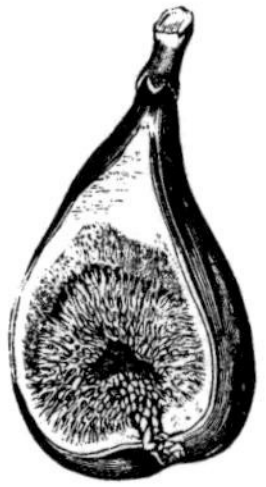

'Anno 1670, not far from Cirencester, was an apparition; being demanded whether a good spirit or a bad? returned no answer, but disappeared with curious perfume and most melodious twang. Mr W. Lilly believes it was a fairy.'

JOHN AUBREY

Oberon House, August 1998

I PULLED on my shirt, trousers and shoes and heaved open the back door to clear my head. The first light was seeping into the sky in the east, the breeze was chilly and damp and the dawn chorus was just tuning up in the distance in Saxon Wood. I breathed deeply, went back inside and tiptoed up the dusty main stairs.

In the gallery, I stared out through the great window for a long time, unsure what it was I was looking for, just as the sun peeped over the hill in the far corner of the glass. I opened the shutters we had unscrewed when I first came to the house. By the time the orange light was flooding across the bare floorboards and onto the walls behind me, where once the family portraits had hung, I saw what I was looking for.

I had never watched through the window at dawn with the shutters pushed back before, and I don't believe anybody had for a century at least. And even then, when they saw the tiny scratches on the far left hand pane of glass, they probably just dismissed them as one of the faults of age – like the creaking roof or the protesting floors. But I knew what they were, because in my half-asleep state I had dreamed them myself.

As the sun rose, the light caught the lines more boldly. With my heart in my mouth and my nose pressed to the window, I examined the tiny lines as closely as I could: '*To EW*,' they read:

Though I expire; though every empire dies,
Though Oberon descends into the slime,
Your beauty, borderless as skies,
Will live forever more, defying time.

She is not old, nor young, yet still there bides,
Within my heart and soul, the keenest trace,
Of innocence and laughter turned to brides,
Of Emma's lips and hair and Emma's face.

There wasn't much of it. It may not have been the poet's best work, yet I knew this was the missing verse of family legend, the verse that I had spent so many weeks searching for. It was engraved into the glass so finely that only the first glint of sunlight of the day – low in the sky and from that sharp angle – could make it visible. It was the most beautiful combination of human and natural I had ever seen. I read it over and over as I stood there, thinking over the events of the past 48 hours and Byron's ironically correct prediction. I've heard since that Queen Elizabeth I used to scratch messages on glass with a diamond. The thought of Byron doing the same, the pleasure he would give with the flirtation, leaning up against the glass as he did so in his boots and jacket, gave me an overwhelming sense of the endless continuity of romance. It seemed such a beautiful thing, and I had found it. In that moment, it belonged to me – the only truly beautiful thing I have ever owned.

Then I thought about how this discovery would fuse James and Susie together – the crowning glory of the relationship for both of them with their collusion and secrets and their bloody

Funny Valentine. In that light, the poem seemed like a final betrayal. If I hadn't lost her to him before, I had now. So as the sun rose inexorably in the early morning sky, I pushed the nearest cardboard box next to the window – right under the small pane that carried Byron's thoughtless words – and, very deliberately, I put my foot through the glass.

There was only a small crash. The shards of glass sprinkled down outside like lethal, historic snow. Then I gathered a few belongings together, flung them in the back of my car, and drove away. I've never been back.

You might well accuse me of the most selfish and blatant piece of vandalism, and you would probably be right. My excuse, having had time to construct one, was that the poem had done quite enough damage in the past couple of centuries without unleashing it again. It had induced the poor deluded daughter of the house to run away, to what fate I still could not be sure. It had sucked the life out of successive generations, seeping into James' will to achieve anything on his own account.

Weigh them in the balance for a second. Those few fragile, dried-out words clinging to the world like mould on the edge of the window – against my passionate, hopeful, life-pumping relationship with Susie as it could have been. What would you have me do? Give up the whole idea for a desiccated antique? An antique that sucks life like a vampire? Give me life not dust every time.

So I gave them both up. I smashed the glass and I abandoned Susie, too, in one simple human gesture against the combined suffocating weight of history and the subterranean part of all of us we rightly suppress. I took my path with the living, and I have barely regretted it.

Still, I have my moments – not perhaps of regret – but wishing the whole event had been different. My life had been intertwined with James' for more than thirty years, and without his company, I have little or nothing that reaches all the way back. I own nothing any more that had been with me that long. I have no keepsakes from my own parents, or photos of myself when young, or supportive relationships stretching back. I sometimes feel as though I might as well have been swapped for a block of wood myself. Occasionally I still find myself wondering how the old house is holding itself together, and about its occupants, too. Not often – I've got a busy life these days: I sell office space and I've got into day trading on the side – but sometimes I wonder about them. I have six employees and two houses. And two women, come to think of it. I don't really know why I still dream about Oberon House. I barely tasted that food in the other world the once, but it has in its own way kept me captive all these years.

In my more depressive moments, I fear I have become like James – or as James used to be. I drift. Neither my contracts nor my relationships seem to last. I float through life without settling. My previous girlfriend even called me 'fey'. But life carries on, and though the weekends are sometimes hard to fill, there are compensations. I've never married, but I've never been divorced either. I've never had to pay a penny's alimony. And there are always more people round the next corner. But I have never managed to get that day out of my mind. I dream about it still – nor have I ever managed to rid myself of Susie's touch and Susie's laugh. Some things do seem to last forever.

Maybe they last forever for James, too. I've never seen him again. I heard through the grapevine that they managed to get government grants to replace the crumbling roof of Oberon House and make it habitable. And she's still there – Susie I mean. There are even children, I believe.

Some people might say this was a happy ending to the tale and maybe it is. But when the nights are particularly dark, or the pubs are particularly full, my mind goes back to that poor beguiled benighted woman, trapped in that place for centuries, still looking for her child.

I don't pray – anything eternal scares me these days. But if I prayed for anything, I'd pray for some kind of rest for Emma.

XXV

'Easy is the way down to the Underworld: by night and by day dark Hades' door stands open; but to retrace one's steps and to make a way out to the upper air, that's the task, that is the labour.'
VIRGIL, *THE AENEID BK 6*

Epilogue I: From the private papers of Byron's solicitor, now in the archive of the University of Pennsylvania.

65 New Road, London
14th August 1812

My dear Hanson,

I was excessively grateful for your letter and the fine feelings expressed therein. I quite understand your difficulty; indeed, I understand why – as you put – it is some months since we corresponded. The life of a lawyer was ever thus! I also understand the need your client Ld. Byron has for reassurance about young Miss Emma Weston. For these reasons – & in respect of your solemn promise to me that the import of this Letter should remain confidential – I have pleasure in acceding to your request for these personal details of the Weston family.

I write it in the knowledge that it was through my auspices that His Lordship first came to Oberon Hse., and I fully accept the responsibility I bear for the Introduction. You will recall how anxious you and I were that My Ld. should have some recuperation after his strenuous Journey abroad. Though, in parenthesis, so to speak, I don't believe any of us could have guessed how much his fame would have spread in these short months, and that may have been recuperation enough.

Even so, I can only apologise, not so much that the visit shd have had such peculiar Consequences, but that his Ldship should have had this added worry. Please convey to him my most ardent best wishes, and convey to him also my complete Assurance that – although I cannot absolutely rule out the existence of a child, even if there be one, he will not hear from my family – or anyone else – concerning its fate.

I realise that this is a Message that, by itself, may not convince. As I have written before, only the Young Lady can possibly know whether there might have been cause for Rumours that the Child is hers, but she remains missing. So I must perforce relate to you the strange events of my recent visit to Oberon Hse., again reminding your good Self that this letter must be for your eyes alone.

I arrived there last Monday night, post haste from Horsham, having dined there on my journey. I arrived somewhat frozen on account of having had to travel outside, and to rely on the kindness of the Coachman for his overcoat during what was an unexpectedly cold journey for midsummer.

I must confess I have in the past found the hospitality of my sister & her husband Mr Weston somewhat overwhelming, so I was surprised that I found it initially hard to make the household aware of my presence at all. The black pot was on the stove in the old kitchen. A fire was laid but unlit in the hallway – though the late afternoon was now quite warm enough I admit. I encountered old Sam as he left through the Parlour, & endeavoured to question him about the whereabouts of my sister, & he jerked his thumb in a vulgar gesture behind him & said 'You'd better ask him'. He said it with some emphasis and strode out of the house.

I was surprised by this – I had hitherto believed I had shared some understanding with Sam, who has served the

Weston family faithfully for many years. Many are the times I have witnessed him rescuing a cart by his quick thinking or directing the harvesting at sundown in his smock, and I had not thought him so casual in his relations with his betters.

Nevertheless, in the Hall by the fire, I found the 'him' I believed Sam had intended to draw my attention to – and a strange sight he was, ageless almost and wearing a leather coat and what I might describe as an innocent look. 'I wonder if you would be so good as to inform my sister and brother-in-law that Mr Austin, her brother, has arrived,' I said, assuming he was the Gardener.

'I'd not like to disturb her now she's with the Babe,' said the man. Then, seeing my open-mouthed Expression, he exclaimed: 'Why, what a glum face is that? – when you're to see the new Babe yourself with his little eyes peering out at the world for the first time? Now, sit your old bag o' bones down here while you wait, why don't you, and dream what those eyes will see in its three score years and ten, while the hens in the village roost & the fox slips by in the night.'

I recall the Speech precisely and relate it here because I had not heard its like before – and with that I turned round and discovered the man had departed. I mention this because I had, and I still have, no idea what he was – & neither it seemed had anyone else. Although I asked all the remaining members of the Household who he cd have been, & there seemed no spark of recognition. Perhaps that was down to the paucity of my powers of description, but it soon became clear that nearly all the servants had handed in their notice – citing irregular goings-on of some disturbing nature in the house. Even faithful Sam held his lips tight. Yet it seemed that some inkling of the manner of the arrival of the Child had reached their ears. It had not yet reached mine.

The Child arrived, sometime in the early hours of the morning in June, left on the front Doorstep, or so it was related to me presently – near the clump of buttercups & the old harness that has occupied its plinth for some decades. It arrived without so much as a Letter attached, nor any indication of whence it came – which was peculiar enough for comment among the Servants and village people. It was an unusual child, with swarthy skin and pronounced ears – more Elf than child, I would aver – and indeed expressed such an opinion to my Sister. Then wd you believe it – normally the most stolid of women – she looked at me sharply & almost with fear.

'Hush, brother! You do not know what you say. This is not a matter for mirth. God bless us and protect us, indeed,' she said & motioned the Wet Nurse from the village out of the room, & spoke to me in a most animated manner.

'My dear brother, you simply must control your opinions in front of the servants, given the unusual appearance of the Child. Even if we believe that the mother is or was poor Emma – who was the father?'

'You mean it was not his Lordship?' I asked. You will note my anxiety that this be made clear.

'Look at him, brother! Look at him!' said my agitated Sister. 'Does that look like Lord Byron to you? With those eyes, those fingers? No, I don't speak my fears about who the parents may be – I dare not. But I see no reason to believe it was his Lordship.'

'Come, come, Sister. This excitement is unlike you. What are you telling me? If it isn't Emma's child, why do you not simply throw it back?'

'Ah, but Jo believes it <u>is</u> Emma's, and who can tell – he may well speak truly. He often does. It is the father that is unknown & about which we must not jest.'

'What a to-do!' I laughed. 'You speak as if the child was bewitched!' And I have to confess that, as the Colour drained from her face, I heartily wished I had not expressed myself so bluntly. She then related to me the unusual manner of its arrival. Not just outside the door, which was unusual enough, but in a tiny Cot woven entirely of Reeds & in the most intricate and beautiful patterns, & with flowers knit together from green shoots and cowslips in a great Canopy over the sleeping baby. It was the most beautiful product of nature she had seen, she told me – though it sounds most unnatural to me.

Since the Babe's arrival, the house has been beset with unusual occurrences. The kitchen was tidied early one morning. The cows in the byres milk'd. The parlour swept &tc. I saw for myself the Crib she told me of, & though it was much dried, it was still a strange sight indeed. I was uncertain how I should reply to her, & I still am, yet it clearly exercised her mind & the minds of the household greatly.

My poor Sister has been beset by troubles in recent years. She lost one child to the Fever one year last March, & another to goodness knows what ailment in May, just before this strange Arrival. I believe her determination to protect it is to make some use of the great & wasted love she bore for poor departed Thomas. Yet even this is not sufficient to explain why she hangs dried bunches of what I believe is St John's Wort around the house. You may know this better than I, but Old Wives say the Herb was used in Olden Days to ward off the Fairies, of all things. Still, if you have such poor luck with children, I suppose one falls back on such remedies, if remedies they be.

I had not by then encountered my brother-in-law & did not seek him out until later in the Evening. He can sometimes be a gruff and difficult man, as you know. I have seen him dismiss minor aristocrats and coachmen alike with the same withering stream of words. In Conversation, he tends to curse & express constant admiration for Wolfe and Wellesley – & who can fault that – as if his profession of gentleman farmer was some kind of branch of the Military. But I digress, the point is that I have never found Mr Weston an easy man. You will recall I had some concerns about how he & his Lordship would understand each other & was surprised that they became such Friends at the start of his visit. I fear such feelings have not lasted on my Brother's part, but perhaps that was too much to expect of him.

I eventually encountered him in the gallery under the great Window overlooking the 'park' and woods. The sun was sinking in the sky and he was standing by the glass staring out as if he awaited some Visitor. I noticed he had permanently sealed some of the shutters to close part of the glass.

'Why fix the shutters, brother-in-law? Is the Window Tax too much for you?' I japed.

'There are some windows I no longer wish to gaze through,' he replied without turning round.

So I stood by him & watched the Twilight gather itself around the house like a blanket. We spoke not at all, and I felt his attention gripped still, waiting – one has to assume – for his missing Sister. The House grew dark behind us, and I could hear the distant clatter of a Baby being settled down for the night. I was about to leave him, suggesting merely that I collect some candles, when I noticed his Expression change.

'What do you see?' I asked him, staring through the gloaming without being able to make out the object of his attention. 'I fear I am not so owl-eyed.'

He ignored me, turned and raced out of the room, leaning back to heave open the grt Oak Door & clattering down the stairs, his boots hammering on the wooden boards. He ran like a foxhound & I cd barely keep up with him, hearing the clang of the Parlour door ahead of me as he plunged on. Outside I could see his shape racing towards the Woods. My eyes are sharp enough, but apart from the fireflies cross-crossing the path, I still could not make out what strange sight had been vouchsafed to him but not to me.

There was, I confess, an unusual atmosphere on the edge of the old Woods. I hope you will forgive what you may dismiss as credulity, but I want to convey an accurate impression of one of the strangest evenings I had lived through. But there was a sound – that breed of humming that, in the sunlight, I would have put down to the heat. If I had my wits on my side, and you will excuse this fancy, my dear Hanson, I would have said it was music. I am a lawyer & was still able to recover the objectivity of my Mind – yet when I heard Joseph shout ahead of me through the bracken, it chilled my spine. I realised he was shouting for his lost Sister – & as I got closer – that he was shaking his fist.

I could hear little of what he was saying, lost him for a

moment, and saw he had double-backed behind me and was standing again at the door to the House. 'Bring her home, damn you!' he was shouting out into the darkness. 'I swear by God, by my Life, by that cursed Cot that lies upstairs, that I will outlive you if I have to – I will see her Home. If I have to live to a hundred, if my heart has to carry on pumping until I'm a hundred and fifty before you let her go, with my wife beside me – by every thing this house holds Sacred – I will do so, and no Poet, no Princes and no damn Robin Goodfellow is going to stop me.'

I must confess to you that, although I understood little of this terrible Oath, as I stood in the Shadows under the leaves, it frightened me. It was almost as if the very leaves felt it would come true, that he would indeed outlive Methuselah just to see his sister returned. And I tell it to you now, my dear Hanson, because I believe it will reassure you about the Babe. Whatever may have passed between His L'dship and Miss Weston, and whether or not there is a Child, you may see from this peculiar tale that he need fear no Paternity claim, no charges and no tittle-tattle from the Weston family.

Believe me, dear Sir,
Your obliged and humble. Sert.
Septimus Austin
Attorney-at-Law

XXVI

'Jack shall have Jill;
Nought shall go ill;
The man shall have his mare again,
And all shall be well.'
WILLIAM SHAKESPEARE, *A MIDSUMMER NIGHT'S DREAM*

Epilogue 2: article in the Surrey Comet, 19 June 2004

MYSTERY SKELETON FOUND
IN NEOLITHIC EXCAVATION

ARCHAEOLOGISTS are scratching their heads after uncovering a mysterious skeleton during a routine excavation in Surrey – and it could resolve a 200-year-old disappearance.

The team from the county's archaeological unit has been investigating a round barrow, thought to be neolithic, near the village of Oberon. But the skeleton they found buried there is about 3,000 years too modern, they say.

'We believe it is 18th or early 19th century,' said excavation director Howard Simms. 'We have absolutely no idea how it got to be there. For all we know it could be a long-forgotten hoax of some kind.'

The round barrow has a traditional local association with fairies, and was known locally as Fairy Mound, but has not attracted the detailed attention of experts before. Historians say it probably dates from around 2000 BC.

The skeleton found in the burial chamber of the mound was that of a woman. What has mystified archaeologists was that the trinkets she was buried with date much more recently – to the time of the Napoleonic Wars.

'A murder seems unlikely, since she was obviously laid here with great ceremony and even – dare I say – love,' said Mr Simms. 'Whoever put her here went to a great deal of trouble.'

Yet there are no contemporary local records of any such burial or event. Local historians are as bemused as everyone else.

The bones and trinkets – even a hair fastening and which has miraculously survived – are now under the care of Surrey County Council, but will probably be re-buried locally thanks to the intervention of local churches.

Oberon vicar Rev Jess Walker says he is determined to give her a proper burial: 'The chances are this woman was a baptised Christian. We are designing a special service involving dancing and flowers. I hope it will re-enact some of the older rituals that took place around these parts and which she may well have known.'

The owner of nearby Oberon House, James Weston, says he believes he knows the identity of the bones – though there has been no confirmation of this from local experts.

'I have reason to think they may be the remains of an ancestor of mine who disappeared in 1811,' he said. 'If I am right, she is – God willing – now at peace.'